A TWIST OF FORTUNE

TONY FOOT

Michael Terence Publishing

First published in paperback by
Michael Terence Publishing in 2021
www.mtp.agency

Copyright © 2021 Tony Foot

Tony Foot has asserted the right to be identified as the
author of this work in accordance with the
Copyright, Designs and Patents Act 1988

ISBN 9781800942066

All characters, places, products and events in this publication,
other than those clearly in the public domain
are the product of the author's imagination.
Any resemblance to real persons,
living or dead is purely coincidental

No part of this publication may be reproduced,
stored in a retrieval system, or transmitted,
in any form or by any means, electronic, mechanical,
photocopying, recording or otherwise,
without the prior permission of the publishers

Cover design
More Visual Ltd.
www.thebookcoverdesigners.com

To Sue,
for your enduring patience

Chapter One

Sefton Mather, Member of Parliament for a largely rural Hampshire constituency was feeling a little jaded after sitting through too many hours of intense, if at times, boring debate. At around six-thirty pm and avoiding the disapproving gaze of a Party whip monitoring proceedings, he left the Commons Chamber in a light drizzle in search of diversion. He headed across Westminster Bridge and focussed attention on his destination and the very warm welcome he knew he would receive there. For this was a place where, on numerous earlier occasions he had gone to relieve the stresses and monotony of parliamentary sessions. The headlights of oncoming vehicles blinked in the light, misty rain appropriately cloaking the Palace of Westminster as he stopped briefly, turned and looked back the way he had come. He continued to a point with the former County Hall, once the lair of 'Red Ken', on his left and where the Mary Seacole Memorial Statue, set in the garden of St Thomas's Hospital, just discernible in the drizzle was below and to his right.

Then, as he reached that part of Westminster Bridge Road opposite the Hospital, with almost balletic precision he negotiated the traffic and crossed into York Road and on in the direction of Tate Modern before turning into Victory Mews. The address proving a very convenient bolt-hole in every sense of the word and from which he could easily slip into the nearby Waterloo Station for trains back to Winchester, the nearest station to the family home in the growing village of Durford. Usually though, when the House was sitting he would instead return to his London apartment. If that was the case then it was the Tube from Waterloo to Baker Street and a short walk to the flat just off the Marylebone Road in Wentworth Street. There was a definite spring in his step and an increasingly warm feeling beginning to flow through his loins as he contemplated the sexual athletics to come. If there was such an individual as an objective observer of his performance and sexual intercourse was ever elevated to the status of an Olympic sport then he would be in strong contention for the award of the 'gold'. As he walked, the cloying atmosphere all around him moistening his hair, face and clothes but doing little to dampen his ardour. Somehow, he mused, it seemed to complement the gloomy mood that had pervaded the Commons throughout this day and many previous ones.

In a few minutes he would be slipping into a different world; one of hot, moist ecstasy but for the moment his mind raced back to the green benches. Morale across the 'Westminster village' was once more low as continuing revelations by a junior branch of the Royal family was only serving to aggravate a country already in turmoil. Indeed, shortcomings over the manner in which a widely respected national broadcasting organisation had dealt with another historic embarrassment concerning another 'Royal' was still rumbling on many months after the event. The Government accused of using the attack on this influential broadcasting institution as an excuse to curb its remit and by so doing, reduce its perceived left-wing bias. Only the 'Press' and the more excitable television studios seemed to be enjoying the current unease the Government and the Broadcaster were suffering. Once again media freedoms were an issue. The Press Office and carefully briefed Ministers were attempting to divert and blunt many sharp attacks and Government whips had hardly been subtle in encouraging all members of the Party to watch their words and be sure during a 'Division', to vote accordingly. Several Cabinet Ministers had walked out of radio and television interviews as the questioning had grown too persistent.

Mather, hoping for elevation to the Foreign Affairs Select Committee before the month was out had been keeping a very careful, low and very quiet profile. Well, at least he had been trying to do that! Certain events happening abroad were issues close to his heart and he had been finding it difficult not to air his thoughts but he was more than pleased that the Government seemed at long last to be switching more of its attention towards the Far East. He had not abandoned entirely his designs on a certain young woman who was deeply committed to a variety of causes including holding the British Government to account in its pledges to overseas aid. As even a very junior member of the Committee, he could ingratiate himself and hope to get into her good books as well as her knickers! Sefton was not totally unfeeling though towards the oppressed and downtrodden of the world but under normal circumstances would probably not have given most of them much more than a second thought. He did consider himself a patriot and the United Kingdom's welfare was a priority but the challenge of Sophie Fortune who had constantly badgered him with good causes since his being elected had encouraged him to think beyond the English Channel. They had attended the same university, Exeter but moved in different student circles during their three years in Devon, other than one hardly memorable encounter. Although he had often seen her at the forefront of many marches, 'sit-ins' and other protests during their time as undergraduates. She had also proved an eloquent speaker in numerous student political debates. Then their paths had certainly diverged. After graduating, Mather was commissioned and served for a short time in 4 'Rifles' and after a brief peace-keeping and training stint in Afghanistan, decided instead to pursue a career in politics. Unlike his brother who continues to serve in the Rifles. One of its battalions was formed from the original Rifle Brigade which has strong historical connections with the Fortunes and Mathers of Durford. Sefton's own family was solidly middle-class and Conservative so it was just a short step to the Commons. His father Gerald, a respected Winchester solicitor and past Chair of the local Conservative Association. His grandfather Ronald had fought in the same regiment, the Rifle Brigade, as one of Sophie's ancestors. Her older brother, Hamish was continuing the tradition and was soon to be appointed Colonel of a 'Rifles' Regiment. Her family, the Fortunes of Durford Hall owe their elevation to the high ranks of the landed gentry to Henry VIII and apart from a few setbacks, mostly the result of death duties, the estate is still a reasonable size. House and grounds now welcome the steady tread of the general public after the impressive iron gates a few years ago were thrown open to all and entrance-fee paying sundry.

Mather's current excursion he judged to be worth any risk to his hopes of promotion and once clear of Westminster Bridge there were fewer security cameras to track his progress. Whenever he had felt that primeval urge to visit the Mews he had also been particularly careful to ensure he was not being followed. Perhaps a guilty conscience breeds paranoia!

He now reflected that even many months after the Prime Minister had declared it was appropriate to shake free from the shackles of that final 'lockdown', a plethora of uncomfortable questions was still being levelled at a Government continuing to suffer from 'post-Brexit' stress, the fall-out from a variety of lobbying scandals including one involving a former prime minister and the impact of the Covid-19 pandemic as it had crashed and reverberated over an unsuspecting and unprepared world and whose effects would continue for the foreseeable future. Mather would not say it publically, not wishing to commit political suicide but like many other people, thought the Government had been slow to respond to those, admittedly unprecedented circumstances. An earlier first 'lockdown' would, he believed have saved lives. The results of the official enquiry during the Spring of the current year into the Government's handling of the Covid crisis were eagerly awaited in some but not all quarters. There had already been personal criticisms by a former close aide, of the way the Prime Minister and others had responded to the Covid outbreak, by their firstly underestimating its seriousness and then not dealing with it effectively. This could lead to further embarrassment and more questions being raised regarding lessons learned, forgotten or simply ignored after the pandemic simulation exercise, 'Exercise Cygnus' in October, 2016. This had uncovered the lack of a co-ordinated overall plan; what plans that were in place varied from region to region. 'Politics', unlike many workers had not been furloughed for the duration and the country still required governing and many hard decisions were and still have to be taken. Of course mistakes had and were continuing to be made but as parliamentary elections were not too far off, such fall-out had to be kept to a minimum and just how differently would or could Her Majesty's Opposition have handled the many crises? Badly, could be the inference if the Tory success in winning a Labour stronghold in a by-election and numerous council seats last year was any guide! Last year's good results some commentators believed only served to demonstrate that Labour was a spent force. Their traditional support in the mining and heavy industrial areas of the country no longer existed; the red wall had been demolished by the Tory-blue demolition ball. There had though been the odd blip even for this Government which had been assisted at the ballot box by many who believed the taming of Covid was down to one man alone rather than the collective response of dedicated NHS employees. One particular setback had occurred late last Spring; a really dark cloud had appeared in that clear Tory-blue electoral sky. In a by-election in an hitherto safe Conservative seat in Buckinghamshire, the Liberal-Democrats had pushed them into second place. Labour, coming a very poor fourth was left looking over the abyss into oblivion. There were for all, so many other more immediate problems though.

Many Scots were increasingly more vociferous (witness their performance in that May 2021 election), in their demands for independence though there had been earlier timely spats between senior Nationalists which could persuade Scotland in the long run to remain in the United Kingdom. There were also a few worrying rumbles from Wales and even from the Unionists of Northern Ireland there is continuing dissent as over five years of 'Brexit' has resulted in fragmentation among those, traditionally, 'more British than the British', Northern Irish Unionists. Mather would have to concede that dealings with Northern Ireland, especially over a sea border had bred suspicion of the British Establishment among even the most patriotic, pro-British in the six counties. It had certainly animated the American President in the Carbis Bay talks of last year. For the first time for many years Sefton reflected grimly, talk of one united Ireland is not idle, wishful thinking among a few fanatics. The continuing reports of plans to strengthen the Union by building a bridge or tunnel linking Scotland to Ireland is, he reflected misplaced. It may be a cliche but we must build bridges of trust to strengthen the call for a continuing United Kingdom before we do anything else. That should and must be the first consideration. Fortunately, if the decision over the bridge ends up taking as long as the one to move parliament to Richmond House, or to the Department of Health building in Whitehall, or to Birmingham or elsewhere when (and if) a Palace of Westminster total refurbishment is ever undertaken, let alone completed, then there would be no problem.

***

As he hurried eastward he realised the anticipation of pleasures to come was having a premature effect. He could feel the red sap rising in his veins and in an effort to control his libido turned his mind towards other matters before it was too late. Mather, was aware that the rampant member tenting his trousers could cause some distress to passers-by. They might misconstrue the situation and ultimately cause him embarrassment leading to a potential stain on his character. This as well as the one he felt spreading just below the waistband of his trousers, so he attempted some surreptitious mid-stride adjustments to his light grey suit trousers. The rain made him regret he had not bothered to take an umbrella earlier in the day and that emission of seminal fluid only added to his cursing his laziness in not bothering to collect his overcoat from its peg in the Commons.

He passed a parked, plain blue van as the front door of the Mews' house came into view and smiled to himself with some grim satisfaction; at least the country wasn't the only one emerging from the first year or so of the 2020s, untarnished. In Russia, Putin's main democratic tormentor, Alexei Novalny, has created a legacy of criticism and dissent is nationwide. China's human rights record is appalling particularly in relation to Hong Kong and in its policy of 're-educating' its Uighur minority whose women continue to be abused in the basest of ways. In Myanmar, Aung San Suu Kyi, though having lost her political way over her failure to help the Moslem minority, the Rohingya is still at odds with the heavy-handed Army junta currently oppressing the country. In the Middle East, millions of Yemenis still live and die in dire conditions after years of war with Saudi Arabia and will there ever be a peaceful solution to the hostility, fear and suspicion that divides the Palestinians and Israelis? Biden's call that both sides need an independent homeland not just Israel, may be the obvious solution. Such an obvious solution seems unlikely all the time many other states refuse to recognise Israel and the latter is more than wary of the establishment of a sovereign Palestinian State. Then there is the ongoing issue of interference by 'those who would do us harm' at the very core of our democracy. GCHQ had confirmed what many parliamentarians had long suspected, that certain countries were accessing a range of cyber secrets.

But if Sefton needed further distraction to add to any conscientious parliamentarian's worries, there was also the issue of 'global warming' which threatened humanity's progress in the 21st Century. This, even more than the possibility of 'nuclear global warring' which had menaced mankind over much of the second half of the 20th! He supported moves by the Government with their policy of electric-powered cars and the phasing out of petrol and diesel vehicles and air travel was being scrutinised too! Vehicle manufacturers had responded positively to the challenge. Mather did wonder how necessary progress can be achieved in time though many assurances had been given at last November's, Glasgow-based U.N. Climate Change Conference.

There are also those who believe additional road building must be abandoned in favour of a cheap fares', rail and bus co-ordinated network. If so quite how would they persuade owners to give up their petrol and diesel guzzling vehicles and take the bus instead! Mather would concede that Britain and other Western countries had enjoyed tremendous wealth from industrial advances. Now poorer countries wanted the opportunity to develop and achieve similar wealth. Could that be managed without them following a similar path? Britain had built its power from coal; this country with others, had also exploited oil. Now, in hindsight the internal combustion engine had proved to be a very mixed blessing. Look at what the exploitation of these resources had done to the planet. Whose rubbish polluted the oceans, whose demand for fast foods encouraged Brazilians to fell their forests?

"I've been watching Sophie Fortune campaigning on too many green issues," he sighed but deep down he realised attitudes must soon change not only in Britain where the challenge he believed had been quite positively taken up but everywhere else as well, or it could be too late!

***

The previous year, 2021 had dawned cold, wet and miserable yet even then amongst all the negativity of lockdown and other burning issues, Sefton had felt a definite twinge of optimism. He was, after all more of a 'glass half full' kind of guy. Especially as there was now a chance for international normality after Trump's assault on democracy. Although the former President has since become the focus for a right-wing backlash that had begun with the invasion of the White House on 6th January of that same year by Trump supporters. His successor, the 46th President at the G7 summit last year in Cornwall declared himself determined to return the country to its former place internationally and restore some backbone to NATO. In the week of the summit the President had warned the Russian leader that Russian expansionism would not be tolerated. The President hoped too that the United States and the United Kingdom could in the very near future return to a 21st Century form of that special relationship. The war years had created the need for an Atlantic Charter to protect democracy; the world now faces even greater challenges! His withdrawal of troops from Afghanistan and ultimately the abandonment of that country to the Taliban has caused many people though, including Sefton to wonder at the President's grasp of foreign policy. What about the many sacrifices by British and other troops to bolster the Afghan people; have these just been thrown away? As for the longer term effects of this decision, only time will tell but early indications from Kabul are that it is not boding well for the Afghan people, not only the hundreds who worked as guides and translators but especially the women whose hard-won freedoms are steadily being repressed! Critics of the new President, anxious to show that his desire to re-embrace old allies was misplaced, did so by suggesting Europe had cosied up all too readily to Russia and China when the United States under Trump had embraced a version of the Monroe Doctrine. Even when the new presidential term had only been a few weeks old there had already been growing concerns that the country would not only be swamped by illegal immigrants on its southern borders but even worse be led into new conflicts. This while other NATO members continued to avoid paying their share towards protecting freedom! Mather, concerned that Britain's forces were seriously under strength hoped that Britain could now invest in the kind of weaponry appropriate to the new technological age. He enthusiastically welcomed Britain's old, special ally back into America's role as leader of the free world. He still had reservations. Chinese expansionism in the East including its likely seizure of Taiwan by force was a topic that had exercised the minds of the attendees at last year's G7 summit. The increasing presence of Russian aircraft close to British airspace and their ships testing British responses in the North Sea were also grave causes for concern especially in the light of that recent report which suggested British soldiers with their out-dated equipment would be no match for their likely enemy, the Russians! The Prime Minister had encouragingly announced a more robust response to events across the world and a military commitment to back it up! Hardly a day passes across the House without there being calls to build even more ships and manufacture equipment for the hitherto neglected British Army. That is, if any home-based steelworks remain in production! The fate of the home steel industry was one of the issues that cropped up with some regularity and one that was of interest to Sefton. During the course of the previous year, short term solutions had been rolled out but the Government flinched at talk of what in many people's view would be the answer at least in the medium term, namely total nationalisation! The future of Britain's steel industry affected jobs but there was also the strategic question that had to be faced, sooner rather than later. If the country was to compete globally just where would the materials for expansion come from? Who would provide the steel for the ships, aircraft and military equipment generally. The wedging of a ship early last year in the Suez Canal caused embarrassment and the loss of billions in trade and the consequential requirement for ships supplying every country north of Egypt to take the long route to Europe, via the Cape of Good Hope. In times of crisis, having to import so much of our basic materials could take up valuable time should any country or Anglophobe wish us ill and if China was indeed a threat we could hardly rely on them for our steel! Mather had raised a question concerning the industry during Ministerial questions; only to be assured that the whole future of the steel industry was under constant review.

***

He winced as the bang of a car door slamming shut somewhere behind him caught him by surprise. This at the same time as he had turned his thinking back to the parlous state of the country's economy lately floored to a level matched previously only by costs incurred by fighting two world wars. Though the Bank of England's prediction of a rapid growth in the economy was almost being achieved as people rushed out to spend their Covid-induced savings and businesses began to feel confident enough to resume investing. That 10% shrinkage caused by the Pandemic had almost been recovered. There still remains however, niggling fears that this growth will only prove to be temporary. That it would all come crashing down. There was, consequently, considerable unease on his side of the Chamber over the long-term repercussions of Covid. Much money had been thrown at the problem which, it had to be admitted, had not always hit the intended target. Spending on such a grand scale and on social areas was very much against traditional Party orthodoxy. Many of his fellow Conservatives continue to blanch at this level of State interference. One such orthodoxy heretic in April, 2020, in a bid to divert the blame if the campaign to defeat the coronavirus failed, had suggested the Government should approach the other parties and form a National Unity Government. This received short shrift from the man who had coveted that 10, Downing Street address for many years and once his feet were firmly under the Cabinet Room conference table had no intention of sharing the prime role with others. The timing though was unfortunate for as the Prime Minister in the early months of 2020 prepared to lead Britain into the sunny uplands promised by the pro-Brexiters, that very unwelcome import from China arrived and changed not only Britain's but the world's plans. As for the pandemic itself, there were many who claimed China was responsible for the outbreak; its origin more laboratory leak than natural! The British Government though was forced to spend those hundreds of billions to support the National Health Service and the country's workforce. Shops, offices, businesses large and small including the hospitality, entertainment, retail and aircraft industries were 'locked-down' and consequently the economy's return to its pre-Covid level will if it is possible to achieve, take time. The Prime Minister, undaunted and with his usual energy and enthusiasm is taking every opportunity to boost morale. The Chancellor's recent budgets are also going a considerable way to restoring some confidence. People have been returning to work but perhaps inevitably, there are still too many shops and offices that remain in darkness. Uncertainty still stalks the country and people who had adopted working from home leaving many of those office blocks under-used, continue to do so. One statistic suggested that at least one million former office-workers would become permanently home-based. This has all created a knock-on effect. Many of the stalls, coffee shops and cafes servicing the pre-Covid work-force with sandwiches, cakes and coffee have not recovered. A few prophetic individuals had suggested the on-line revolution in consumerism that had been slowly impacting from the 1980s would ultimately destroy the traditional shopping centre and high street anyway but this downward spiral was then accelerated by the pandemic.

***

These and other weighty thoughts were put to one side as he reached number 21, Victoria Mews. He looked squarely at the camera eye above the door before turning his own key in the lock and entering. Serena greeted him in her usual manner by kissing him full on the lips and placing her right hand on the bulge that had returned to his nether regions. The evening then proceeded along a familiar path. As Mather padded dutifully after her, he stopped at the hall table, where two or three small, carefully sealed cardboard, clearly addressed packages lay, no doubt awaiting posting. One of the names and addresses on one of the packets, 'someone' in television he recognised. Seeing his interest, she informed him they were the basis of a new but potentially very lucrative business.

Serena led the way to her bedroom where two champagne glasses, filled seconds after she had seen him on the front door's camera monitor, stood chilled and waiting on a bedside table. The room was tastefully furnished, the lighting subdued and the bed, its soft pink duvet thrown back, invitingly! They sipped their drinks and Mather quickly undressed, the tip of his hot, rampant cock dribbling as it sprang out almost at right angles to his groin as he released it from the confinement of his boxers. He gently unzipped Serena's dress and it fell to the floor. He deftly removed her bra and cupped his hands beneath her firm but not over large breasts before squeezing them gently and rolling her hardening nipples between his practised fingers. Then his right hand reached down to her thighs which parted and within seconds he was stroking the plain cotton gusset of her dark blue knickers; then two fingers were inside the material and teasing her from clitoris to vagina before rolling those digits their full length inside her in search of a certain spot. He pulled her, his two fingers still in situ towards the bed and positioned himself comfortably before moving his hand and those thoroughly soaked fingers to Serena's bottom. Then, a hand on either side of her hips, he lifted her up towards his face and for a moment or two kissed her mouth then nipples before tilting and sliding her up his chest. Her legs were either side of his shoulders as he reached down and pulled the gusset to one side again and then his fingers were probing around her clitoris before he gently licked, sucked and kissed that too. He then tenderly eased her back down until she was lying full length on him. Fleetingly, a thought crossed Serena's mind and she smiled to herself. In her pursuit as a modern forward-thinking woman for equality in all things she had interpreted the expression, 'putting a woman on top' quite literally in this and her other very exclusive couplings. She bent her legs at the knee as a signal for Mather to remove her knickers and that achieved, he began again to explore her intimate places with his hands before guiding her right hand to his throbbing length of manhood that she could feel hard, warm and wet stretching up from her finely groomed pubic hair to her navel. Teasing him she moved its tip around her swollen inner labia and almost breathlessly, he urged her to take the plunge. At last, she guided it in and began slowly and rhythmically to engulf him completely. Then she increased the pace and began to roll from side to side as well as thrusting up and down. Sefton Mather was not entirely passive at this stage as this quite beautiful young woman pleasured both of them. Hands ran across her spine and down to the backs of her thighs, then his right hand was eased underneath her and carefully down to find and stimulate her hooded lady as she raised her body to allow him easier access. Somewhere, deep inside she gave thanks for those hours spent in the gym and for the attentions of her personal trainer. Then hands found her breasts once again just as her whole body began to tremble in an ecstasy of pleasure as she anticipated and waited to feel his hot semen splashing into her. Mather, who no doubt was also grateful that he too kept himself in good shape including regular sessions on a rowing machine that provided an all-over workout, was also approaching that exquisite moment when all the cares of the world would stream from him as he ejaculated over four millilitres of sticky, creamy-coloured liquid into that special receptacle.

One evening with little better to do and curious he had researched on the internet just how much semen was involved in the sexual act. The relatively small amount surprised him and he recalled those many times when after an ejaculation in the privacy of his own room, he had examined the pool of thick liquid glistening in a tissue, the result of flicking through his comprehensive selection of adult magazines or at the hand of an obliging female friend. He had been convinced the volume in his own case would be measured by the cupful rather than one to two teaspoons! Sefton's teaspoonfuls now splashed high inside her but then the explosive release was over. That primitive act, the exchange of bodily fluids, the intimate touching, the extreme feeling of pleasure that had left their skin tingling was at last slowly ebbing away. Both lay exhausted on the bed ; Sefton on his back and Selena now on her left side, her head on his chest with her lips just brushing his right nipple. She let her right hand stray to his scrotum where she gently, playfully, began stroking his balls. He half-turned towards her, lifted his left arm and let his fingers trace the carefully trimmed rectangle of dark hair, some three centimetres wide and five centimetres or so long whose lower end pointed the way to her genitalia. It was wet with a few drops of his semen mixed with her own secretions. Just as she lifted her right leg a fraction to allow him access, he licked his forefinger and returning his hand down that same furry path toyed once again with her own little member before reaching a very wet, tunnel entrance. He had risen to the occasion more than once a few times before with her but as this was how they generally wound down from their horizontal jogging, he was not dismayed that this particular encounter was almost over. Those last minutes though had been gentle, sensual and demonstrated they were aware of and responded to each other's needs.

He also remembered that he must leave by nine-thirty pm as he had arranged to meet a member of the Foreign Affairs Select Committee in a Soho restaurant at ten. Sefton also had a question on the Order Paper in tomorrow's Prime Minister's Questions as part of his campaign to make a good impression where it mattered. So when he had emerged from the shuffle of questions to head the pack, he intended his supplementary question would be to ask the Prime

Minister what Britain's response would be should the Chinese invade Taiwan. There had been barely a few opportunities for him to shine, following the customary uncontroversial tone of the maiden speech he had made many months ago. He was interested in China Seas politics as one of his cousins, a journalist had been kicked out of Hong Kong, declared, 'undesirable'. Britain's need to expand in Asia's markets and the belligerence currently exhibited by the so-called People's Republic of China was therefore of great interest. He had first become aware of Chinese influence in the region ever since reading the diary of a great uncle who had fought in Korea to save the South from the Chinese backed aggressive North. South Korea remains free though they maintain an uncomfortable, almost surreal but potentially deadly relationship with their racial kin to the north. Then he read Heinrich Harrer's book about Tibet and after discovering the cruel treatment of that country by the Chinese decided that China's prime aim was to dominate the whole region. This would threaten not only British interests there but potentially create another 'Cold War' or even a very hot one!

After nearly ten minutes of giving their bodies time to recover, Serena playfully ran her hand up his now flaccid and very wrinkly member. Then she moved across to kiss Sefton and rolled to her right and moved off the bed. Sefton looked across at her taking in the sight of her beautiful, well-formed slightly oval buttocks as she reached the end of the bed and headed for the shower room. Mather swung his legs off the bed and with his right foot deftly lifted her recently discarded very flimsy, dark blue knickers from the floor. Then, holding them inside out and with their sticky, creamy, stained gusset aimed in Serena's direction, he waved them at her. Grinning, but with a sudden thought occurring to him, he asked if this garment too would be in tomorrow's post. She looked at Sefton with a withering stare and dismissed his remark by declaring that only an exclusive few were ever allowed to inhale or lap up her cream. He dropped them into her hand. She bent forward to catch them and very gently the long fingers of both hands were soon pulling the gusset apart. Only slowly, reluctantly did it yield its moist, sticky secrets. Then she lobbed them into his face. Soon his nose and mouth were engulfed in the warm, musky, almost indefinable but intimate feminine smell mixed with the scent of that expensive French perfume that Serena earlier had lightly sprayed strategically over the more intimate and certainly more tantalising parts of her body.

"If you're desperate for them as a reminder of me they can be yours for a price and even a discount. I'll pack them up and post them to you," she said, giggling.

"Ah, so that's it. I guessed as much and that's what's in those little boxes downstairs," he declared, a note of satisfaction in his voice and confirming what he had deduced earlier.

"Yes," she replied amiably, "merely supplying a service. In part thanks to Royal Mail and their 'Click and Drop' service, a boon for the entrepreneur's expanding business."

"How does it work?" he enquired.

"It's all very simple. I was idling through the internet one day and came across a tabloid headline declaring that housewives unable to make ends meet were advertising their soiled underwear for money in order to put food on the table. Intrigued, I looked a little further and happened upon this page of companies offering used women's kit. I sent for a few items just to see exactly what was on offer. Then with Jemima, you've met her," she said, "I set up my own company, 'Gemma's Gems' after we had recruited about forty women. Now that Jemima is doing less escort work especially after several bad experiences she is running it day to day. During those first few weeks we began to discover just what our clients wanted and widened the shape, size, age and ethnic range of our donors."

Sefton's eyebrows raised in some incredulity though he had seen enough adult magazines to know that almost anything could be advertised for there was a big market to satisfy out there. It was likely that thanks to Covid those who ordinarily would have sought satisfaction by visiting prostitutes had turned to the many varied websites offering an alternative range of services.

"By the very nature of the goods supplied there are no returns," she volunteered, "which would be difficult anyway as we only include the recipient's address. I suppose if anyone could be bothered they could find us via Companies House. Tracing our donors though would be more difficult as any pictures sent are more often than not taken from the shoulders down. In exchange for their promise to maintain the privacy of our clients we in turn guarantee anonymity for our donors."

"So there are no complaints?" he asked

"Just a few," she admitted. "The last one several months ago involved one of our packets being opened and some photographs being removed and the garment being taken out and put back before the container was resealed. In that particular case, very badly."

"Bit of a surprise then down at the mail depot when someone pulled out a pair of smelly drawers, Serena," he asked, picturing the scene in a busy sorting office.

"Yes, I imagine so but worryingly, if someone wanted to cause our client mischief," she replied. "Anyway, in order to placate the customer, we sent, by way of a different carrier, some replacements and as he has re-ordered on various occasions since, then we assume all is well. Perhaps I should have also given scented candles a whirl too."

"Candles?" Sefton asked. "I thought the market's saturated enough with those damn things already. Can't move at home without choking on the smell of 'em. I suppose mother thinks they disguise doggy smells after the Labradors have rolled in fox shit or splashed in puddles."

"Didn't you hear about," continued Serena, "an American actor, a real 'A-lister' and her company who were attempting to expand the range of candles their business offered. When they tried one particular range of scents and smells, she remarked that particular product smelled just like her vagina. So that's how they marketed the new range. Sold better than hot cakes."

A bemused Sefton innocently asked why Serena hadn't tried something similar.

"No, thankyou. As you should know by now, some things even I don't want to share," she said.

In her mind's eye however, she could see such a product. Candle wax, a deep red in colour and available in a range of jar sizes. Once lit, any room would be flooded in that deep musky scent that was exclusive to her; more specifically her vagina. She pictured a colourful, enticing label on each jar that read, 'Serena's Secret Sex'. Underneath instructions, 'light the candle, lay back, relax and breathe in my innermost secrets, Love, Serena'. What man or woman could resist? Then savouring the image, she burst out laughing.

Sefton countered with:

"I'm surprised no one's tried to market, 'semen scent'. Or have they?" he enquired, not entirely joking.

"Not that I know about," Serena replied still finding the whole sexy candles concept amusing. "But Seffy, if your political career goes tits-up then 'Sefton's Semen Specials' could make your fortune. On second thoughts, better make that 'Sefton's Spermy Specials' in case punters think you've misspelled the word and you're offering some sort of deal with sailors down in Portsmouth. Either way though could be your entry to fame and fortune. Perhaps a friend of mind with contacts in television and marketing could fix you up with an appearance on 'Dragon's Den'."

"Might be worth it just to see the look on my mother's face if I set up a few in Mather's Mansions back in Durford."

They both laughed at the sheer absurdity of it all.

"Mind you," Sefton added, "could be just the thing for the independent woman after a stressful day. Light the 'semen-special', lay back and switch on the vibrator and let those masculine smells overwhelm the senses."

Remembering he needed to leave earlier than usual she left him still holding her underwear and quickly showered and after washing away all outward signs of their coupling, piled her hair high under a towel, quickly dried the rest of her very toned body, pulled a long dressing gown on, slipped her feet into soft house shoes and moved to the kitchen where she prepared coffee for herself and the soon to depart Mather. She intended taking a more leisurely bath or shower, after a reviving bowl of cornflakes. He, in the meantime too had quickly washed away the more obvious physical signs and smells of their sexual encounter, dried himself and was soon padding back to the bedroom. He stood looking at himself in the wall-mounted, full length mirror on the wall at the end of the bed. He looked up and to to his left where there was another wall-mounted mirror. Serena had dismissed it when many months before he had noticed it saying she used it to do her hair. But this one, unknown to him, differed from the first, as it was a two-way mirror. Serena had installed it to record the activities of that exclusive circle of sometime lovers. Not necessarily with any intention of blackmailing them but for her own protection. He returned to gaze at himself once again and lifted his now very flaccid member but could not resist saying out loud:

"Who's a lucky boy then?" before returning it after its earlier, vigorous contribution, to the confines of his boxer shorts.

Sefton continued to put the rest of his clothes back on, pausing only to pick up the contentious pair of knickers that he had eventually left on the edge of the bed. Grinning to himself, he folded them neatly and slipped them inside his jacket pocket. If all else failed in moments without female company over the next few days, then perhaps they might offer some alternative comfort.

Then after finishing his dressing, and a quick brush of his hair with one of Serena's brushes, joined her in the kitchen, drank his coffee, kissed her lightly on the cheek and was off. First to Waterloo to take the Tube to Oxford Circus and then on to Soho to meet Marcus Browne at 'Gianna's' an Italian restaurant where he is a frequent diner.

Chapter Two

Serena MacDonald, as she had lain by Mather's side resting from their earlier exertions had been mulling over all that had happened during the last decade. Days after completing her 'A'-levels she had returned home from visiting an elderly relative with her mother Rachel, who had gone on by herself to Oxford Street to shop. Serena had expected to find her father, Antony alone in the house and in what originally had been a billiards room but which he had converted to a multi-gym. At one end there was a mat and a net for him to practise his golf swing. For, unlike his older brother Daniel, he had not followed their father into the City but playing off 'scratch' by the age of fifteen and winning amateur competitions and filling a sideboard with cups, salvers and medals, he soon turned professional. He then spends most of each year travelling the world on the professional golf circuit still making a very comfortable living winning less prestigious events but also finishing in a respectable position on the leader board in the 'Majors'. Serena did find him in the old billiards room but naked and astride Teresa, one of her mother's friends. There followed a succession of apologies, red faces and months of argument and recrimination and whispers of domestic abuse of her mother suffering at the hands of her father. It seems he was less than understanding as his wife suffered the discomfort, indignity, anguish and unfairness that was the menopause. Eventually her parents did divorce after months of acrimony but with her mother retaining the family home.

In the meantime Serena had gone to university and would achieve a first class honours degree in modern languages. Towards the end of the evening of her final term while attending the summer ball, Serena squabbled with her boyfriend, Callum Winters and left the venue just before the end. As she walked away, a little unsteadily on very high heels, she was confronted by a familiar figure; one of her tutors. He pushed both his hands on her breasts, squeezed them roughly before wrestling her towards some bushes. The thin straps of her long, green dress, chosen to offset her rich, waist length, chestnut-tinted hair, were pulled down and before long both breasts exposed. He forced her to the ground, her head striking a paving stone. As she struggled to remain conscious she felt one of Doctor Webster's hands at her throat, while the other attempted to pull back the bottom half of the dress. This for him, was made easier as the dress had a fashionable slit rising high up on the left thigh. As his full weight fell upon her he attempted to kiss her and the memory of that whisky-fuelled breath would stay with Serena for a long time. One of his hands left her throat as she gagged and retched as he attempted to prise open her thighs and rip off her underwear. Frightened for her life she raised her hands but as she prepared a last desperate attempt to scratch his face, the sound of laughter and giggling some metres away caused her assailant to pull himself off her and run. The voices melted into the darkness as she forced herself up and into a sitting position. For a full five minutes she sobbed uncontrollably then thought what might have happened had it not been for that vocal but unseen interruption. She rose unsteadily to her feet, repaired the straps of her dress as best she could and began to move unsteadily off in the general direction of her digs. She passed under a lamp standard and in the light saw and touched small flecks of an off-white sticky substance. Realising that she had been only seconds away from being raped and feeling utterly desolated and violated, Serena began to sob once more. As she reached the end of the street where she had been living during her final year, she tripped as the heel of her left shoe broke off. She staggered forward. Then an arm reached comfortingly around her shoulders and a soft, female voice spoke soothingly to her.

***

Sophie Fortune had booked a taxi to collect her from the Ball. As the car made its way towards Ide, the village where Sophie lived during term-time, only minutes after setting off home, she had glanced out into the night and noticed a figure lurching along; possibly drunk but certainly in distress and in need of help. Now, as they shared the backseat of the taxi, Sophie managed to persuade Serena that she must go straight to hospital to check for injuries. There was clearly a head wound for where she had fallen, the skin looked angry and bloody. She must also report the crime. Serena recognised her 'Good Samaritan'. She had attended debates chaired by Sophie and knew her to be a great supporter of many causes including that of the rights of women. Sophie's soothing tone and calming presence began to allay those earlier fears. Although she had not been penetrated, and that had been down to chance, Serena realised that in the interests of women everywhere, her male abuser must be brought to account. The taxi-driver was instructed to drive to the nearest hospital, the Royal Devon and Exeter at Wonford and wait for further directions on arrival. Sophie accompanied Serena to the reception desk and they were soon ushered into a cubicle where she was carefully examined. Photographs were soon taken of the bruises to her forehead, neck, shoulders and inner thighs. The police in the form of two female officers arrived shortly after Sophie's emergency call and documented Serena's story. The latter's clothes were placed carefully into an evidence bag for forensic analysis and Serena persuaded to remain overnight to recover from her ordeal. Sophie, before leaving for Ide promised she would leave a note in the letter-box of Serena's digs for the others who shared the house so they could bring a change of clothes to the hospital. As a precaution, Sophie asked for Serena's phone-number and said she would phone the house in the morning in case her scribbled note was missed. An exhausted Serena after thanking Sophie for her help sunk back on the pillow and before her saviour reached the door, she was sound asleep. Sophie looked back as she reached the door at another victim of man's aggression.

***

Serena frowned as she thought back on the events that followed the attempted rape of her. Two of the three detectives who interviewed her subsequently were mostly very supportive and had encouraged her to proceed with the case. The exception was a male sergeant whose almost permanent expression exuded disbelief. The alleged, attempted rapist had been interviewed and although he admitted he had met her where the incident had taken place, maintained that Serena had willingly kissed him. He had gone on to say that she had placed one of his hands on her breast and seemed ready to have sex. It was then, he asserted, that she had tripped and fallen backwards. He agreed that he should not have just run off at that point but had not thought her badly injured, just drunk. Hearing voices and not wishing to be found in a compromising situation he felt it best to go. Serena was assured by the female detectives that the photographs and the forensics would tell a different story in court. Nothing short of the court case being over and Webster beginning a prison sentence would go anyway to removing that nervous, depressed feeling that immediately after the assault had begun to envelop her. She couldn't eat and was losing weight, she slept barely a few hours each night and was frightened to go anywhere alone or after dark. When one of the detectives contacted her to inform her of a new development, Serena involuntarily as a result of feeling in despair, poured out her heart. Detective Constable Andrews concerned for Serena's well-being, especially in the light of the regressive news she was about to impart, ensured that a car was sent to bring her to the police station in an effort to reduce her present stress, as well as the increased level she was about to suffer! The police officer who met her at the door was just about to tell her about this 'development' when her mobile sounded and she motioned Serena into a nearby interview room promising to return shortly. Detective Constable Sheila Andrews in her rush to answer the phone left the door ajar and soon Serena was hearing two voices.

"Don't worry, Jeremy, there'll be no case to answer now. There was the possibility of contamination and anyway, the evidence bag with the dress and her flimsies has gone walkabout. Even if the pictures turn up, what will they show. Serena's tits out to here and if ever a dress had the welcome mat out with a slit up the side inviting you to stroke pussy then I don't what does."

Serena sat rooted to the chair and her blood ran cold as realisation of the significance of the overheard conversation dawned on her.

She remembered her response as Andrews returned to the room and barely had the detective said:

"Now where were we?"

When she rounded on her, hysterically shouting and sobbing:

"It's not going to happen is it? You've lost the evidence. That's why I was brought here today. To tell me it's gone. That creep is going to get away with it."

Serena remembered too getting up and storming out of the station then arriving back at her digs shaking with anger and frustration. The following day she returned to the family home in Hampstead but did not come back, weeks later to Exeter for the awards ceremony in the Great Hall. Instead, by this time she was turning her attention to ways of ensuring that such a degrading act would never be perpetrated against her ever again. She then concluded that as the distaff side of humanity had since time immemorial been screwed in every sense, then it was high time women fought back and were recompensed for all the shame and degradation heaped upon them and for those opportunities not denied to the male of the species. As a teenager having suffered like so many of her sex, the crude, unimaginative and clumsy gropings of young men and witnessed her father, 'in flagrante delicto' she decided to exploit the male's apparent inability to control the contents of his underpants.

Just to keep herself financially independent of her mother and to maintain her adulterous father at arm's length, she took a succession of temporary jobs including stints at major Oxford Street stores including Selfridges. She did meet her father briefly, awkwardly at her brother Jerome's wedding to Brooke Kinnear four years after that unfortunate encounter in the multi-gym. She was also pleased to be Auntie Serena to their twins. Both parents claimed the arrival of Chiara and Cosima exactly nine months on from their honeymoon was down to those warm, sensuous, Chianti-fuelled Florentine nights. To augment her income Serena also accepted commissions to translate books and documents and was tempted to accept an appointment in Brussels, working for the European Commission. She had during her time at university spent many happy months between Paris and Berlin fine-tuning her French and German. Then, left property by Aunt Ursula who had doted on her, she returned to an earlier plan. It took a few years for Serena to make the right contacts and build up the appropriate businesses. But within five years she was achieving her twin ambitions of asserting her equal place in society and taking control in the bedroom. By satisfying those quirks and foibles that men seemed unable to resist but on her terms, she regained much of the confidence that had poured out of her during that attempted rape. She had also come to the conclusion that as she was being used as a whore, albeit a very expensive one then she might just as well take the money as she was behaving like one. After all, she reflected, men were like very naughty, curious, guilty children. They are a confused species, weak, needy, full of contradictions but with an insatiable drive to be in control and maintain their societal monopoly on power. The 'caveman effect', she called it. Now she stood shoulder to shoulder with them as women took to the streets to protest about the way society categorised and compartmentalised them. She had even been arrested and brutally handcuffed during a silent vigil on Clapham Common over the murder of yet another woman. The Establishment claim that the vigil breached 'lock-down' rules still in force in March, 2021, which in technical terms it did, cut very little ice among those who saw the actions of the police as yet more evidence of the violence suffered by women.

All her enterprises by now, which included a very exclusive escort agency, were proving to be extremely lucrative. In the first few years she had acted herself as an escort to extremely wealthy business men, oil and internet magnates, Arabs, politicians and senior police officers and judges. That's when she had come across Sefton Mather again, after first noticing him at Exeter. To protect herself henceforth, she decided to employ a private detective to vet each client and to build a dossier on each of them, just in case! At intervals, she asked Jemima to take such files and lodge them with her mother's solicitors,

Morehouse, Greaves and Arnold, in Holborn as her business partner made her way home to Kentish Town. Sometimes the role of 'escort' merely required a companion for the evening but often it ended up in the bedroom. Clients though were left in no doubt as to what was acceptable. Serena had said when taking the bookings that if they wanted more or were into acts that required their partner to be overly submissive or indulge in violence then there were plenty of tarts and agencies out there willing to oblige. Now she employed others to offer similar, highly expensive companionship that she herself had once regularly provided. The Covid pandemic had reduced turnover as a result of social distancing but not stopped it completely.

Two other businesses not requiring face to face contact helped fill the financial hole left by the coronavirus. One was via the telephone as men phoned special numbers luridly advertised mainly in male, 'top shelf' magazines. These sex lines, enabled them, a non-contact outlet through which to fulfil their desires. Serena employed over thirty women of varying ages to listen to men talking out these fantasies. Alternatively, it was possible for men to listen as women on the other end of the line engaged or pretended to engage in activities guaranteed to arouse the caller. The phone business was successful but the venture that was really expanding was the one Sefton Mather had seen an example of downstairs. By contacting the web-site, a client could order a selection of underwear worn for varying lengths of time and soiled in particular ways. Serena had though, drawn a line underneath the offering of some of the more bizarre requirements some men desired that she had seen on other sites during her feasibility study. Some of these she felt were quite repugnant and not only demeaned the women willing to provide anything but more than demeaned those who received them. Some bodily functions exclusive to the female really were private! Gemma's Gems arranged for each donor to be kept regularly supplied if they wished to subscribe, through direct debit each month. Or, just pay for a single order to supply the appropriate garment or garments and/or other sundry items including photographs of the item being worn and other poses, if required. It was then sealed in a plastic bag to be posted in a small box or bubble wrap envelope using a label with the client's address. On receipt he could carry out whatever fantasies he liked in the privacy of his own home, while Serena pocketed 20% of the invoice once expenses had been paid leaving Jemima who ran the business, to share the balance with the woman who had fulfilled the order. Gemma's Gems' price-list ranges from a modest fifteen pounds to over one hundred pounds. Some men took it to the next stage, the 'Gemclub' where for an additional fee they could contact a particular donor for 'online chat' but NOT for meeting in person! Serena did not want to risk prosecution for living off immoral earning as her previous employers had done.

***

Serena allowed the water to flow gently over her body ensuring that all the smells and the sticky bodily fluids left behind after her time with Sefton were completely washed away. As she stood there she thought back over the events of the previous seven or eight years. She had spent the first couple of them employed as an escort. Providing men and on several occasions women willing to pay a large sum for the company of a beautiful and articulate dinner companion. Or even a larger sum if they wanted to take that same woman on and into the bedroom for some horizontal companionship. Those years and the men she 'escorted' provided Serena with very useful contacts and when some two years after her first engagement she set up her own escort agency she carried with her some influential people. Now she would only allow a penis inside her when it suited her; now she felt in full control. She recalled the favourite quote of a much liked and respected 'A'-level teacher, George Samuels. Barely a day would pass without him repeating Ludwig Wittgenstein's, 'The world of the happy is quite different from that of the unhappy'. As she stepped out from the shower she certainly felt happy in her world.

***

Serena who had first met Alysha at a mutual friend's party ran into her again in the West End a few months before the onset of the Covid-19 pandemic. Feeling very comfortable in each other's company with that special frisson that only women seem to possess, they soon became firm friends. Thereafter they met quite regularly for coffee and occasionally dined together in some of the more fashionable Soho restaurants. The coronavirus pandemic struck and it became obvious to Alysha that she would no longer be able to afford to pay the high costs of her studio flat near Kennington Oval. An address which pleased her father who had played cricket for the West Indies against England and for Essex against Surrey at the Oval Cricket Ground. He would have preferred her to have remained living with family and commute but time, costs and inconvenience ruled that out. When work colleagues had recommended she follow up the chance of a flat she had been very pleased to sign the lease of that small but well appointed studio apartment; although until she had begun to ascend the promotion ladder, those early days in the flat necessitated thrift.

***

It was around seven o'clock one evening towards the end of May when they met again. Lockdown had affected everyone in so many ways. Alysha had phoned and although attempting to remain calm was unable to prevent that giveaway tremor in her voice. Sensing a problem Serena asked if they should meet at once:

"Shall I come to you, Darling?" Serena asked.

"No, there's no need to drag you across London. I'll come to you. It's a lovely evening. Let's meet at Bankside, by Southwark Bridge near the Globe Theatre at 8pm."

Serena readily agreed, then slipped into hoodie, jogging pants and trainers but to pass some time as she lived not far from their rendezvous, filled the dishwasher.

She arrived to find her friend distraught and looking wistfully across the Thames in the direction of St Paul's Cathedral. Much against those coronavirus rules current at that time, they embraced before Alysha, in response to Serena's concerned but gentle questioning admitted that she was no longer employed. Consequently, as she would no longer be receiving what had been a very good salary plus the many fringe benefits that went with the role of Personal Assistant to the Special Events Senior Co-ordinator, she would soon be homeless.

"What shall I do? I don't really want to go back to Essex much as I love my parents. I feel I belong here!"

"No problem," her friend exclaimed. "It's obvious. Why don't you move in with me, at least until things get back to normal. We can be part of the same bubble. I have a spare room and I'm sure we can work things out."

Serena added this as an afterthought because it suddenly occurred to her that those of her other activities might alarm Alysha, especially if a naked QC waddled past her or found her sitting on the lavatory when he needed a pee. Or would a lock on the door help? Then there was Sefton, a much more regular guest. Yes, social distancing rules were being bent but Serena was a social not to mention sexual animal.

Before the week was out, Alysha had moved in and halfway through the following week was sharing Serena's bed. Serena enjoyed sexual relations with men because it empowered her as she ensured she was in control of proceedings. She also savoured it as there was not much that really compared with fifteen and preferably many more centimetres of rampant flesh and blood thrusting away inside her. As Alysha cuddled her though, she felt really contented. If she had to choose a man it would almost certainly be Sefton for he knew just how to please her. She had once remarked that for a man he possessed quite a beautiful body. Muscular but not grotesque like some body builders and quite the firmest buttocks she had ever seen (or felt). He had challenged her when she had said it:

"Isn't that sexist?" he had remarked but only in jest.

"Now you know how it feels to be a member of the underdogs of the world, women," she had laughed.

Yes, Sefton would be her choice but with Alysha she felt contented and secure in the knowledge that she did not have to compete to prove herself. The two of them came to the bed as equals.

Soon after moving in and to augment her greatly reduced income Alysha became one of Gemma's Gems donors. Indeed, one of the boxes Mather had seen that Tuesday evening was one of Alysha's contribution towards satisfying one male's fantasies. Another item was under preparation as the white thong she was wearing was soon absorbing her exclusive warm, moist emissions that increased as the two lovers settled. They did this on those evenings when Serena was not otherwise engaged, before sleep overtook them and just long enough for arousal to occur and stimulate their juices. Then they would turn, face each other, kiss, then sleep. The following morning, Alysha's thong would be snug inside a plastic sleeve, along with a photograph, from the neck down to protect her identity, of her wearing the garment, showing a finger inside the gusset indicating the way to the delights in store. A 'Click and Drop' Royal Mail label from the printer in Serena's little office would be produced, glued to a cardboard box and soon another of Gemma's Gems would be on its way to another expectant male, or perhaps female!

Chapter Three

As the underground clattered westward, Sefton thought back to his first sexual encounter with Serena MacDonald. This was during a fellow Army officer's stag party just before Sefton resigned his commission. Sefton recalled that Kieran's evening certainly did go with a bang as the six young men after the regulation drinking in a popular pub, found themselves in the company of six beautiful women. Kieran, in his formal invitation to his five friends promised them something special and to appease them because they would believe it ought to be they who should be paying for the evening's entertainment, asked them to stump up the modest sum of one hundred pounds in cash each, towards 'expenses'. It was Kieran who intended making it an evening to remember but strictly on his terms. By taking control of arrangements he hoped to avoid the usual fate of the bridegroom, either handcuffed naked to a lamp post with whitewashed testicles on display, or drunk and unconscious on a ferry to France!

After necessary visits to test the pub's porcelain, they took the luxury minibus Kieran hired, using the others' contribution to a very well known and very expensive West End hotel. In the hotel lounge bar comfortably seated on plush armchairs with champagne bottles and glasses to hand, Kieran produced a sheet of paper from an inside pocket:

"Ready guys? Each of you pick a number from one to six. Sefton, as I've known you the longest, this may be your lucky night so you go first."

"Number three," Sefton announced with a little caution, curiosity and concern creeping into his voice as they had all been victims before of Kieran's practical jokes.

"Ah, good choice," the soon to be married Kieran replied, consulting the rather crumpled piece of paper that he had pulled from an inside pocket.

Sefton, sitting closely to his friend could see two columns of figures. Down the left hand side, numbers one to six and opposite them on the right hand side of the paper another list, a series of six sets of three figures.

"You're in Room One Six Five. Here's your swipe card. Off you go and enjoy. No need to rush though. Everything, and I do mean everything is booked, bought and paid for until mid-day tomorrow," he added, his eyes shining and a smirk spreading across his face.

Sefton walked a little unsteadily, the champagne kicking in, towards the lift. He turned to see Kieran repeating the process for the other four men. The lift opened noiselessly and he stepped in and pressed the button for the second floor. His head was 'swimming' a little as he stepped from the confines of the lift onto a brightly lit, grey carpeted corridor. He reached the cream-coloured door to the appointed room. A growing curiosity had overtaken that slightly uneasy feeling and he swiped the card and pushed open the door. In front of him stood a small rectangular glass-topped table. An ice bucket containing an opened, still bubbling bottle of champagne and two glasses. Just beyond was a selection of nibbles including crab cakes, garlic biscuits, mini quiches and fried chicken legs.

Then a soft, female voice cooed an inviting:

"Hi, don't be shy. Come on in."

Sefton followed the voice and there she was, standing, looking absolutely ravishing, in a red, low cut dress that revealed enough of her breasts to excite any red-blooded male. And Sefton, was certainly a red-blooded male! He managed to move his gaze from those enticing mounds to take in her other attributes. From the French plait down to the very high heeled shoes on her feet. He lingered for more than a moment on the dress material as it clung to her body from belly to the tops of her thighs forming a 'V', the point of which, to the very keen-eyed Mather more than hinted at the presence of the gap to her as yet unexplored secrets. He looked at the perfect face, from long eyelashes, delicately applied blusher and bright red lips and matching red fingernails. There was a hint too of nipples just pushing against the dress's soft fabric. It was those two buttons that also caught Sefton's attention. Something about those pert but hidden points inflamed his imagination and stirred a fire deep in his loins.

"My name is Aurora, and I'm yours by special invitation," she smiled so invitingly that his knees all but buckled under him as he began to imagine the pleasures to come.

Sefton was also rendered speechless, if temporarily but after that initial view he could not shake the feeling they had met somewhere before.

"I'm," he began, as he moved towards her.

"Sefton," she said, before he could complete his name, "but names don't matter here." She smiled and added, "When all this was arranged it was agreed that sex only, was on the menu. There is a special place reserved for you but if you're into whips, rope and handcuffs you certainly won't need them tonight. There are some things I will not or have no need to do no matter what the fee. So just lay back and we can begin; there is absolutely no need to rush. We have the whole night in front of us; I'm yours until mid-day tomorrow if you have the stamina," she said, continuing to smile.

Aurora, as she called herself when carrying out her professional duties for Exclusive Escort Services slipped out of her dress. The sight of this woman standing in front of him in bra, lacy, diaphonous knickers, suspender belt and sheer black stockings was proving irresistible. Sefton, like many men preferred his women wearing stockings. There was now a growing bulge underneath his trouser fly causing him a little discomfort. This was relieved as she carefully unzipped his trousers but being extra cautious not to catch even the smallest portion of delicate skin in the track. Now his already dribbling erection was free and she bent to place her lips firmly around it just below the rim of his purple-reddish pink helmet. Then she raised her head to admire the red lipstick line encircling the very ample circumference of his glistening penis.

He fumbled, unusual for him to rush things, to remove his trousers; his suit jacket having already been flung to one side as he had moved towards her, discarded along with his highly polished black shoes. After casting aside her dress, Aurora then slowly and deliberately teasing him, unclipped the suspender belt but the stockings remained clinging warmly to her long slim legs.

"Don't rush," she repeated quietly, as he attempted to grasp her breasts and encourage her to fall back.

She would have none of that and pushed him firmly on to his back while she stepped out of her knickers and very deftly allowed her bra to follow them to the carpet below. All this while Sefton was holding his throbbing dick at right-angles to the world desperate to push it home. A condom was quickly and expertly rolled down its length by Aurora though after leaving that earlier red marker perhaps its introduction was a little late. However, so expertly was it put in place that Sefton barely noticed it. Now she very slowly and deliberately began to ease down and fully accommodate its not inconsiderable, rubber jacketed length. Then she rose and fell, steadily accelerating and watched as Sefton's face, neck and upper chest began to redden. She gripped his right hand and directed it towards her pubic mound and on down. He used two fingers, though with a little difficulty. For even though she had adopted a more upright posture while rhythmically continuing up and down in order to find and squeeze, firstly its protecting hood and then the fun button itself, the pose was a little awkward. This was stiff too as he began to gently roll, pull and rub it. Then the two fingers continued down the slippery path to her puffy inner labia. Everything he touched was wet and just like the base of his dick which was still thrusting away pushing and stretching those pink vaginal walls as Aurora regulated its speed of movement and controlled how deep it went. Then she eased off his erection and turned; her back was now to him and she manoeuvred back down on him and began to rise and fall. The movement of her vagina 'riding' his urgent member creating a 'schlurp-schlurping' sound. Much like the movement of a piston inside a well-lubricated cylinder. Utterly amazed by this change of position he determined to take full advantage of it. His hands reached forward and began to squeeze her breasts carefully rolling her aroused nipples between his index fingers and thumbs as she continued to rhythmically rise and fall. He dropped his right hand from its stiff bud to another stiffened but very intimate part of her anatomy, her clitoris or as he had heard the men in his platoon call it, 'the little man in the canoe' and timed his manipulation of it with Aurora's sliding up and down motion

"Here's a man," thought Aurora, "who seems to know the way to a woman's heart is via her clit."

This just as matters finally followed their natural course, for a jet of man's milk filled the teat of that thin rubber addition and Sefton bucked and groaned, unable to control his response. Aurora muttered, "Yes, yes," a few times as she too reached the summit of her own sexual arousal. During some of her other professional engagements she had felt some obligation to make a few appropriate utterances as proof of the man's sexual prowess. Men were such ego-trippers believing women couldn't survive without them. Many men seemed to work at the level of, 'wham, bang, thankyou, ma'am', giving little or no regard to female needs but not this particular man.

Feeling fully satisfied, she even wondered if there could be a re-match in the future. If, as she planned she went freelance and set up her own agency she would be sure to seek him out.

***

That violent encounter, those years before had for a time rather soured her view of most men and increased her determination to remain in control thereafter. Some might consider this was difficult especially for her after that attempted rape, as the essence of the sexual act between men and women was the former's penetration or invasion of the woman's body. Yet women throughout history managed to have some mysterious hold over men and had manipulated them to do their bidding. It had been Helen's face and no doubt other beautiful aspects of her body that had launched those thousand ships. And Anne Boleyn, a cock-teaser if ever there was one had kept Henry VIII at arm's length for many years before allowing him access. Though that story did not have a happy ending either. Aurora once more would have to admit that it was only a rare man who could inflame her sexual desires rather than just his own.

**

Sefton Mather reached Gianna's Restaurant in Soho just seconds before the arrival of Marcus Browne.

"Good evening, Marcus, how are you?" he asked more mechanically than with genuine interest for the other man's welfare as he tried to sound upbeat.

He hoped this mood would prevail and continue the success he had enjoyed during the earlier part of the evening. The only way to top that pleasurable horizontal shuffle he had engaged in with Serena would be to have the day rounded off by his being confirmed as the eleventh member of the Foreign Affairs Committee. He did on the other hand, have reason to be grateful to Marcus Browne; a friend of his father Gerald, who had rather taken Mather Jr under his wing as a new Member of Parliament. There were many rules and customs and do's and don't's for the newcomer to negotiate; for example, voting in the wrong Division Lobby is not popular nor is sitting on the wrong bench in the Chamber! One other very helpful contribution Marcus had made was to suggest he shared his 'Administrative and Research' Assistant, Alicia Tomlinson, whom he paid for twenty hours a week's work, helping keep up to date with the rising amount of paperwork, literal and electronic as well as pursuing research as necessary. Sefton employed her for ten hours but was realising that he either needed to raise this to fifteen or employ an additional person, an intern, perhaps a politics' graduate as an unpaid researcher but one keen to gain the experience. Most Members employed, paid or otherwise, part-timers, work experience and or interns but there was no set pattern of employment and it varied from one MP to another but as long as the MPs adhered strictly to the Independent Parliamentary Standards

Authority, or IPSA, then any arrangement privately entered into and agreeable to all parties was acceptable. Marcus Browne had not particularly been very subtle when advising him not to attempt any 'fooling around' with the very attractive Alicia as the Party was still smarting from the fallout concerning a Tory MP who had won in spectacular fashion a long-held Labour, 'safe' seat. Then soured it all as he had soon after been accused of inappropriate behaviour towards a female intern as well as a male employee. The Member concerned felt obliged subsequently to resign and Labour had regained the seat at the ensuing by-election.

"I'm fine," Marcus replied, "but no doubt like you, Sefton and everyone else in these very challenging times, looking forward to returning to some sort of normality. How's old Gerry by the way, haven't seen him for years?"

For a second or two Sefton did not comprehend to whom he was referring when Browne had said, 'Gerry'. It was the first time he had heard his rather staid father called anything other than Gerald by folk outside or for that matter, inside the family.

"Yes, he's well," he managed to say.

"You a bit of a chip off the old block, eh?" Browne said with a knowing wink.

Sefton, bewildered, merely nodded his head.

The pleasantries over, Sefton asked if they should order.

"No, if you don't mind, can we hang on for ten or fifteen minutes? I've asked a friend to join us. Still, nothing to stop us from having a drink. What's your tipple?"

Mather found it very difficult to suppress his disappointment over the imminent arrival of a third party, especially as the potentially good news he was waiting for, would now be delayed even more. But he could do nothing; he certainly did not want to rock any boat so he voiced no objection. He rather lamely suggested that as they were eating 'Italian' then what could be better than a good Chianti.

"A bottle of Felsina Berardenga Chianti Classico if you please, Andrea," he told the waiter who was hovering within earshot but not too close. All good waiters should not be too near the table and certainly not eavesdropping but be ever available.

For a few moments Sefton remembered with affection his first university vacation. Was it really a decade and more ago? With a girlfriend he had driven down through France to Tuscany and to the province of Siena. They had rather lost their way and fetched up in the principality of Castelnuovo Berardenga about fifty kilometres south-east of Florence and fifteen, east of the city of Siena. It was there he discovered that particularly fine Chianti. Now, the first of several bottles was arriving and soon, encouragingly, large glasses would be filled.

"Cheers," they said in unison.

"Now, before our duo turns into a trio I need to bring you up to speed over a few matters, Sefton," said Browne.

Mather just knew that something ominous was heading straight at him. A certain tension seemed to be building up between them.

"In Commons' terms you've made a pretty good start," began Marcus Browne in a very confidential tone, "but you've managed to upset a few of the wrong people too."

Sefton's expression was changing from concern to what was fast becoming a look of disappointment and he lowered his eyes like a naughty schoolboy up before the headteacher after being caught smoking behind the bike sheds. To compensate him a little for his growing anxiety he poured himself another generous measure of wine.

Seeing Sefton's quizzical look Browne shifted his chair a little nearer to the table and attempted to explain.

"Do you remember some charity bash at Durford Hall just before Christmas not long after the 2019 Election?" he asked.

A rather crestfallen Sefton, nodded as events of that evening flooded back at about the same speed as the blood had travelled to his now very red face, no doubt though assisted by the wine.

"Seems you upset one of the guys down on the Embankment. Ranulf Faulkner is not a man with whom one trifles! He mixes with a very odd bunch of people and rumour has it, runs agents on both sides. Little for him evidently is beyond the Pale. Didn't seem to care much for your 'tupping' his wife, Athena. Not that you've been the only one. Put it down to her being conceived in Athens and all that hot Mediterranean blood coursing through her veins." At this, Browne paused before continuing to impart yet more damaging information.

***

Sefton certainly did recall that particular fund-raising 'event' that he had felt obliged to attend. He and his father shared a taxi the short distance from their home to the Hall but he determined to lose him at the first opportunity. His mother had 'cried-off' attending and not for the first time she had developed a convenient headache. Sefton happily though discovered long ago that such 'evenings' provided every opportunity to 'meet' the opposite sex. His roving eye soon settled on a slim, very attractive, auburn-haired woman perhaps fifteen years his senior. She in turn had returned his look with a faint smile but there was the promise of very much more to come in those large brown eyes. As the guests wined and dined quite extravagantly, Sefton doubted if anyone else would notice him slipping away. 'Brown eyes' was already gliding from the room and heading towards the broad staircase leading to the bedrooms of the East Wing of Durford Hall and in particular, to one of the rooms set aside for the convenience of attendees. To the right of the staircase one was marked 'Gentlemen' and to the left, a room marked 'Ladies'. She emerged from the latter two minutes later just as he caught up with her. She smiled encouragingly at him; at least that's how he interpreted it and very soon after was steering her towards what he hoped would be an unlocked, empty bedroom. The door opened easily to his touch and he fumbled for a light switch and before they had gone many steps towards a large duvet topped bed he was slipping her dress off her shoulders. This action made all the easier thanks to the spaghetti-thin design of the dress's straps. He moved forward to switch on a floor standing light that shone its beam over the near side of a bed before moving back to turn the main bedroom light off. While he was thus engaged she obligingly stepped out of her dress that dropped down by her ankles. Then he was standing behind her, he cupped his hands under her breasts pushing her bra up before kneading gently the firm, smooth skin upwards and then squeezing, hardening nipples between the thumb and forefinger of each hand. He bent down turning her slightly in one smooth movement and kissed her right nipple then lightly nibbled it with practised teeth. She was whispering:

"Go on, go on!"

Sefton needed little encouragement.

Sensibly, she was wearing very silky and smooth, expensive hold-up stockings. He was pleased, for he found tights so tedious. All too often by the time they were down and off the moment could be gone.

Stockings on the other hand, left that sensual, smooth strip of skin between the tops of them and the frilly, elasticated edge of panties that were oh, so pleasurable to slip fingers under. Sefton now remembered that moment only too well for as he sat opposite his Parliamentary colleague he could feel a slight wetness inside his underpants. Briefly he recalled the moment when his right hand had glided over her surprisingly smooth belly crossing that section of skin he also found so arousing to touch just above the pubic mound which in her case was a generous V-shaped bush of dark hair. Then it was down and over the hood, pausing to give her happy lady underneath, as some women called their clitoris, a tweak. His hand, from bulging inside her knickers and slipping inside her wet vagina moved to grip the gusset and pull them down. He then turned her round to face him once again but bending her across the side of the bed while encouraging her to open her legs. By this time they were both breathing heavily as he alternated between squeezing her breasts to running his hands from her pubic hair and along the inside of her thighs then through to gently part her buttocks. As this felt a little uncomfortable she turned herself round lifting her rear towards him and only inches from his face. Looking down he saw a small, almost perfectly round hole, not unlike lips pursed for whistling. For a a brief moment he was tempted to lick it but almost at once he was drawn back to the second orifice. The fingers of her right hand gently pulling a 'petal' back to fully display this one. It was now glistening pink and was more than ready for him as he stood erection in hand, oozing with its transparent pre-cum. He dropped his hands and stroked her swollen labia before grasping his member again with his right hand and poised to plunge it between them. He was barely fully inside and ready to begin thrusting when the door burst open. The shock of this interruption made him pull out but not before sending a stream of his ejaculate across the back of her thighs, buttocks and back.

"You bastard," the intruder yelled, his dark, usually cold eyes now blazing with pent-up rage, "what are you doing with my wife?"

Mather later reflected on this ill-timed entry of an irate husband and had smiled to himself thinking that it was pretty self-evident what he was doing to the man's wife.

The question however had been followed by a threat.

"You'll pay for this, Mather. I promise you," he snarled.

With that he pulled Sefton back with one arm while the other aimed a blow at his face but the fist caught him near his right eyebrow. Then a highly polished 'Oxford' style shoe was kicking him in the general area of his naked and very vulnerable scrotum. Fortunately, for scrotum and their delicate contents the pulling of Sefton off his paramour had caused him to fall back and sideways. The blow consequently missed its rugby ball shaped targets and grazed his hip instead. Sefton landed on the carpeted floor dazed but not too stupefied as to leave his genitals on display any longer than necessary or to allow another attempt at damaging them by the cuckolded husband. His dick now shrunk to half its earlier size and still reducing with balls close behind but encased, not in a loose-skinned flapping scrotum as before but now inside a shrunken much smaller sphere, were thrust back into his boxers. This item of clothing together with trousers had been decorating his ankles during the encounter but which were soon hastily being pulled back into their correct position.

The wife while this had been occurring was busily returning breasts to their soft nests; the 36B cups of her black bra. This followed by straightening her stockings, the easing of her matching black knickers over those swollen labia and saturated vagina, wiping Sefton's creamy donation from her body and putting her dress back on. To Sefton's immense relief the husband turned his attention and ire away from him and towards the woman. She had been stunned by the force of his appearance but most of her dignity seemed restored for when the man started to shout at her, she calmly replied:

"And Serena?"

Then both of them left the room without a backward glance. Sefton retrieved his jacket. He checked that fly and shirt buttons were in position and left after a five minute interval and was down the stairs and slipping into the night to walk down the Hall's long drive to negotiate the homeward journey. In all the excitement he made no connection between the 'Serena' mentioned by his intended conquest and 'Serena' of Victory Mews.

Sefton remembered that his mother was still up having watched an old movie on television. She was surprised to see him back so early and alone. Then she gasped as she caught sight of his face with an ugly gash running along his right eyebrow and his rather dishevelled look.

"That needs stitching," she said in a rather resigned tone before slipping into the kitchen to bring warm water and cotton wool. She dipped the latter in the water and began to bathe the wound.

"What trouble are you in?" she asked thinking the worst of her rather wayward son. Rumours of his many 'flings' had reached her ears long before.

"You've not been dallying with Sophie Fortune, I trust?" she added, a note of anxiety creeping in.

"Dallying," he repeated. "What a deliciously old-fashioned word. What do you mean and why are you always so against, Sophie?"

"What happened?" she persisted.

"Oh, nothing really. Just a difference of opinion," he replied, his face looking blank. "I'll give old Hargreaves a call in Harley Street in the morning and see if he can patch me up. He charges enough so there shouldn't be a scar."

His mother was hearing too many stories concerning her son's philandering ways and look at him despairingly.

"You really must be more careful or you'll ruin your political career before its really begun. "Mistakes," she uttered wistfully, "may haunt you all your life!"

At breakfast the whole sordid story was aired again as Sefton's mother had been told early that morning by her husband of an incident at the Hall. A woman who had been found 'in flagrante delecto', had slunk off. Sefton's mother had met his:

"Good morning, Ma," with an icy stare and the words:

"It's high time you started to act responsibly."

Sefton was lucky for early the following Tuesday, after a few deft touches of the surgeon's scalpel at Mr Hargreaves' private clinic, the damage inflicted by that irate husband on that eventful Friday was barely noticeable. More evident was the size of the cheque in payment!

***

"There's also that faux pas earlier, at another social evening," Browne continued, "and word of that soon drifted back to Party HQ regarding a few ill-judged jokes. Perhaps what could turn out to be even more damaging could be your association with a certain young lady over the river not far from Waterloo Station. Not to mention another one even further east."

He realised who the first mentioned woman could be but was stumped as to the other one. What had Browne meant when he had said 'further east'? As for that gaffe at the social evening, he remembered that only all too clearly as well.

Sefton had been invited to host a charity auction just before the election which saw him elected to the House of Commons. Of course he was regarded as something of a local celebrity and so the role of host would not be a problem. Indeed, any opportunity to be in the public eye was good, free publicity. Perhaps it was the free drinks or his mistakenly believing before the evening opened that the audience would be predominately male that contributed to his misreading of the situation. Sefton and a small clutch of helpers occupied centre stage. Below them in a hall darkened to add mystery and atmosphere to the evening, was the audience. There were a few speeches to begin the evening after which Sefton decided to regale them with a few jokes. The first of these were innocuous enough. He began with:

"A horse trotted into a bar. The barman looked up and asked, why the long face?"

There was a ripple of polite applause. Heartened by this he continued until he asked the audience if they knew the difference between a circus and the Follies Begeres. There was no sound, so he continued:

"Well, a circus is full of cunning stunts."

Sniggering began, a little applause followed but suddenly the atmosphere chilled. Somehow he managed to bluff and bluster his way through to the end but the odd thing was the evening raised the largest amount ever and Sefton Mather was returned at the election with an increased majority. It is perhaps fortunate for all however, that Sefton decided against joining the ranks of the new wave comedians!

***

Browne looked at Mather and continued:

"Certainly the one with the address near the station is very well known to you in the Biblical sense but you are not the only one sharing those expensive favours."

Mather thought it best not to mention that he no longer paid to enjoy Serena's particular skills and yes he was aware of others; he didn't like it but considering what he got from her, yes he would go along with it. She was a free, modern woman after all. Apart from which most of them were not that frequently in her bed with her. He and Serena enjoyed what could be regarded as an 'open' relationship. Sefton certainly enjoyed her opening her legs for him.

Browne sat waiting, either expecting some sort of verbal response or for him to wriggle uncomfortably. It was certainly striking deep but Sefton tried to remain expressionless but he could not prevent a cold shiver from running down his spine.

"Look, Sefton, if you can't keep the trouser snake in your pants then for God's sake don't get caught. A Member consorting with an 'escort'. Think what the tabloids would make of that."

Then Brown's face looked solemn as he added:

"As Committee Chair I must just mention that you were not successful in the ballot earlier today."

Browne smiled briefly as he saw Sefton's face fall.

"Actually this is no bad thing in the long run. Most Select Committee members tend to find themselves in a kind of advancement, 'No man's land' with little chance to climb the career ladder. You have an interest in Foreign Affairs but a better strategy would be to pursue the Parliamentary Private Secretary's route. I understand there will shortly be a vacancy for a PPS; it's within the gift of the Foreign Secretary. A bit of an unpaid dogsbody but at least it'll get you noticed."

Sefton managed to butt in with a few words:

"Yes, Marcus but you must admit that the Committee exerts considerable influence and gets things done."

"True. There was a recent case when we managed to persuade the Home Secretary to bar entry to the UK of a doctor intent on performing FGM operations. You know Sophie Fortune don't you? Doesn't she live near you? Anyway, she appeared before the Committee and gave a very good account of herself and was largely instrumental with the evidence she brought, in barring the guy. Again, when she was called as a witness she also gave the Justice Select Committee a rough ride over the overall way rape cases are being handled by the Crown Prosecution Service."

"We were at Exeter together, well not exactly together, more at the same time and I caught one of her meetings and I know how intent and sincere she can be," Sefton agreed.

"Yes, she can also be a pain in the ass. Forever petitioning or lobbying for this or that cause. Shouldn't wonder if the Justice, Home and Foreign Offices haven't dedicated a whole suite of filing cabinets just for her correspondence. However, you must watch yourself. For example one of the ten current members of the FAC is a strident advocate of 'women's rights'. She's very hard-working, well respected but a real ball breaker and tipped for Number 10 as the new 'Iron Lady' once she moves on from the Committee. It's Honourable Members like her that you must keep on side even if you're not one of that team. We can't risk any more problems in that direction. If your amorous adventures reach her ears and she takes any notice of them, then your chances for advancement in whatever direction will be dead in the water at least for the foreseeable future. Remember Edward Edwardes and his fooling with an intern? Yes, I know your private life's just that and far be it for the Party to interfere but not when you are in the public eye; your life's no longer your own."

Sefton groaned inwardly and thought:

"This sounds like my mother talking."

He was managing to draw some comfort from the knowledge that people did come back from the dead. There were several politicians who had fallen from favour but were now rehabilitated. Though there were certainly some who were not, including Edwardes, who had sexually propositioned that intern! Yes, and of course there was that even bigger upset towards the end of June last year, when a senior Government Minister though initially supported by the Prime Minister was compelled to resign. This however, was less to do with sexual misconduct than with misbehaving in other ways. More particularly when he was revealed, considering his role, has having blatantly breached social distancing rules during lock-down. The tabloids relishing the whole affair as they splashed pictures as proof of his hypocrisy across their front pages. The impression he gave was of one rule for him but another for the rest of the country. Yet misdemeanours, sexual, hypocritical or otherwise were not the sole preserve of the Conservatives. In living memory, from the Profumo Affair through to the Duck Island Expenses Scandal there had been too many instances when Members of Parliament had been heavily criticised. Consequently, respect for them, if there had ever been much, had fallen. The other parties too, had fallen short. The Labour Party had suffered and continues to suffer its share of problems from the John Stonehouse incident through to accusations of anti-Semitism, stalking, suggestive e-mails and inappropriate touching. Not to mention problems faced by Liberal-Democrats and Scottish Nationalists. What was it that President Lincoln had said about power corrupting?

Marcus Browne had thoroughly warmed to his task and this showed by the ever increasing lightness of his tone as he asked Mather, if he had found the stroll across Westminster Bridge that afternoon, 'bracing'.

Mather was left in no doubt that Browne had known all along where he had gone and what he had been doing. A thought crossed his mind, which he voiced:

"Is the Party having me followed?"

"Yes, probably. Partly down to a loud whisper in Security circles that you pose a risk and partly down to some of the company you have been keeping. The two may be linked but remember what I said earlier about crossing a particular person? Though some of the aides in Downing Street do have big eyes, ears and influence too," Browne said. His voice almost purring as he hinted at 'behind the scenes' intrigue.

Then he added:

"You realise that the trick in all this is not to be found out. Be like Caesar's wife. Difficult in these days of prying newspapers, cameras on every street corner and social media. Snoopers, spies and all manner of nosy undesirables have never had it so good," he declared.

Mather of course had long since realised that even at the best of times it was an almost impossible balancing act protecting the public from the terrorist bomb or biological or chemical nasty yet not infringing personal freedoms. Covid-19 restrictions had tested Government and public almost to the limit. There had been violent clashes in several cities as protesters complained the Government was riding roughshod over human rights and seemed hell-bent in turning the country into a police state. But the outrages on Westminster Bridge and the Salisbury Novichok poisoning were fresh in the minds of those charged with protecting that same public. On a more personal level he was concerned that he was under scrutiny. Or was he simply a victim of a Security Officer's personal vendetta? If so, was he really under any sort of threat?

"Sefton," Browne, continued, "one thing you must try and do is play the long game. Who knows in twenty years time you could be there in number 10. You know as well as I do that several of the current Ministers did have very shaky starts so everything is still up for grabs."

By this time a soberly dressed, middle-aged, slightly stooping figure had reached their table. An attentive waiter moved silently behind him and pulled out a chair for him. Marcus Browne stood up and introduced the newcomer.

"This," he announced grandly, "is Mr Grey!" Then added, "let's eat and then we can discuss cases."

Chapter Four

The meal was excellent as it always was, from antipasto through to the classic Tiramisu and the reason why Mather dined and lunched there regularly. The lateness of the hour might have suggested a lighter meal. Had that been the case Sefton would have chosen another real favourite, Spaghetti Aglio Olio. All three men though were used to keeping irregular hours and eating accordingly. He decided that as he felt like a condemned man then he might just as well eat like one and have a hearty meal. All washed down with copious amounts of Classico Chianti; then brandy just as Sefton's ordeal was set to resume He was still trying to come to terms with the listing of some of his indiscretions but the pouring of the brandy accompanied his being bombarded, as he had anticipated, with more revelations.

Mr Grey, who had sat largely silent throughout most of the previous sixty minutes of the meal now shifted in his chair enabling him to look Sefton squarely in the eyes. His only contribution so far had been to affirm the quality of the food and thank the waiter for pouring the very drinkable Chianti into his wine glass.

"Mr Mather, have you come across, Bahira Abadi?"

"Yes," he replied, a little surprised by the question, "she was with some UNESCO mission or other in Afghanistan during 2013 when I was there with 4 Rifles."

"How well did you know her? Intimately?"

Grey's face barely showing any flicker of emotion at the implication, though his ears were pink and probably more the result of Italy's best and Napoleon's finest than anything else.

"Well, yes," admitted Sefton. "There was a moment when we met in the Serena Hotel in Kabul. We were both lonely, far from home and as terrorist groups had been busy elsewhere in the city we were at risk of being caught up in the bombings."

Browne pursed his lips and thought to himself:

"He'll shag anything with a pulse."

Grey continued to question Mather:

"Was she already in the hotel or did you arrive first?"

"Not sure. It's a few years ago now. I think she was there, in reception just as I was dropped off," a very puzzled Mather, answered.

"What were you doing there?" Mr Grey asked.

Mather could stand the tormenting no longer. He was feeling irritated.

"Is there a problem and why are you both interested?"

Browne cut in:

"Mr Grey is with Sis!"

But he said the letters as a word instead of saying the initials, S.I.S and seeing Mather frown, went on to explain:

"Secret Intelligence Service."

Sefton though close to being overwhelmed at what amounted to an interrogation as well as the baring of his soul, the food and the many glasses of alcohol was now cursing this modern obsession with acronyms, when Browne seemingly not to be outdone, followed it with another.

"He's MI6," he said.

This snippet of information added to Mather's aggravation for he was still unsure why he seemed to have been singled out for such treatment but it may account for him thinking before Browne had confirmed it that he was probably being followed.

"There's also some interest on the domestic front among the boys and girls down on the Embankment at Thames House but as there is a possible foreign connection, '6' is interested too," said Browne, waving his right hand in Grey's direction.

He continued:

"Not to mention some twitching among the folk at GCHQ. It's all about, 'cyber-creep' these days. Everything from infiltrating the Economy to undermining our military preparedness."

As the two serious-looking men continued to look on gravely at the brandy glasses on the table in front of them, Mather ever keen to find humour in any situation began to postulate that if MI5 and MI6 dabbled in secrets then why were their headquarters so well known? He had thought little of their work hitherto, other than it was necessary in order to protect our freedoms to sometimes poke into every nook and cranny to root out anyone who threatened those same liberties. Then he turned to thinking about the SIS building by the Albert Embankment at Vauxhall Cross. He did know that it had been built on the site of the old Vauxhall Pleasure Gardens and to him that seemed ironic and brought a smile to his lips. When passing the building down by the river on occasions, he had also thought that its design had been conceived by an architect with a sense of humour. Many sightseers and critics said this post-modern edifice resembled an Aztec Temple and was deserving of the nickname, 'Legoland'.

Grey continued:

"This woman, that you were friendly with in Kabul, when did you last see her?"

"About three weeks ago; maybe less. I'd left the House and as it was a fine afternoon decided to walk along the Embankment. I took a left up Northumberland Avenue and just as I reached Trafalgar Square saw her walking towards me. I…"

Grey interrupted:

"Had you been meeting up before this?"

"Yes, I'd met up with her on four or five occasions after the last lockdown and I think twice before. I remember asking her what she was doing in London. She said she had left UNESCO and was working for a London-based children's charity."

"What about during Covid? Where was she?" Grey asked.

Mather was tetchy and bored. He snapped:

"We met just before Christmas when the restrictions were lifted temporarily. I was about to return to Hampshire when she called on me. I delayed going home until the following day."

Grey persisted and asked whether during any of their conversations the topic of domestic and international politics had come up. No, only two things had come up but Mather mentioned just the one concerning coverage in the News, of a bomb outrage in Syria. He felt disinclined to say that the only other thing that had arisen had found a very satisfying home and any talk between them that night had probably included:

"Don't stop," and "Yes, yes, aagh," as they fucked the night away.

This reminder of their passionate nights together mellowed Mather a little and other than frowning he was preparing for more questions. He was asked if he had ever visited where she lived but he had to admit that after offering to see her home on a few occasions had never been there.

"Where did she say she lived?" he persisted.

"Actually, I'm not really sure. She was always a bit vague. Just mentioned she lived near London Wall and as my flat was never too far from where we met up, it didn't really matter too much. But that's it. I've done most of the talking and answered your questions, so what's it all about?"

"The woman you know as Bahira Abadi is not Iraqi but an Iranian called Derifa Asghar. Her twin brother, Bahram, which incidentally means, 'victory over resistance' is an especially nasty type. Torture, beheadings, bombings; you name it, he's done it. Although Iranians speak Farsi, he'll have enough Arabic from studying the Koran to get by as an Iraqi. There's also a cousin, Farzad Asghar but he seems to have dropped out of sight."

His two companions let Sefton sit for a minute as, tired, 'tight' and in some torment over someone with secrets who had recently shared his bed, he seemed dazed and rooted to his chair.

"We also think he's managed to involve himself in county lines drugs distribution to fund more of his operations," Browne added, "and," he paused, "this is strictly confidential, we think he has a contact somewhere in MI6, which Mr Grey here is trying to confirm. This contact has probably links too with a police officer or officers in the West Country and a tie-in with drugs. He or they are about to undergo an investigation. The MI6 officer responsible is about to be reined in too."

Under his breath, Browne muttered:

"With any luck!"

Sefton turned his thoughts back to that Iraqi/Iranian link. He knew enough about the two countries, Iraq and Iran to know they spoke different languages and that most Iraqis were Arabs but only a few Iranians were of Arab extraction. The majority were of Persian ethnicity. A few months before he had given his support to a petition organised by Sophie Fortune, calling on the Iranian Islamic State to treat British-Iranian joint passport holders currently incarcerated, more humanely; especially one particular woman cruelly detained on very flimsy charges. Curious, he had delved deeper with Alicia's help into the situation of women generally in Iran; but supporting anything that Sophie backed was never one simple issue. Sefton was surprised to discover that since the Revolution of 1979, women at least in theory were equal to men though under Khomeini they had faced serious setbacks and under Sharia Law adulterous women faced death by stoning. A change since then in attitudes to women may also account for why Bahira seemed very much to be a modern, even 'Westernized' woman posing as an Iraqi. Women in Iran are permitted to hold public office, drive cars, go to university and even run for President. Yet, according to Sophie, they are still being arrested for offending 'headscarf' and 'dress code' laws. So things may have changed but in many ways they remain the same.

"Of course, there could be a perfectly innocent reason why the sister of a terrorist, drugs dealer and contract killer found her way into your bed, not only in Kabul but here in London," offered Grey, barely concealing the sarcasm in his voice. Then he added:

"May just be for your charismatic personality or," he continued, "your sleeping with a known terrorist's sister may leave you open to blackmail; to be pressed into doing them a favour in return for not ending up as front page news with your trousers around your ankles and pumping away inside an enemy of this country!"

Sefton was almost discounting the thought that the man whose wife he had all but 'shafted' would trouble himself into seeking revenge on a lowly MP when there were such potential terrorists as Asghar on the loose. It was instead his own bedding of this man's sister that had brought about his having 'spooks' follow him.

Browne took up the narrative:

"This particular guy on the other hand has no qualms about using his sister and is not motivated if ever he once was by religious zeal alone. Drugs as I said just now and robbery keep him in funds and he enjoys his work and for the right price will augment his income by taking anyone out. To complicate matters, '6', or rather one of its Department Heads has almost certainly used him when no other course of action has been open for them to infiltrate terrorist organisations. Our American cousins still want him for the shooting of some of their key people."

Sefton, now rather confused, managed to interrupt before Grey took up the grim liturgy.

"Are you saying Bahram Asghar has worked for us to betray other terrorists?"

Grey nodded in agreement and added:

"Yes, under various names but remember what Mr Browne said a minute or two ago; Asghar will do anything," he paused, "for a price and sacrifice anyone as a means to suit his own devious ends."

He continued:

"About the only positive contribution by Covid-19 in an oblique way was the restriction on movement including those who bear us ill.

Few ferries, fewer aircraft movement has meant fewer undesirables managing to slip into the country. Though along the south and east coasts efforts to keep an eye on them had to be ramped up when the asylum seekers took to their little rubber craft. Who knows who was trying to creep across the Channel along with those poor souls who had shelled out their life savings to the scum who took their money for a seat in a leaking dinghy."

"In the meantime, Sefton just go about your business as normally as possible. Though," Browne added solemnly, "if there is anything out of the ordinary let me know and I'll pass it on."

Then, leaning across the table, his parliamentary colleague added:

"For God's sake though, be careful. We think they may be planning something big but exactly what, we don't know. I need hardly say be wary with whom you associate and watch travelling alone late at night."

Grey added, "We know brother Bahram is in London somewhere, having used one of his collection of faked documents to slip back in. Where his sister is, he's not going to be too far behind."

"What shall I do if we happen to meet casually? Do I ignore her from now on?" Sefton asked anxiously.

"Rather depends where you are. If you're in a crowd, rather than lurking in a dark corner then behave naturally. If she's with anybody, make your excuses and go," Grey said.

With that, hands were shaken and the other two drifted off into the night. If Sefton had not been worried before then he certainly was now but how on earth could he be of any possible use to a terrorist other than providing them with the kudos on the international terrorist scene by falling victim to a terrorist bomb or bullet. Blackmail had been mentioned but how could there be any photographs. How else could blackmail be achieved? Apart from that one very lively session in Kabul, most of the other sex sessions between them had taken place in his London flat. Desire may have overcome caution he conceded but that, he reassured himself was unlikely. There was just the one other occasion when he had taken her to bed in an address that was not his own but that was months ago.

***

He began to recollect that very event. He had been walking along the Embankment near The Temple having strolled from the Strand where he had met up with an old friend from his Army days. His intention earlier had been to walk back to the House. As he neared Cleopatra's Needle he met Bahira, or as he now knew her, Derifa. She had flung her arms around him in greeting.

"Oh, Sefton, fancy meeting you. What a lovely surprise," she said, very enthusiastically.

"What are you doing here?" he asked.

"I've just been to a charity meeting in Pimlico and needed some air. So here I am."

Sefton's mobile rang and he groaned inwardly until he recognised the caller's number.

"Excuse me, Bahira. I'd better get this. Hello," Sefton said.

"Hi, Sefton," a familiar voice replied. "Sorry if I've caught you at an awkward moment but I wondered if you could do me a favour?" Jemima asked. "Only I'm out of town for the rest of the day. I stopped overnight at the Mews and left after Serena this morning. She's away until Sunday. The thing is I have this horrible feeling I've left the cooker grill on. I'm away and so is Serena but as I don't want her returning to a smoking ruin wondered if you could pop in and check."

"Yes, of course," Sefton replied cheerfully.

Sefton's face was soon glowing at the prospect of a golden opportunity that had, if not by chance but thanks to Jemima's absentmindedness, now presented itself to him. Hadn't Grey suggested he treat her 'naturally? Nothing more natural than what he had in mind.

"Just leave it to me," he added, managing to hide his delight at the possibilities only minutes away.

"Thanks, Sefton, I owe you one," Jemima replied.

"Fancy a coffee and a snack?" he asked his companion. "I need to do a favour for a friend. The house is only a shortish walk away. We can collect a drink and food and take a Tube or a taxi."

Sefton steered her towards the Embankment Underground and they caught a Tube to Waterloo. Then it was a short step to Victoria Mews via a well known coffee shop.

He would have been very surprised to have seen from where Jemima had made that call to him. She was at the time sitting in the kitchen of number 21, where Serena lived and where occasionally she stayed over. Just before she left the house she carried out two tasks. The first was to go into the second bedroom that contained a wardrobe that was always locked. This she now unlocked and checked the camera equipment and set the timer inside to run in sixty minutes time to record the activity in the main bedroom that she was confident would then be occurring. Satisfied that all was ready she hurried into the bedroom on the next floor. She always slept there when staying over with Serena when they discussed their business interests. After checking the room was reasonably tidy, Jemima scooped up her handbag and returned to the kitchen. There she turned on the grill and for good measure left on one of the hotplates heating a saucepan of water. Then she left the house thirty five minutes before Sefton Mather and his sometime lover arrived and set off for a meeting with a tall, dark suited man at their rendezvous point close to the Albert Embankment.

***

The two new arrivals ate their repast in silence but it would have been obvious to any fly on the wall or spider in the centre of its web present in the kitchen, what their intentions were. Their snacks duly finished, the coffee drained and the debris of coffee containers, sandwich wrappers and crumbs consigned to recycling unit or waste bin accordingly, Sefton led the way to the main bedroom; he knew the way! The way to Bahira's secrets were all known to him as well and he could barely contain himself to renew their acquaintance. After stripping the duvet off the bed he turned his full attention to his companion. He kissed her full lips and began to drop her outer clothing to the floor where it joined the bedcover. His jacket, trousers and shirt followed and before long they were kissing and fondling. A long, slim hand reached in to free his rigid member but before she could release her grip his hand closed over hers and began gently to masturbate him while his other hand ventured down and over her pubic mound and between her fast-moistening slit. He removed his left hand, reclaimed his right and then pushed her back and over the side of the bed. His glans were gliding between her labia and being pushed into the resisting entrance to her vagina. Then he pulled her back up. His left hand grasped the right cheek of her buttocks and pressed her into him. They resumed kissing; she cupped his balls and he gasped with surprise at the suddenness of it. He turned her so he could more easily knead her breasts. He returned a hand to plough the length of her vulva then pressed her face down on the bed opened her thighs wide. His hand an instant later guiding his dick into her glistening pink entrance before he began to steadily rise and fall. His hands now free played with nipples and breasts in unison, or one dropped to squeeze and tease one of the stiff buds. Bahira began to rear as that moment came and as Sefton's seed shot out of him. He pulled himself out from her and tenderly turned her over; then both lay on their backs before recovering and then dressing. Bahira turning down the opportunity to shower saying she would do that once she reached home. She dressed and said that she must go but no he didn't need to accompany her there. She had a few errands to run on the way and did not want to change his plans anymore than they had been already. Sefton was disappointed but could not really complain. He, well they, had enjoyed spontaneous sex so what could be better than that. She promised to phone him during the following week and left the house.

Sefton remained naked on the bed putting off that moment that he knew he must tidy up and remove all evidence of that unexpected session before Serena's return in a few days. They agreed they were free agents but freedoms as far as Serena might be concerned probably did not extend to his having sex with another woman in her bed. He decided he would do the necessary remedial housekeeping before returning to the House. In a few days time, irrespective of what Messrs Browne and Grey had said he would give Serena a call and then come and see her.

***

So it was that Sefton Mather following that call to Serena found himself those several days later reaching inside his pocket for his key ring and for the one that opened the front door of 21 Victory Mews; as he did so he reflected on his responsibilities. Of course his first duty was to his family, then country and then to Party but how could he give up those searing sessions with Serena? No other woman satisfied him in quite the way she did and he had been trying his best with other women just in case. She also performed oral sex in the most extraordinary way, extracting every millilitre from his balls. Though usually a 'spitter', occasionally she swallowed but had once told him that she usually got her protein in more palatable ways than from his mildly salty flavoured creamy solution. For her, Sefton had suffered the discomfort and indignity of the waxing of his nether regions including his scrotum, though leaving the hair below his navel intact down to the base of his penis. Serena had insisted on hair removal further down and underneath before opening her mouth and taking in his genitalia. She had declared:

"I'm not picking your short and curlies from out of my teeth after sucking your nuts!"

Serena herself, years before and to encourage a select few to venture between her legs during their sessions and reciprocate the licking and sucking to bring her to heightened ecstasy, had visited Salon Carmen for a 'Brazilian'. All that remained of what for years had been an untamed forest of lush growth was now a neatly trimmed and manageable thicket. On several occasions she had been tempted to remove it all but her men friends seemed to prefer running their fingers through those pubes. But a rectangular strip, over four and a half, almost five centimetres long and three centimetres wide but tapering to a point to show the way to that special place between her legs was all that remained. Of the favoured few only Sefton and one other, opted to fully satisfy her in this way.

***

Sefton's thoughts returned to his present circumstances. He was after all a Member of Parliament and his party was in Government. Yet it was a dazed Sefton Mather who presented his credit card to settle the not inconsiderable bill for the evening's repast. Bidding Andrea and Enrico, the waiters who had both been most attentive, and the proprietors a good night, he left the restaurant and walked as briskly as the food, chianti and brandy would allow. He turned into Old Compton Street, then a right into Charing Cross Road and down to Cambridge Circus where he hailed a black cab. He was not really scared; he had been a soldier but this was different and he found himself as he walked, looking round for anything out of the ordinary. It was with some relief however when the cab dropped him outside the apartment block where he lived.

***

He had much to think about after brushing his teeth, peeing and then flopping on to the duvet strewn untidily across his double bed; just as he had left it earlier in the day. Obviously his failing to join the Foreign Affairs Select Committee had been a disappointment but in one way it was a relief. He had been told that he had made quite a good impression and he could build on that. There was also PMQ's. Messrs Browne and Grey had made him feel as though he was walking around with a target pinned to his back so perhaps keeping a reasonably low profile at least for a little while was not such a bad idea after all. As for other diversions, surely a few more visits to Victory Mews could make little difference. This thought began to lift the thin cloud of depression that had settled around him since meeting up with Marcus Browne just after 10pm. This mood had deepened soon after their eating at Gianna's. Now there was an encouraging stirring in his loins as he conjured up a picture of Serena's body in his head. As he moved from those exquisite, firm breasts to the warm belly curving down to her slit, his thoughts then turned back to that first intimate contact with Bahira or Derifa or whatever her name was, over eight years before, in Kabul. If he had ever given it much thought then it was to consider it was merely circumstance that had thrown them together in the hotel. Three days earlier than that meeting with her, he and the ten riflemen and a similar number of Afghan National Army under his command had been carrying out what should have been a routine patrol in Helmand's Nahr-e-Saraj district. They had left their armoured personnel carrier to climb a very steep ridge that would afford them a spectacular view of rebel-held territory in the mountains, twenty kilometres away. Lieutenant Mather ordered his men down the other side of the ridge in the direction of a deserted village several hundred metres below. In traditional Rifles fashion, two men scouted ahead of the rest of the patrol who were strung out across the slope. As those first men reached a line of rocks they noticed what looked to be a light flashing in one of the ruined buildings below them. Ever on the alert for booby traps, ambush and the like, one of the riflemen, Sergeant Jayden Williams, a Welshman from Cardiff, dropped to his knees and ordered Rifleman Westbrook to return to the patrol and alert them as to possible movement in the village.

"Boss, we think we've got company. Down there, to the left of that black door. Maybe a weapon," Westbrook said.

Lieutenant Mather required no further prompting and ordered the patrol to move right and to cover behind the rocks.

Sergeant Williams had re-joined the main patrol by now and was sent with an Afghan soldier to cover their right flank while Westbrook and another man were sent to the left. Mather decided they were in a good position and hoped the enemy would be foolish enough to launch a frontal attack up the hill. No such luck, for the enemy realising they had betrayed their own position sent up mortar and machine gun fire, effectively keeping the heads of the British and their allies down. The soldiers watched as shapes began to move from building to building. Mather ordered his men to train the GPMG into the conflict-stressed buildings nearest to his patrol where he could clearly see more armed men excitedly pointing towards his position. The riflemen, interspersed along the National Army men stood ready with their SA 80s poised while Mather waited with his Glock 17 automatic pistol hoping for an opportunity to open fire. This 9mm, seventeen round pistol, with an option of an extra one in the barrel, was a great improvement on the Browning which it replaced and Mather had found he was quite a good shot with it.

"Well done the Austrians," he had thought when blazing away on the range at Aldershot, "more to them, than 'Sound of Music' and Wiener 'Schnitzel'."

But Mather cursed the poor intelligence regarding the occupancy of the village but decided he could not risk breaking cover to run back up and over the ridge.

"The good news," he muttered to his Sergeant, "is they can't reach us either without being plastered all over the hillside but we can't just wait here for them to stroll away. Let's call for some help. I'll give HQ a 'sit rep', that we've encountered a strong enemy force."

Mather had been in this inhospitable terrain long enough to see what damage can be caused to flesh and blood by a relatively small, scruffy force of determined men. Earlier that same week a suicide bomber had exploded his device in a crowd of civilians and the country generally was still littered with improvised explosive devices.

What added to the problems of the forces trying to bring the country to some sort of normality was that civilian and would-be bomber dressed identically. His men like the crack regiment they were had to always remain alert and keep a very wary eye on their bearded adversaries. Sadly violence and death was not the sole preserve of men. Too often women and children were used to carry bombs and weapons to remote villages or to detonate suicide bombs in crowded areas! As Mather carefully swept the village below through his binoculars several of them tried to outflank his force behind the rocks and were shot dead by his small force of British and Afghan soldiers; the dead remaining motionless in the long grass. While he and his men waited for reinforcements, the conversation inevitably turned to discussing the various merits and attributes of the women they knew back home in England. They quickly lowered the tone of their discussion when they considered what they would do with their respective girlfriends once their tour of duty in Afghanistan was over. Rifleman Robert Westbrook, casually mentioned the name of a local girl, not unknown to others in the Battalion, that he had been 'seeing' who was great for a night out and as he put it, regular 'afters' but not a girl to take home to meet the parents. As he delicately phrased it:

"A bit like throwing a sausage into the back of a four tonner."

This did bring a smile to Sefton's lips and it helped reduce the stress but then he reflected on what comments would be levelled against a young man of similar sexual proclivities.

"Nothing would be said," he concluded under his breath.

Although a dedicated womaniser he believed women should be treated the same as men but that was still somewhere in the future, even far into 21st Century Britain. It did occur to him that it was women who were the butt of most sexist remarks; then he smiled to himself at the one way women could get their own back. This was the special way they had of humiliating a man by indicating his sexual inadequacy by waggling their little finger in the air! Sefton and the two married men of the patrol made no contribution to the other riflemen's sexual musings. Sefton's main concern was to keep them as focussed as possible as they were in enemy territory, a land sown with IED's and his patrol, likely to be attacked at any moment.

Thirty minutes after the call for support was sent, an Apache AH1 suddenly appeared above the top of the ridge behind them and then angled down towards the village. Two Hellfire missiles were fired in quick succession into the heart of the village. A few of the intended targets could be seen running. A machine gun clattered above their heads and the men on the ground fired rifles and a 'general purpose machine gun' in support. When the smoke, dust and debris settled, little remained in the village below, certainly nothing living!

"Well done, guys," was all Mather needed to say to his men as he ordered them back up and over the ridge and down to their vehicle where driver and two other riflemen, riding 'shotgun' had been waiting to take them the eight kilometres back to base.

Three days after this skirmish Mather was ordered to Kabul to assist in the training of more Afghan National Army Officer recruits. On arrival he found the start of training was delayed so after his recent adventures he decided to treat himself to an overnight stay in a luxury hotel, the 'Serena'.

***

As he lay on his back a decade later he thought, in the light of later events this must have been something of an omen of things to come. Serena Hotel offered many comforts; Serena MacDonald offered even more! He was also remembering that first encounter with the stunning, raven-haired beauty in the foyer of the Serena. Immediately after the first time they met, it had been his intention to immediately coax her into bed. Sex to soothe the nerves after that patrol was just the tonic he prescribed for himself. She proved very willing; perhaps in the light of his recent experience in Soho, too willing. Below the dark hair underneath a headscarf and her almost coal-black eyes and very full luscious mouth was a surprisingly pale skin that had an almost milk-like quality. As the air-conditioning in the room carried out its role, Sefton entered into his. He ran an appreciative hand over breasts, having unbuttoned her blouse and unclipped her bra to release them. They were full and yielding and rose to firm points above the rich tan-colour of her areola. She had been reluctant to drop her skirt. Perhaps this was shyness but to create an appropriate ambience as soon as he had entered the room he had pulled the drapes across. He then switched off the main electric light which had made the bed below look like an over-enthusiastically lit stage. A warm glow from the sun, kept sufficiently at bay outside the building produced the intimate glow that Mather had been seeking.

She lay on her back with him on his left side next to her. Then he reached across and felt for the first but certainly not for the last time, a luxuriant growth, a veritable bush forming a distinct 'V' before his fingers continued on and either side of her vulva. He moved on through the dampening slit, pausing to circle, then gently squeeze her clitoris before venturing on and finding the slippery entrance to that gloriously, glistening gash. He slipped a forefinger, then a second digit in and up five or six centimetres of the front of her vaginal wall. She responded by wriggling and twisting; then she began to arch her back. She bent her knees and slowly, quite deliberately, raised her buttocks up to present Sefton with a ready target for his ever-eager erection to gently thrust down. He looked down appreciatively at the pinky-red furrow perfectly framed between dark folds of skin contrasting so flawlessly against those milk-white thighs. Seconds later she was groaning and he intended withdrawing and then easing his helmet back into the clenched entrance but she had been brought to the top of her sensual mountain all too soon and he felt a rush of liquid splashing his genitals. Surprised but delighted and approaching so urgently, his own special moment he realised he had bedded a real gusher. Not just someone who squirted a few drops but a stream when that joyful, intense moment was come. If only this was London and not Kabul and they could meet regularly! Little did he realise at the time that their paths would cross in the future.

Chapter Five

By the time Sefton was downing his third glass of Chianti Classico in Gianna's Restaurant, Serena was tucked up and back in the same bed where both had enjoyed their earlier coupling. Neither Serena nor Sefton referred to it as love-making in the romantic sense. It was the act itself they both loved and both were good at it but it was that and the occasional companionship and nights out together that seemed sufficient. Serena had no intention of being tied to one man and Sefton was looking elsewhere for that ideal 'wife' material. Yes, their couplings were certainly energetic and satisfying but did she really continue to indulge him in her bed mainly for the level of his intimate ability or was the fact he was a member of parliament the real reason? Such a contact could be quite useful and was probably why she occasionally over the years allowed five other men, potentially useful contacts into her bed though at decent intervals in between. This exclusive sextet including Sefton, numbered some quite influential people though only one other besides Sefton enjoyed anywhere near the length of time or number of appearances under her duvet as the most recent occupant. He was Gareth Valentine, a senior police officer. The others, Vivian Sage-Bedford, a barrister; Ranulf Faulkner, a senior civil servant, then there was Farouk Nassad, a very wealthy banker. The latter, he had told her was a banker but he was rarely in the country and even when he appeared at her front door always seemed to be in a great hurry. The last of the super six was Bertie

Jameson, a television producer and director. Serena had entertained Bertie on many occasions in her professional capacity and he had tried to help her in his.

***

Bertie Jameson left school in the early 1990s but with little ambition to follow the advice of his staid and somewhat controlling parents both of whom were teachers. His boyhood was not particularly happy as his mother and especially his father expected a lot from him, their only child. By the time he began secondary school the stress and pressures he was feeling contributed to a growing streak of rebellious behaviour including petty thieving from local shops and supermarkets and vandalism; spraying walls with aerosols and smashing car mirrors and lights. A visit from the local police did prove enough incentive to abandon at least for a time a prospective life of crime. In mitigation he cast the blame on a gang of boys who he claimed had bullied him into theft and damaging property but he would not name names. His parents continued to try and persuade him to accept responsibility for his actions. His was overall quite a lonely childhood and he had according to him, only behaved anti-socially in an attempt to gain acceptance by the other gang members. Then he fell foul of the neighbours, for over one weekend, the now fifteen year-old Bertie had developed a sudden liking for astronomy. On previous evenings during one particular week in June the night sky had been particularly clear and so it was on the Friday; indeed it was a stargazer's heaven! He borrowed his father's very powerful, Skymaster 25 X 70 binoculars. Instead of gazing up, Bertie gazed across from his bedroom which was directly opposite and looked down on the one occupied by the neighbour's eighteen year-old daughter. That evening she was standing dressing in front of her window. The binoculars brought her breasts almost within touching distance as she stood there in just black, lacy knickers and nothing else.

His sudden, excited movement in response to those visual delights must have caught her eye. She looked up and momentarily caught sight of this figure looking down at her. She crossed her arms over what Bertie considered were her very shapely boobs. She moved to one side; the blind shot down and the bedroom light was switched off. She pulled on a sweater to cover her chest, then wriggled into tight jeans before rushing off, fuming, in search of her father. The latter, two minutes later was knocking at the Jamesons' front door. Twenty after that, a police car pulled up. Bertie was summoned; an angry neighbour shouted accusations at him as he stood just inside the Jamesons' hallway. As the police officers managed to calm the situation down the boy was ushered into the living room. The Clements were invited to return to their home after assurances that their complaint would be thoroughly investigated.

As well as alleged voyeurism Bertie was also accused of stealing Esther's underwear from the washing line the previous afternoon. He vehemently denied both charges and railed against his parents for even thinking he could do such things. His room was searched but nothing incriminating found other than the binoculars. He dismissed the spying complaint by admitting that he had been looking out of his bedroom window but was about to begin a sweep of the night sky when he had been distracted by movement in the bottom of the garden. He claimed he had then seen a fox on the prowl before sweeping the 'glasses' up and in the direction of the night sky. Yes, he may have swept the binoculars up and beyond the bedroom opposite. He apologised if it had appeared to the half-naked neighbour that he had been looking at her. At the time he had not really noticed she was unclothed; it had only been the fact of Mr Clements uttering threats about his spying on her top half that he knew about it. The police officers and the parents, begrudgingly considered his explanation to be reasonably plausible. Then there was a knock at the door which interrupted further discussion. It was Esther's mother; she stood at the door looking embarrassed.

"Sorry," she said to one of the police officers, "but I took in some of Esther's washing yesterday as it was dry and as it didn't require ironing, just put it away."

The officer deduced the significance of this statement:

"You didn't tell her that you had brought it in, did you?"

"Well, no; she must have come home from college, gone to collect her washing, thought it had been stolen but had gone out before we had time to chat. I had gone to a friend's. It was only when we were discussing a possible peeping-tom, that she mentioned the so-called missing underwear that I in fact had put away."

"Just for the record though," the second officer asked, "have any underclothes gone missing before?"

"Yes, a few times," Mrs Clements replied.

"Well, as we haven't found any evidence regarding missing clothing and it's the young man's word against Esther's and with no corroboration there's little we can do," the officer said.

"My husband said that in the circumstances perhaps we should give him the benefit of the doubt over the binoculars incident," she said.

"Yes, probably best all round," the officers agreed but glancing meaningfully in Bertie's direction; certainly one of them not taken in by his innocent demeanour having noticed him grinning slyly.

Things certainly returned to normal in the Jameson and Clements' households though Esther never seemed to be able to find a set of matching bra and pants, that early one afternoon she had hand-washed and pegged out on the washing line. Bertie, having gained the moral high ground by shaming his parents into thinking ill of him, determined to adopt a far more cautious approach to his interests and hobbies and avoid being caught out in future!

***

This unfortunate interlude had occurred at what turned out to be quite a propitious time for Bertie who had had reached that time in a boy's life when a daily inspection of his chin for the first signs of whiskers was a necessity. He had after all as a result of those powerful binoculars discovered the enticing soft curves of the female form. All the while his pushy parents hassled him over his lack of effort at school. The 'binoculars incident' had only driven him to carry out the barest minimum to avoid aggravation from his teachers and ensure parental zeal that hitherto had caused stress and pressure, was now ignored. Suddenly though at the beginning of Year 10 he began to show an interest in acting. This was prompted by the arrival at his school of a new girl, Arlena Rich just weeks before the end of both the term and Year 9. Very soon after the start of the Autumn Term she began to appear in school plays and musicals. Bertie had first caught sight of her during the very warm last few weeks of that Year 9 when she had been playing tennis in her white tennis kit on one of the school's courts. He was smitten! Not overly keen on sports, what was the point of it and having loathed P.E., he did join the Drama Club instead, in order to be close to her. Twice a week after the club Bertie walked home with her to the new-build estate close to the former Guards Depot site where she lived and in their hometown of Caterham. During these walks she told him of her determination to making acting her career. An aunt, Cheryl Langston regularly appeared on television in dramas and 'commercials'. As the last months of Year 10 arrived, he returned to deliberately walking past the tennis courts just to see her in that sexy, skimpy tennis dress. He managed to contain his excitement and not cheer when, as she chased a ball her dress lifted to reveal white sports pants at the top of very long, slim legs. Tennis he would describe as a boring game but certainly not under those arousing circumstances. While Arlena continued to perform in school productions, Bertie volunteered for any backstage task including making, painting and shifting scenery and prompting lesser cast members with their lines merely to be close toa her.

Year 11 was all too soon upon them and the end of compulsory schooling loomed large. As that gloriously awaited date fast approached, pastoral staff focussed on ensuring students were making the correct 16+ choices. When Arlena had spoken to Gisele Gorman her drama teacher on joining the school about her acting ambitions, the teacher reserved judgement. As the terms passed Gisele fully supported her plans and now Arlena's choice to do Drama, English Language, Literature and History at A-level, at Sixth Form College was fully endorsed by Miss Gorman. Usually when a student declared an interest in becoming an actor, especially when they announced, 'to be on the telly', she groaned inwardly and then spent time trying to persuade them to look in a different career direction. In Arlena's case she had no need for the girl had talent, a fine singing voice, was determined, hard-working and very glamorous in or out of tennis kit. Bertie so influenced by Arlena's presence decided to follow a similar careers' route having just about managed the necessary grades at GCSE. Not a choice that pleased or impressed his parents. It also caused his class tutor to groan for although he knew of Bertie's efforts backstage he had always wondered why the boy was keen to put so much effort there but managed to use only a small percentage of his undoubted talents elsewhere. When names cropped up in the staff room or at meetings, Miss Gorman made her feelings known and other staff's attempts to dissuade Bertie from his choice, also failed. Gisele's P.E. teacher colleague, Dennis Trueman felt just the same when mostly boys stood before him saying they were set on a career as a professional footballer. During the whole of his own six years to date, teaching career he could only recall two boys from this comprehensive school going beyond the 'apprenticeship' stage. Only one of them managed to be signed by a professional football club and that in Division Two of the Football League. Football, like acting, attracts so many but few, very few are chosen!

Still in pursuit of Arlena, Bertie continued to follow her home when their paths crossed as school finished. He had been disappointed in July when his suggestion they attend the School Prom Night together was turned down. She had been offered over the days leading up to and beyond that final school 'rites de passage', thanks to a good word from her aunt, a role in a t.v. commercial for a pizza company. Reluctantly but with her future career in mind and the sizeable fee that accompanied the job, she chose that instead. Another opportunity to 'make out' with Arlena gone forever he decided. Soon after and marking time to begin sixth form, Arlena secured a Saturday job at a coffee shop in Caterham Valley. On numerous occasions Bertie would appear outside, then sometimes even venture in to buy a cup of coffee and a cake but then only as an excuse to drool over her.

At college, Arlena continued her upward trajectory towards stage and screen. There was more work in television and she played a leading role in the College's Drama Department's productions. Bertie trailed along behind her, very much cast in her shadow. She was playing 'leads' while he was doing 'walk-on' parts as a butler or chaffeur. Then he was asked to help with the direction of a short film the Department was making for an entry in a short feature film competition. He carried out the role of 'second unit' director in a different part of town very well and received praise from his tutors for the way he had taken control of the scene and his fellow students. Bertie having been controlled as a young child by his parents had enjoyed the chance to manage and organise others and seemed to have a natural flair for achieving what he wanted. When it was finally time to apply to university he once again followed Arlena; this time to Bournemouth but there was also something for him as well. The other side of the camera was appealing more and more to him. It offered huge possibilities in others having to do what he wanted rather than the opposite. So he chose a degree that had some acting but really focussed more on stage, television and movie production and direction. As Arlena continued to shine he was emerging as a directing talent. After graduating, she was cast in a four-part period drama. From that to a West End musical.

***

Bertie's acting career, unlikely ever to set Hollywood green with envy stalled. This was more than compensated by his applying for and being successful in a vacancy for a job as an assistant director working in regional news and current affairs for local television. He showed a knack for working well with people on both sides of the camera especially women. Two months before his twenty-fourth birthday he was directing a children's television mini-series set in Southampton. Then his big break came and he was invited to interview for a vacancy offering an opportunity to head up a team producing documentaries for BBC Television. Offered this role he soon began to show considerable flair.

One documentary he was heavily involved in concerned the controversy surrounding 'extraordinary rendition' and the degree of collusion between the United Kingdom and the United States in the detention of nationals purported to be involved in terrorism. Their confinement and subsequent transfer without trial or any recourse to any form of due legal process to the United States Detention Centre at Guantanamo Bay prompted the programme to raise many awkward questions of the British Government. Doubtless some of the men 'snatched' in this way, Afghans, Iraqis, Iranians, Libyans and others were terrorists but both governments faced a vociferous and hostile backlash over the whole matter. The U.S. Government claimed that the greatest nation on earth was powerless in combating terrorism in the orthodox way. It offered the only means of protecting its own people and Western Democracy from terrorists who were prepared to use whatever measures no matter how base to achieve their warped ends. They claimed they had no other choice to adopt extraordinary measures including rendition, or to 'fight fire with fire' as one security spokesperson put it. For his contribution in exposing 'rendition' Bertie received a major television award. His plan to produce a 'follow-up' was thwarted. Certain individuals and one in particular, in the British Security Service brought pressure to bear suggesting this would not be in the Nation's best interests; a move no doubt supported by their American counterparts.

By 2016 and Brexit, Bertie had still managed to carve out a very successful career. His parents who he rarely visited did bask in their son's reflected glory. A neighbour (not the Clements) had asked them if a credit, 'Director: Bertie Jameson', on a television programme was any relation. They positively glowed with pride and had the temerity to suggest that his success was down to their encouragement.

On a whim and at a loose end one evening after being given a business card by an acting friend, Dickon Colgate who was appearing in the studio next to his own, he made a telephone call.

Dickson had said earlier:

"Try this Bertie. She'll put hairs on your chest. Not cheap but worth every one of your expense account pennies."

Colgate and several others in his immediate circle had been wondering about Bertie Jameson for some time. He appeared to like women and at awards evenings always seemed to stroll down the red carpet in the company of a young woman. Dickson had appeared in plays directed by Bertie but was curious as to why many of the female cast nearly always seemed to be quickly replaced. At first he had not believed it when one aspiring actress accused Bertie of wanting sexual favours in exchange for acting parts in his productions. Not yet convinced though and prompted by curiosity that Bertie was much of a ladies' man he had given him Aurora's card. Later, Colgate began to change his mind

Bertie too was curious though not for the same reasons as his friend. He was certainly more intrigued than eager or desperate for sex when he had rung, 'Dating Delights Escort Agency' and arranged an evening's company in a discreet hotel. Very soon his professional life was uncomfortably close to his private life.

He was commissioned to examine claims that some women were being forced into prostitution, escort work or selling their underwear and a range of personal articles in order to feed their families. One evening he found himself in the company of beautiful women as he began to pursue a possible subject for a new probing documentary. One of these women he had met several times before. His office had been sent some details concerning an escort being the subject of a brutal attack as she had plied her particular trade. This unfortunate escort was advised to pursue the case in the fervent hope that it might result in the lid being lifted on the widespread sexploitation of women by a cross-section of Britain's great and good. Bertie was introduced to 'Laurel' who had sent her story to his office; later he would discover this was her working name as she generally answered to 'Jemima'. Serena, first known to Bertie as Aurora confirmed Jemima's story:

"Yes, covered in bruises after being punched and kicked by not just one man but a second who fancied a violent threesome. This was hardly the first time this level of violence been done," she replied.

They were just getting into their stride when Bertie's mobile rang. It was his studio and they needed him back to sort out some editorial technicality or other. It was agreed they would meet in a few days time and allow him to continue with his probing. Bertie before he rushed off suggested there could be a story in what he had heard so far. That could very well result in a programme that would bring violence against women under public scrutiny. The following day he received a call suggesting a time to meet but suggesting a different venue. Instead of a hotel why not at Serena's house near Waterloo? A couple of days later Bertie found himself rushing from his office deep inside Broadcasting House. He knew the Waterloo area well for various reasons. He had been an occasional visitor to Television Centre to the north of his current destination. Word around the BBC was that ITV planned to buy the freehold of the Centre and before long sell it off for re-development. Built in the 1970s it had once been the dynamic hub of London Weekend Television. This was confirmation that the world of television was changing radically.

The cab delivered him to 21, Victory Mews; he paid the driver off after securing a receipt for his expenses and moved towards the front door.

"Do come in, Bertie dear," Serena invited.

"Thanks, love," he replied; trying not to appear too theatrical but that's how the words made him sound.

Already seated was Jemima and another woman that he knew by sight having seen her on television being interviewed on various women's issues and at the head of protests and demonstrations and through her growing reputation for her energetic support and promotion of women's rights. Before Bertie had a chance to introduce himself to her, she had moved towards him with right hand outstretched.

"How do you do, Mr Jameson?" she said formally but continued, "we have actually met and you were helpful in a campaign I was involved in concerning FGM. I'm Sophie Fortune."

Yes, he remembered, he had met her but quite a long time ago but knew of her investigating and championing the plight of the desperate, deprived and disadvantaged. Her star was in the ascendant and her success measured by the level of pain and irritation her crusading thorn was causing the collective side of those in authority.

"In case you're wondering why I'm here, Serena and I do go back a long way but we're hoping that you may be able to embarrass and prod the Government into action over the continuing shameful treatment of women no matter what their occupation. Little seems to have improved since our university days," she said, waving her hand in Serena's direction as the latter headed in the direction of her kitchen.

Bertie nodded his head in recognition but Sophie as passionate as ever about the causes she espoused took his acknowledgement as a signal to continue.

"Government cuts," she added, "in recent years to the CPS, the reduction in police numbers and the consequential loss of dedicated teams of officers investigating rape cases has dramatically cut the numbers of cases being prosecuted. Many women just think it a waste of time reporting their rape. We have asked the Government after their lame review of rape incidents, to look again but this time not just apologise for the shortcomings but take real action and give many wronged women justice."

Bertie thought after this social statement that it was his cue to utter something encouraging but for once felt a little uncomfortable in the presence of such a strong-minded woman; but what a woman! Feeling stunned and with a grave responsibility settling on his shoulders, he heard himself rather lamely replying:

"We'll see what we can do."

She smiled but added:

"Not that it was great under the previous regime. For God's sake, we are half the population and deserve better."

Bertie was beginning to wonder if he had wandered into the inaugural meeting of a 'women's action group' or some such, after Sophie's diatribe but Serena's re-appearance with an impressive range of drinks on a large tray meant they could now return to the original purpose of the meeting. Hopefully, Sophie's intense gaze on him would shortly be diverted elsewhere.

Serena opened proceedings:

"Where to begin?" she said, looking a little puzzled. "Well, let's start with Jem's story. While she was working for another escort agency she was constantly propositioned to perform all sorts of acts that clients had been told were not provided. This was made abundantly clear at the time of booking their appointment. One instance was after Jemima had accompanied a client to the theatre and then back to the hotel where he had forced himself upon her. There he slapped her and threatened the poor girl with much worse if she did not allow him to carry out anal and oral sex on her and then take him in her mouth until she gagged. She at first refused, reminding him of the t's and c's mentioned before."

Bertie looked a little incredulous and appeared to have no control over his eyebrows.

Serena noticing their rising continued:

"Yes, I know this sounds ridiculous; escorts talking about terms and conditions but women ALL women," she said emphasising the word, "are potentially vulnerable."

She looked across at Sophie who was nodding vigorously in agreement. Sophie Fortune who harangued and encouraged the Government to introduce measures to effectively protect women from the violent behaviour of men. Sophie who marched, campaigned and protested on behalf of all women.

"What happened?" Bertie asked as his faced switched from incredulity to concern.

"Her arms, thighs, buttocks were very badly bruised as well as internal organs and," she hesitated before adding, "pooing was extremely difficult and painful for days."

"I managed to distract him and grabbed my things and ran for the door. I reached the lift where I pulled on my clothes. A group of men jeered as I passed them but not one of them tried to help. I reached the street and caught a cab back here and called the police," Jemima said.

"What action did the police take?" Sophie enquired.

"None, well only the bare minimum even though I had given them the name of the man, a Jamail Hallet; I had also met him before when I worked briefly for the other agency. He had been a bit rough then and now I think about it used the same name; though it's probably not his real one. I was interviewed by detectives but nothing else. Though," she said, "when I mentioned the name I'm sure I didn't imagine it but one of the officers raised his eyebrows as though either the name was familiar or he just didn't believe me. I asked Serena to take pictures of my injuries and she came with me to A&E where I was checked over for signs of permanent injuries."

"Just to clarify, you heard nothing after this visit from the police?" Bertie asked.

"No," Jemima declared adamantly, "nothing at all. Apparently my job description, 'escort' means my injuries are either, self-inflicted or deserved. Anytime they do help they want a 'freebie' in return," she added bitterly.

"It's one of the reasons why I originally decided to go freelance and try and have a little more control but nothing, I suspect would have stopped him in this case," Serena said. "We offer a limited range of very exclusive services," Serena only just remembering to stop herself from saying to Bertie, 'as you know', "but," she continued, "at very high prices in an attempt to sort the wheat from the chaff."

"Surely though, violence and less savoury practices are not confined to the thuggish end of society?" Bertie suggested.

"No, not at all. Some of the nastiest British womanising bullies are in the police and often want something, as Jemima suggested, or are lawyers or bankers. No, that's not necessarily a euphemism," Serena replied smiling thinly. "As further protection for my team, I employ a private detective to 'vet' potential clients."

"What about this Hallet, guy?" Bertie asked.

"Nothing. According to Mr Hargreaves' investigations, Hallet doesn't exist. Which seems suspicious in itself. No trace of him entering or leaving the country and both Home and Foreign Offices very tight-lipped. Come to think of it though, when later we again brought Hallet's name up with the police, one of them said best leave it!"

What Serena failed to mention was that one of the police detectives in question had availed himself of her very bountiful services and furthermore was a very accomplished lover. Gareth Valentine was a senior detective with the Metropolitan Police and indeed in Olympic terms would be in serious contention for 'gold' in the mattress marathon!

"We mustn't forget the other end of the 'sex' as a commodity spectrum or that for women generally, violence against them is nothing new," added Sophie and continued, "periodic economic down-turns don't help and too many women and girls are forced to sell themselves to feed a cocaine habit after being exploited by men."

"Yes, I think we've some scope here to begin an in-depth expose. I've a pretty free hand and have been giving some thought, as you were speaking, to a working title, 'Sexploitation and violence in 21st Century Britain', just to get us started. My research assistants, Rowena and Sienna will be in touch soon."

He looked across at Sophie's deadpan expression and added:

"It is only a working title so any thoughts and suggestions are always welcome. This is a very sensitive and contentious area after all and any probing may cause a few of your past and present clients Jemima, to worry about what may be revealed."

Bertie could have added that he was relying on Serena's discretion as he would not like it to be generally known that he, a respected television producer and director had bedded an escort or that he enjoyed certain diversions while doing so.

His thoughts were distracted as Sophie apologised for having to leave as she had a very early start the following morning and would need to work late in order to prepare documents for a case at Westminster Magistrates Court. Jemima left soon after leaving Serena and Bertie together.

"The usual?" Serena asked softly.

"Yes, I could certainly do with some of your tlc after that session," he replied.

"Do you think you can do something to help?" Serena said.

"We'll certainly try," he answered simply, quickly downing the drink she had given him before she headed upstairs and to the bedroom with Bertie just behind. As he reached her dressing table he placed a wad of notes under a photo frame. He preferred a motley range of banknotes to other methods of payment as they were less easy to trace. Conversely, Serena didn't; cash struck her as being so sordid though in this particular case it did allow her a few steps up the slope to the moral high ground. He was a big name in television while she and the others she employed were very expensive escorts or call girls. She resented the use of what she regarded as the rather coarse word 'prostitute' with its lowly connotations. She consoled herself with the thought that she was good at her business but increasingly needed to perform less and less herself as she diversified into other businesses. When she did act as an escort and to bed then it was only to indulge a few special men, her super sextet! Even several of them were becoming rarer visitors. There was also the fact of an 'edge' offered by her filming her couplings and those of Jemima when they were at number 21. Years before when an escort for liaisons had been arranged it always took place in specific rooms of a select number of hotels. It had taken Serena some time to work out that celebrity clients were filmed by the agency she was then working for to give them the option of blackmailing them. When she started her own business and used her own address she had set up in one of the rooms, film equipment not for blackmail but as a means of protection, purely as a safeguard should any of the sexual transactions go awry. Much easier nowadays with the small but ingenious instruments that were so simple to operate.

***

Bertie was not overly demanding although he did like to be in control and so far in their sexual couplings she had been content to fully oblige him. After the first few visits Serena was certainly able to give him the impression that he was in charge. This was achieved after he had asked her for a particular favour. Serena was pleased to dress in white tennis kit; this included a white sleeveless dress. In order to carry out his fantasy, she had cut the shoulder straps with scissors and then joined them with two strips of Velcro. As Bertie's excitement rose the Velcro enabled Serena to release the dress held in place by that material. As that garment slipped to the floor Serena who had invited Bertie to remove shirt, shoes and trousers, then moved forward and released his uncircumcised member from his shorts. She then began to tease him by slowly, deliberately removing her sports bra. Serena pulled him towards her so he could run his dribbling penis up towards her navel. Then she pushed him back on to the bed and wriggled out of very skimpy, very white sports pants. Soon it was time to manoeuvre down on to his erection before he suffered a premature emission. She rose and fell, gradually accelerating until he climaxed. Then she extricated herself and rolled by the side of him. It was hardly passionate for there was never any foreplay not even fumbling; Serena had long decided that it was the skimpy tennis knickers that were the trigger though invariably he did seem to enjoy sucking her nipples. He had become a regular and was never rough and always paid the required fee without a quibble. Later he would even subscribe to 'Gemma's Gems' and a particularly favourite purchase was white and skimpy! Serena, on further reflection decided that he liked the idea of sex rather than the act itself. She knew he had never married but seemed to enjoy the company of women. Later when a scandal broke in the United States concerning a Hollywood Movies producer expecting sexual favours for acting roles, an acting friend of Serena suggested that Bertie had looked worried when similar accusations had been levelled at some of his peers in the industry on this side of the Atlantic. Somehow he would manage to ride out that particular storm but before then pressure was brought to bear on him and his team to modify the incisive investigation he was planning on the subject of violence against women. He did at least have the good grace to ring Sophie at her office and explain that he had run into what he referred to as 'editorial difficulties'. In an odd sort of way she drew some comfort from the fact that the programme soon to be broadcast was not to be quite the in-depth investigation originally envisaged. Underneath though she was seething at a missed opportunity. She suspected external meddling but to her at least it was proving the cause of women was advancing when the Establishment was having to take such steps to protect itself by curbing them. Bertie was annoyed but unless he wanted his private life plastered across the tabloids could do little but comply. He did settle for one course of action and that was to keep copies of scripts and 'programme rushes' of what would have been broadcast. If details of his private life did become public he would pass them on to a 'tabloid' editor he knew. He also felt better too when he kept copies for Sophie Fortune who would be sent them if he became front page news. She would certainly recognise the names of several of the men who would have been exposed had Bertie not been 'persuaded to toe the line'. Until something else cropped up that he could tackle without fear or favour, Bertie directed several dramas.

***

During early 2019 Bertie, still wary after his earlier experiences received an anonymous tip-off suggesting he look into the activities of certain members of the Security Services. Somehow the latter heard about this, a source from his own office had put them on to it and he was warned off. A frustrated Bertie turned to other projects; hopefully ones that would cause less upset to senior figures in HM Government and elsewhere. Certainly one other investigation that Bertie had chosen to pursue did irritate certain sections of the Establishment. This was an attempt to trigger an enquiry into the treatment of former Jihadists in Syria and other countries including Britain, France and Spain. There was always the possibility of further awards and the accolades that accompanied such recognition by his peers for such quality, investigative journalism. His declared intention though was to uncover the inhumane ways in which people, mainly women and girls had been abandoned not only by their former Jihadist partners in the short-lived Islamic Republic but by their original countries too. Some of the women had turned to law and one of the lawyers trying to fight for their right to return to their former homes was, Sophie Fortune. When she had finally calmed down after being informed of the change to the format of the investigation into violence against women she did not so much blame Bertie as consider it another example of how women were regarded in Society. Hearing about this projected documentary she contacted his office and sent on some evidence including specific examples of stateless, non-persons languishing in tented refugee camps in Turkey denied citizenship. Sophie was informed that he was to shortly meet the brother of a victim of this injustice at a friend's address near Waterloo Station; she asked if she might tag along, though with little expectation. Of course, Sophie remembered a previous visit to this same address and hugged Serena who stood framed in the door. She followed her in and was delighted to meet Serena's friend, Jemima again too. Sophie was then introduced to the relative of a young woman denied a British passport and stranded far from home. Ten minutes later they were joined by Bertie Jameson. Sophie Fortune, not a person to bear grudges and, believing Bertie had had little control over that 'women and violence' episode greeted him with a warm smile and:

"Hello Bertie, how are you?"

He smiled back and simply replied:

"Fine. Thankyou."

Three hours later after hearing harrowing testimony the meeting finally broke up leaving Bertie, Serena and Jemima quite drained after those stories of the life of those who had travelled to Syria, the fighting and soon after cruelty, hunger, and their abandonment and rejection by their native states. For Bertie it was forming the basis of a hard-hitting documentary but ahead there was to be quite the opposite than thinking about misery for him that evening. The relative and Sophie had already gone their separate ways when Jemima announced she had plans for later and excused herself too. This left Serena and Bertie sitting alone and just like on other occasions they were soon sharing a bed.

***

Soon after Sefton's departure, Serena had pulled the duvet around her body, still glowing in the aftermath of those earlier exertions but eagerly awaiting the arrival of Alysha to get in beside her. Men were useful but women in many ways made better lovers for they were thoughtful and gentle. The two women had found little need in their loving relationship so far, to resort to artificial aids or toys. Their love-making was deep and satisfying. They were equal lovers and each came to the love-bed with only their own red-blooded equipment including lips, tongue, fingers and the inter-twining of their bodies and certainly no ego. There was one really enjoyable position which made them feel particularly connected; it began with them face to face, then one woman would go head to feet, then turn on her side and lower herself down so her genitalia were opposite her lover's; she would then open her legs and slide up bringing her wet vulva into moist, arousing contact with the other's eager clitoris, sopping labia and vaginal entrance; fingers were often employed to assist them in their progression to that ultimate moment. Then both would gently rock in unison until they invariably reached orgasm.

***

Now moments after arriving home her lover entered the bedroom, stood at the end of the bed and allowed her dress to fall to the carpet. She unfastened her bra and allowed that to follow the discarded dress to the luxuriant pile that she could feel between her toes. Still wearing a white, silky thong she got into bed. Serena could not help but give a gasp of pleasure as the beautiful Antiguan's body with swelling nipples eased close to her, half turning so that warm breasts were pushing against her own warm mammaries sending an electrifying tingle through Serena's already aroused body. Oh so gently, Alysha kissed

Serena full on the lips. Serena moved slowly, deliberately from left to right so that her small, firm breasts and their hardened tips moved and gently massaged Alysha's mounds with their sun-kissed hue bequeathed to her by her ancestors toiling under a blazing Caribbean sun. Then she rolled Alysha over and ran a hand down her shoulders and waist then eased the backs of her thighs apart. Soon she was fingering her way over her lover's tight anus and finding the moistening folds of her labia that in turn was transferring her feminine wetness to the thong's gusset. This was very timely as the next day that little garment would be in the post to an eager client in Birmingham. Then she rolled her onto her back and slipped head first down the bed removed the thong and was soon breathing in Alysha's unique feminine scent. Perfectly positioned in the '69' position both young women began to first lick then suck each other's hooded ladies before gently pinching engorged labia in their teeth. Within five minutes both women were sighing with pleasure before returning to the more orthodox position for sleep, side by side. They turned to each other kissing softly, lovingly those lips now tasting of each other's special place. Then it was a whispered, 'Good night', before sleep came quickly to both of them as they lay, with Alysha cuddled into Serena's back; both at ease with the world.

***

The Antiguan beauty had first come to Britain with her mother to join her cricketing father, Tomson. He had initially toured England with the West Indies then returned to play in Test Matches in successive years. His prowess as a very fast bowler was in great demand not only by the 'Windies' selectors but with numerous English county teams. Eventually he joined Essex County Cricket Club. Weather apart the move was a very successful one and he sent for his wife and children;

two year old Alysha and three month old Cayman to join him. The family settled in Colchester. Many more appearances followed for the West Indies and for Essex. His was among the first names pencilled in on the team sheet After years of sending stumps, bails and occasionally batsmen in different directions he was appointed first team coach.

In time Alysha studied, 'Business Studies', 'Economics' and 'English' at Colchester College and applied for a position at 'August Sandor Promotions'. A company promoting a wide range of corporate events. One afternoon she was part of a team involved in a product launch at Tottenham Hotspur Stadium in North London. To add to the glamour and excitement of the occasion, stars of film and television and a new breed of 'wannabees' from reality television, were in attendance along with some very well known names from the host venue. Including Jethro Boateng, a very talented footballer and a regular in the 'Spurs' first team and a stalwart of Ghana's national side. The only blot on his particular landscape was being subjected to bouts of vile racist abuse both on and off the pitch. When playing away from home at some football grounds it persisted and too often on social media he received not only that same abuse but threats too. When playing for the National team in Eastern Europe a section of the crowd had booed and chanted the foulest of insults. At its inception he had fully supported 'taking the knee' during the pandemic but after a few months performing it to empty stadiums, in his mind it became a meaningless ritual and achieved nothing. Ridding the game and society of racism was a long-term project requiring new and vigorous practical ideas.

A leading television personality, Xanthe Cuthbertson acted as host as the great and the good mingled to contribute to yet another success for 'ASP'.

It also launched a new relationship as, in the words of the romantic novelists, 'their eyes met across a crowded room'. Alysha, who had risen steadily in the company was now Assistant to the 'Director of Events', Kieron Melrose, a role which kept her busy ensuring that such events as the one at the football stadium ran smoothly. As Xanthe, waxed lyrical over the merits of the new product, Alysha glanced around the room and her eyes soon fixed on those of a tall, very athletic young man who was staring right back at her. Though most people in the room had all 'scrubbed up well' to coin a phrase, he wore his clothes particularly well. He was wearing an exclusive, nearly five thousand pounds worth, of one of Savile Row's finest suits but with an open neck shirt revealing a heavy gold neck chain. He stood out from the crowd not merely because of the bleached tips crowning the long hair of his classic Mohawk with its shaved sides but all the way down to his expensive, two thousand dollar imported casual Berluti leather boots. He also had a presence, a definite charisma; he radiated confidence, bordering on arrogance both on and off the football field. Alysha was smitten by Jethro but so was Jethro with Alysha. It was the end to a perfect day. Firstly, she had been impressed by the football stadium itself with its four, tiered stands, hospitality accommodation and the perfect playing service The stadium frontage shimmered in the sun hinting at the gladiatorial, high quality football contests played out within.

As the afternoon came to an end and guests melted away, the promotions' team hovered as their technical and construction units removed all their equipment, television screens and product promotional material. Then Alysha noticed Jethro standing near one of the exits, his face split into a broad grin.

The day's tasks fulfilled, a good job done she moved towards him.

"Fancy a lift, I'm going your way," he said.

"You don't know my address," she replied, smiling.

"Will do, when you show me," he answered.

Two minutes later they were heading south in his red Aston-Martin.

They stopped for supper in the West End before as promised he took her home to her studio flat. Alysha invited him in for coffee and would not have minded more but he said he must be in for training early next morning and had to leave. He explained that after their defeat earlier in the week, their rather world weary Coach had ordered them in early on subsequent days. They had thrown away a two goal lead to lose by three goals to two. Now that defeat was being addressed; each player's shortcomings discussed and an earlier curfew and other restrictions imposed.

"You sound like naughty children," she commented.

The look on his face confirmed this as an accurate summation of how he felt he was being treated.

"I'm out of contract soon and have had offers from a couple of American clubs as well as a Chinese one. It's been a very difficult time recently. May have to follow the money and go east but before I do that I'll go home and spend some time with my family back home in Ghana," he explained.

The football world including Jethro, was still recovering from the Super-League saga. Six of England's leading teams, or rather their rich owners seeking even more wealth had thrown the football world into confusion over one weekend last April. Behind closed doors they had been bidding to be part of an exclusive European league; but only the twelve or fifteen signees would be playing each other. In that league there would have been no promotion or relegation just the same teams involved but as a consequence, they would have been banned from other competitions. Even the Prime Minister commented on the likely outcome. Most commentators agreed that if that small group of teams left, irreparable damage would be done not only to the Premiership but every league down to football's grass roots. Not only fans but players too would have been affected. Those who might play in the new league would be banned from representing their countries in future. By the middle of the week, the six very embarrassed English football clubs, the 'shameless six' had withdrawn from the project, overwhelmed by criticism directed at them from all sides. It left many questions and recriminations and only added to Jethro's feeling of uncertainty. A cynic might still be reflecting, now some of the dust seemed to have settled, that regardless of all the shock and the horror of an attempt by rich clubs to get richer, little had changed. Money, big business, power, a select few, television and not the fans were the ones who really controlled the 'beautiful game'. Was football any different to any other big business or to the game of politics?

**

He left Alysha after a long, lingering kiss, promising to phone her in a few days. He proved as good as his word and even arranged for her to watch the next home game from the comfort of one of the very plush hospitality suites.

She had been brought up in the world of cricket but could appreciate Jethro's contribution. He scored one goal and 'assisted' in two others. After the game he drove her south-west to his house near Richmond Park, then they went out to dinner. As they relaxed and watched, 'Match of the Day' on 'playback' and the presenter and pundits enthused over his contribution to the Spurs win, he slipped an arm around her, pulled her close and began to explore the contours of her dress. She had seen him that afternoon play quite aggressively and once again in edited highlights. He tackled hard but was tackled hard by opposition players and she began to realise this was quite a confrontational sport but his physique was well-suited to the game. Yet as a lover, there was no sign of that aggression. He was quite gentle although as her sexual experience was limited and his physique was not restricted to muscles alone, his first penetration of her was quite painful. Her body was soon quivering and a thin trickle from her was beginning to form a stream as she rolled off Jethro's straining member. This, as a ribbon of semen from him jetted across her pubic mound. It continued its upward trajectory coating her left breast and its very erect nipple then on towards her armpit. Her groin still ached with desire though and fortunately, his hand soon moved to play with her pink-brown petals and maintain her level of arousal. He rimmed the entrance to her vagina then eased several fingers inside before removing them and stroking the length of a very wet vulva which gave them both much satisfaction. Feeling she had let him down by abandoning their coupling and for the first time with any man, she bent forward to take his slowly shrinking member in her right hand, rubbed the glans and slipped his helmet into her mouth. Then she withdrew it, with a sucking, slurping sound, leaving a thin trickle of semen and spit trailing from mouth to penis. Her response this first time had been amazing and so unexpected. In future he would be very careful not to plunge in too deeply! The very next time and ever the considerate lover he turned her on her side, lifted her left leg gently and penetrated from behind which caused her much less discomfort. As their meetings increased he returned to the frontal approach where he could kiss her breasts and gently knead her buttocks towards him and push into her increasingly more receptive groin.

Their romantic attachment continued for many months but she did not move in with him. That would not have been acceptable to her church-going mother. They did alternate between their respective properties where the sex continued to prove very satisfactory but it suited them both to maintain their separate addresses. Everything seemed to be going well then Covid arrived but she still did not want to move in with him. Alysha was desperate to maintain some degree of independence; somehow Serena's offer was perfect. Pandemic normality began to return but very reluctantly once travel conditions began to improve, Jethro realised that he must make a professional move and their love-making became a rarer event. An offer had come in from an American Soccer Club. The US soccer, as they insist on calling football, scene was changing. Twenty and more years ago they brought in European football stars at the end of their careers but now they needed younger players if they were ever going to succeed at international or even at club level. Stimulate that at the appropriate level and it will encourage progression in the national team. Jethro decided to follow the dollar. A footballer's career is a short one; even shorter if injury intervenes. He did ask Alysha to accompany him but she did not want to leave her now ailing mother. It was with great and mutual reluctance they broke up.

***

Sefton sat back in his chair considering just how things can quickly change. Just after 'A-levels' and during his first undergraduate years he had edged curiously along the drugs path. The four usual outlets for 'wild-oat sowing' had all, saving one, largely been rejected. The first, sex, he continued to pursue enthusiastically; the second, drinking, in more recent years, he had adapted and now generally drank more moderately, after falling into several potentially career-wrecking escapades. The third, gambling, was now a very rare vice and the fourth, drugs, had come to an almost abrupt end after a 'heroin-fuelled' evening that had resulted in the death of one of his companions. Occasionally he and Serena like so many of their contemporaries did indulge. As always they were looking to add something special to their sensual adventure.

The Walpole twins were at boarding school with him and the three friends had shared adventures. On many occasions the trio could be seen climbing the wall back into their school after visiting the local pub and taking it in turns to share the favours of the local girls. One in particular, in Sefton's words, 'knew the score' and in great measure had put their interest in the female form gleaned largely from top shelf magazines into more practical knowledge and certainly a more pleasing form. For services regularly rendered the lads contributed equal financial shares. Sefton was an especially eager learner and very quick to turn that two dimensional theory from those pictures he had drooled over, into three dimensional practice. Soon Sylvia Worthington's vulva and the ample contents of her brassiere were as familiar to him as those of the plastic-surgery enhanced beauties of the much thumbed magazines. It was Sylvia who had first led him to discover the clitoris.

Victor Walpole, nicknamed for his initials, 'the Beetle' and Arthur Walpole, known to his intimates as, 'Horace' were Sefton's friends since childhood. They were all keen sportsmen. The Beetle and his brother played in the school's first fifteen but the Beetle was certainly expected to go on beyond county level to represent his country. When it all started to go wrong was not clear. Sefton and the Beetle became irregular users but Horace began to descend deeper into a regular cocaine habit. On the day he should have been sitting the first of his 'Finals' a worried student who shared his digs broke into his room only to find him dead, a needle still in his arm.

His twin, who Sefton remembered with a grimace, had dated Sophie Fortune during those university days at Exeter, was devastated by his brother's death. Sefton would have grimaced even more if he had known that it had been 'Horace' who had had actually bedded Durford's most eligible virgin, months before university. Not that the young man remembered much about the de-flowering as it had taken place during a cocaine-powered haze. Even worse, if Sefton had known, would be Walpole's response to Sophie's sharing her concern that she might be pregnant after that encounter. When she confronted him, his response was brutal:

"Well, you can get rid of it can't you?" he said, shrugging.

Verity, Lady Fortune, concerned that her daughter had suddenly gone from being a lively, spirited, fun-seeker to a morose, irritable teenager almost overnight, asked to see her in the Hall's Library; a place of refuge and a room to share secrets for generations of Fortunes.

"Are you pregnant?" she asked bluntly

"I'm not sure," replied Sophie, taken aback by her mother's directness.

"Not been fooling around with Sefton Mather, I hope," she added.

Sophie shook her head and wondered again why her mother seemed so set against Sefton.

Happily, for all concerned, it proved to be a false alarm and nothing more was said on the matter.

Arthur Walpole's untimely death left his brother almost inconsolable; he dropped out of sight for months and on his return to Durford seemed to have changed totally. It was strongly rumoured he had undergone some sort of conversion of Damascene proportions.

His taking to religion was complete, after training for holy orders. The last Sefton heard of him was that following ordination he went on to serve as curate in a string of Lincolnshire parishes.

Sefton's consolation was he was some distance away from Sophie.

***

He was in his place on the green benches in the Commons, the very top row directly behind the Prime Minister at the Despatch Box, just after 11-00am the next day, Wednesday. He was feeling just a little nervous, even though he had spoken before and asked questions of various Ministers. This would be his first time asking the Prime Minister one. Just before mid-day, the PM walked purposefully into the Chamber. Somehow, even after the most torrid baptism of fire faced by any Prime Minister since Churchill in 1940, the current tenant of Number 10, Downing Street, still radiated his usual, bubbly unflappable personality. He reached the Despatch Box, placing papers and files before him and sat down.

The Speaker called out, "Mr Sefton Mather."

"Number one, Mr Speaker, Sir," and promptly sat down.

The Prime Minister rose to his feet, looking round him, savouring the moment and then responded in the customary way.

"This morning, I had meetings with Ministerial colleagues and others. In addition to my duties in this House, I shall have further meetings later today," Then he backed away from the Despatch Box and sat down.

Sefton Mather rose once more to his feet to ask his supplementary question:

"Does My Right Honourable Friend, the Prime Minister believe that the recent activity by Chinese naval forces in the East China Seas is a feint by the Chinese Government to disguise their continuing barbaric treatment of their Moslem minority, the Uighurs, particularly women?"

As Mather sat down, the PM rose and turned through almost one hundred and eighty degrees in order to acknowledge the questioner.

"I thank my Honourable Friend for his question. His interest in Chinese and women's affairs," he hesitated and then changed his statement slightly, "His interest in Chinese affairs and women's rights is well known. I can say to him that we are continuing to monitor the situation in the East China Seas and doing all we can to take the Chinese Government to task over their appalling treatment of the Uighurs and other persecuted minorities within their borders."

For the twenty five minutes that followed, the Prime Minister answered a varied range of questions and the usual criticism from the Leader of the Opposition before finally rising to his feet and leaving the Chamber as quickly as he had walked in.

Chapter Six

Sefton, on Friday afternoon, left his London flat and set off for home and his constituency. There was nothing like his mother's cooking and being waited on by her on a lazy Sunday before returning to the hurley-burley of London. Furthermore the au pair his mother had recruited might still be looking after his brother's children at home. He was wearing a dark suit for the train ride home but carried, along with his dirty washing the grey suit last worn to the Commons on Tuesday, then to Serena's and then Gianna's later that same evening. His mother always urged him to bring anything requiring washing or dry-cleaning home. Durford seemed to be one of the few towns left in the county boasting a dry-cleaning shop.

As the train clattered westward through stations and green countryside scarred by an occasional new-build housing estate, he thought ahead to the following morning. When he was back in the constituency for the weekend, he spent most of the Saturday morning, holding a mobile surgery. He towed a specially converted caravan as his travelling office behind his much-loved black Range Rover that would soon, with rather mixed feelings be replaced by a 'Plug-in Hybrid' model. Not that these days he drove very much but Sefton felt compelled to full in line with Government thinking on 'climate change' and driving an electric car would also silence a few of the more vocal and very 'green' critics in the area. His routine for his surgery now was to just turn up and park in whatever town or village he had decided to visit on that occasion. For his first ever surgery his agent had arranged for him to meet his public in the community hall of one of the small towns within his constituency. Publicity in the form of a notice in the local newspaper, flyers in letter boxes and a mention on local television stations was arranged. On arrival at the venue he was amazed to see a long line of people waiting to see him. Some were merely curious, others wondered who he was and more than a handful thought they were queuing to see a local celebrity. Too many though posed very pertinent questions and complaints regarding local services. The advance publicity gave those old hands in the art of attempting to embarrass their political opponent time to prepare. That first session had spilled over into the middle of the afternoon as he valiantly attempted to answer all the questions put to him. This caused him some discomfort as he discovered that charm alone is not enough. His overrunning also aggravated the 'antiques fair' stallholders who were forced to delay their setting up of their trestle tables in that same hall. The Hall's caretaker did little to disguise his annoyance at over two hours lost. From the moment he climbed wearily back into his car he vowed never to repeat that mistake. In future he would turn up at a random town or village set up for two hours and then leave much as he had done when canvassing. When descending on part of his constituency then, his local party workers who had done much of the legwork beforehand would hand out leaflets to the locals. He had also addressed small captive audiences in school and village halls where he assured them of his commitment to serving the community. This included several female Party helpers he had managed to serve particularly well. He had also dutifully sat on 'question and answer' panels, appeared on local television as well as BBC1's, 'Question Time'. It was rumoured that in one community hall, a Labour supporter was heard muttering in a voice dripping with envy:

"Don't know why they bother to canvas here. Just stick a blue rosette on a sheep and it'll be elected."

Now after the respite Covid-19 had provided, Sefton just turned up, stood outside his caravan, smiled, shook several hands and answered a few questions.

***

The week had been one of mixed fortunes. There was of course Serena, then that disappointing meeting at the restaurant but there was potential too and overall he felt hopeful. He had showered and now lay naked on his bed in his old room at the family home in Durford. He looked down at his genitals which were a constant source of interest and amazement to him. He stared at the smooth, loose folds of his scrotum and a rather wrinkled length of penis topped by the shining surface of the glans. He reached down and pulled his foreskin, or prepuce back. He smiled as he recollected those visits to the library in Winchester as a very curious twelve-year old to look up all those 'naughty' words. The glans was glistening with clear liquid oozing from its slit-like eye. He chuckled to himself as he remembered an old 60s movie. In its flaccid state between his thumb and forefinger, for some unaccountable reason it reminded him of a scene from that same film, 'War of the Worlds', starring Gene Kelly, no, not Kelly but Gene Barry. Based on the H.G. Wells novel, the Martians have landed hell-bent on destroying all human life. Their machines are roaming the countryside laying waste everything in their path. One extra-terrestrial machine lands near a cottage having detected human movement. A thin, tubular probe with a coloured eye at its tip, snakes down from underneath the craft and moves towards the wrecked cottage where Barry and a female companion have taken refuge. In comes the eye looking for its prey! Now as the blood began to rush to his own tube,

Sefton wished he had a suitable receptacle for it. Perhaps the au pair, Oriane would be a sport and oblige him. She was looking after his brother's children at Mather Senior's Durford home while Major Julian Mather and his wife, Eliana were in the United States during Julian's attachment to the American Marines. As they had sat at the dining table, his mother, father, his niece and nephews, Oriane and himself, earlier that evening, the French girl had looked at him with some interest and brushed against him as she had left the room. Encouraged, he thought it worth a try and pulled on trousers and dressing gown before quietly padding up the stairs to the floor above, the former servants' rooms and tapped on the door.,

A sleepy voice called out, "Entree, Monsieur Sefton."

He pushed the door open desperately trying to think up a reason for his appearance.

There was no need; she pulled the bedcover back, smiled and asked him to join her as she removed her right hand from teasing the inside of the shorts she was wearing and pulled her tee-shirt off. This was followed by the removal of those shorts which revealed a shaven pussy.

He pulled off his trousers and slipped out of his dressing gown to reveal a very rampant erection. He slipped in beside her, the two kissing and fondling. Then she carefully arched her body and eased on to the tip of his dribbling shaft. Then he was fully in and pushing down into that warm, wet and rather tight sheath. He carefully withdrew, then thrust down again. This exquisite action was repeated three or four times. Each time she assisted her penetration by pulling his clenched buttocks firmly down on her as she lay on her back. It continued a little longer, this sensuous rising and falling. Then waves of pleasure seized her and the muscles of her vagina gripped his manhood, encouraging him to ejaculate and spray that stretched chamber with a thick, sticky solution.

***

The following morning without a care in the world but after exchanging meaningful glances with the young woman sat opposite him, he ate a very good breakfast and set off to carry out constituency duties. Though not before thinking that his mother had given him some odd, curious looks. These expressions, he reflected had become a common occurrence in recent years. As Sefton headed towards the front door she suddenly appeared before him holding his grey suit in one hand and dangling from one finger tip of the other hand something she had found in one of the pockets; a flimsy pair of dark-blue knickers.

"Sefton," she sighed, "when are you going to settle down?" With that she flung the underwear, unable to hide her disgust, at him.

After that confrontation with his mother and with his ego a little bruised, his earlier decision not to stray too far from home now seemed to be a very sensible one and he parked in a small car park just off the high street in Lower Durford. He set up a hinged board with a picture of himself and surgery times close by, returned to his caravan office and waited. It had been an exhausting week in more ways than one so he had decided to go to where he was generally well-known, as a 'local boy'. All was going very well; several locals had sat down at his table inside the caravan. He had taken notes over the issues they had raised; one concerned the threat to the local environment not to mention house prices if permission was given for a company to extract gravel to the south of the village. The not unrelated, second issue concerned the proposed spread of house building across many nearby fields. One of his constituents much exercised by the thought that if building continued at its present rate and with a rising population, would enough arable land remain to feed the country without importing even more than presently. This had caused Sefton some concern too for it made the United Kingdom even more reliant on foreign countries. What if there was an international crisis? There was also the still unresolved issue regarding the extension to a nearby airfield. Sefton listened sympathetically but there was little in practical terms he could do. He would though contact the appropriate Local Government Departments and invite them to investigate each case and report back to him as well as contacting the appropriate constituent.

He glanced at his watch and with some relief noted it was 11-58am and two minutes away from returning home. As the board outside the caravan stated, 'Sefton Mather, Your local Member of Parliament. Surgery here today

10-00am to 12 mid-day. All welcome', his time was nearly up.

Then he heard a voice.

"Good morning, Sefton. Can you spare me a moment?"

There, standing on the steps leading into his caravan stood Sophie Fortune, dressed casually but looking, oh, so stunning, Sefton thought. She wore clinging, black leggings, a light grey hoodie unzipped, beneath which clinging to every curve was a white tee-shirt. Printed in large black letters across her chest, the legend, WOMEN MATTER TOO!

Sefton could not help noticing that the letter 'M' and the letter 'R' of the middle line were each perfectly positioned over the respective nipple of each breast. On her feet she was wearing burgundy coloured trainers which had a distinctive white stripe running from the top of the heel and turning down into the sole beneath the bottom of the laces. Her long, blonde hair was pulled back into a simple pony tail.

"Saw you drive past the gates of the Hall and decided to follow you. Stopped in the coffee shop over there," she said pointing to a shop of a ubiquitous national coffee franchise, "just to kill a little time. It's been a while since we've had a good chat, so here I am, your devoted follower but I do have a few questions."

"If only you were devoted," he thought but braced himself for what was to come.

"What have you and your fellow, mostly male colleagues done this week to help prevent violence against women and the harassment and exploitation of schoolgirls by their male peers? A concern that was again voiced over a year ago," she asked, never one to mince her words, then paused to see what effect the question was having on the hapless male in front of her.

His mind flew back immediately to the March before last when along with the Covid-restricted rump of parliamentarians in the Commons, he on a particular day had sat in rapt silence. Their attention captured as a very well-respected Member on the Benches opposite solemnly read out the names of over one hundred and twenty women killed by men during the previous twelve months. Sefton Mather who liked women felt really moved and humbled. He sought out that particular MP to thank her for such a sincere contribution to the debate and pledged his support for the on going campaign in pursuit of securing the safety of all women and girls. He was also at the time rather surprised to discover how well he got on since those, his early months, as an MP, with many of the Members opposite.

That Honourable Member's speech and much more he communicated to Sophie including the speech he had made in support of the Government's pledge to provide thirty million pounds for additional street lighting and closed circuit television cameras where they would be the most effective.

"Let's hope unlike other Government assurances this one sticks," Sophie said dryly. "I'm beginning to believe what a friend said to me the other day."

"What was that," Sefton asked but dreading the answer.

"That the Government and your Party consists of 'shape-shifters'; able to adapt to populist clamour just to secure their votes," she replied.

Sefton chose to ignore the charge and went on to offer his own support for Sophie's work in attempting to rid the world of the scourge of Female Genital Mutilation. Sefton had described it in a letter to one of the broadsheets as 'barbaric, medieval, cruel with no place in the modern world'. He loved women but he believed women should be equal in all matters including sex. No man had the right to inflict this barbarity on women and young girls so men alone experienced the joy of sexual intercourse or put them through the pain and indinity for any other spurious, cultural or religious reason.

Sophie sighed, "It's a very long road ahead until this practice is abandoned. We're up against fear, superstition culture and religious prejudice."

"Secondly," she persisted, "what action has the Government taken lately to demonstrate that the, 'Black Lives Matter' campaign is still alive? And lastly, how is the Government planning to dissuade the Chinese Government from persisting in the ill treatment of its Moslem minority? "

Sefton reminded her that the 'Black Lives Campaign' was still high on the Government's agenda. Again, he was supporting many initiatives to combat racism. Too often ignorance breeds prejudice through fear so perhaps a good look at introducing a more robust programme in schools is long overdue. Footballers 'Taking the knee', is undergoing something of a revamp too and he had this very week asked the Prime Minister a question over the Chinese problem.

"Yes, I heard you on Wednesday's, Radio Four, 'Today in Parliament'. After hearing that, it occurs to me that you and all the politicians in all the democracies across the world face a potential problem," but Sophie was not quite done yet:

"There is a strong impression too that the bar of acceptable behaviour among Ministers has been lowered. The public has been lulled into thinking that if a senior politician, who may indeed show other talents, can get away with deceit or impropriety then that's all right. Politics has mislaid its moral compass." A grim-faced Sophie was still not finished yet but Sefton managed to interrupt.

'Sophie, why are you so pessimistic? We are addressing many of those issues but it takes time and may I remind you that we're still recovering; the world is still recovering from an unprecedented crisis."

She was quick to respond:

"And what's your excuse for pre-Covid problems. Wake up, Sefton; you may face unrest unless confidence is restored and everyone begins to believe they have a stake in the country. If not, you're merely postponing the day of reckoning. You also appear to be accepting a new Cold War with talk of increasing spending on nuclear warheads. Incidentally, if the Scots' Nats get their wicked way and the evidence for that is growing daily, where will you base Trident? There is also that rising tide of nationalism and populism. This Government seems hell-bent on promoting a 'Disunited Kingdom'. Perhaps, ironically, thanks to Covid, people are no longer content to accept what they are told and are on the march. Mass, instant communication is amazing but a potentially dangerous revolutionary tool. There's a rising tide of dissatisfaction across the world!"

Sefton thought that some of this sort of anachronistic socialism had been rejected along with 'Corbynism' but gauged this was now an excellent time to change the subject and suggested that if she was free this evening, he knew of a very good pub near Botley that offered an excellent Michelin Star cuisine.

Much to his surprise, particularly after her comments, she agreed and after a quick phone call to the manager; he did know the right people; to book a table, they arranged to meet at the public house rather than him collect her from Durford Hall. Of course, they had known each other since childhood but their paths had rarely crossed since then and he had often thought this was quite a deliberate ploy but for no reason that he could imagine. It was however, only since around their sixteenth birthdays that he began to take any real notice of her. It had been some social event or other when he had bumped into her. How she had filled out and in all the right places and by the time they were poised to leave for their respective universities this interest had grown. Though he was hardly reserving himself solely for her.

***

"Did you have a good evening?" her mother asked as Sophie walked into the room where she was eating breakfast served as usual in that small dining room by Mrs Edwards, one of the Hall's permanent staff.

"Yes, pleasant enough," her daughter replied but with no enthusiasm for developing the conversation.

"Why the disagreeable look then, Darling?" Verity asked.

"I'm a few days late, that's all," Sophie said, regretting saying the words as soon as they were uttered for she knew she was in for an interrogation.

"Sophie, when are you going to settle down like your brother? Who's the father; not Sefton. Please tell me you've not been sleeping with him?" she said, her voice almost desperate. "Was it him you were with last night? How pregnant could you be?"

Sophie sighed, feeling a little irritable as she prepared to answer the questions in the order they were asked:

"I'm quite happy with my work; there's still so much to do. Are you aware for example, mother, that over the last three centuries there have been only around fifty-five prime ministers, only two of whom have been women? No, it is not Sefton's; yes, I did spend the evening with him but no we did not in any Biblical sense; must be over six weeks ago, yes I did have sex but not with you know who, that unmentionable Sefton!"

"Thank heaven for that at least," her mother said, sighing with relief.

"Why are you so against him. You've never really said and I'm not completely stupid. He does have a bit of a reputation, so is that the problem?" Sophie wondered but realised that Sefton had long been regarded, certainly by her mother, as a 'no go area'.

"What are you up to today, Darling?" her mother asked, pleased for the opportunity to change the subject.

"Last time I was home, I promised Spirit Monroe that I would go and see her new home in Hinton Ampner; also be good for a 'catch-up' with her," Sophie said.

"Who calls their child, Spirit?" muttered Verity.

"Oh, I don't know, it's always rather suited her," Sophie mused, "always so full of life and a truly free spirit," she added defensively.

The following day, Sophie returned to London and threw herself into her work.

On the Wednesday of that week she was feeling uncomfortable as well as a little twitchy and rather brittle and felt it sensible to leave work a bit earlier than her more usual 6pm and rush home. She dashed into her bathroom and was very relieved to see a very dark reddish-brown stain in her underwear. Emergency over, although like many of the women she knew she thought Nature was rather unfairly disposed towards the female of the species. Of one thing she was certain and that was, she was going to be very careful there were no mistakes the next time she decided to go to bed with a man!

Chapter Seven

Saskia Van de Berg's boyfriend, Kelvin Fenwick, a very talented footballer for a North London club has also made five appearances for the England national team. He would have pulled on many more club and England shirts had he not arrived on the Senior footballing scene at a time when both sets of team selectors are spoilt for choice. England pundits enthused on 'Match of the Day' that the wealth of so much talent should take the national side a long way over the following four or five years of international competition and lay to rest once and for all, over fifty years of failure. Even going beyond what had already been achieved! The national team had certainly bettered the efforts of the Government, in uniting the country, certainly as far as England was concerned, by reaching the 'Euro 20' finals. That evening's disappointment made far worse by the vile and vicious racist attacks via social media on the three unlucky England players who missed penalties. The competition played last year; the delay a consequence of Covid! The tabloids are still hoping for an even better outcome in November of this year, the World Cup but one that avoids a penalty shoot-out!

Although not relishing the 'wag' (wives and girlfriends) tag, Saskia was pleased and flattered to be wined, dined and seen on the arm of such an athletically fit young man. Yet, for some inexplicable reason, sex between them had yet to hit the heights and too often was rushed and uncomfortable. If only his disappointing attempts to satisfy and please her in bed could match his desire to score on the football pitch! There were also a few warning signs of Kelvin's growing possessive and aggressiveness. Increasingly, she was realising that his demands for sex were less concerned with love than with trying to maintain the testosterone-fuelled 'macho' image he carefully cultivated on the field, or demonstrated during television interviews and 'chat' shows. Kelvin always appeared to be in a hurry in his pursuit of money, fame, fast cars and fulfilling his own rather limited sexual gratification. He was growing increasingly more angry and jealous. After a Saturday night out together, at a casino where he had spent the evening losing money and altogether ignoring Saskia, they returned to the flat they shared but with him bristling with irritation. A chance remark by Saskia on the folly of gambling sent him into a rage and he grabbed her by the wrists, slapped her face and threw her into a chair.

"Keep your nose out," he snarled. "If you don't like it, then piss off."

She should have done just that but thought he would be full of contrition the next day and in a better temper so she went off to bed and waited for him to calm down and join her. An hour passed during which time he consumed a third of a bottle of Scotch; not the best preparation for a game of football or much else!. Finally he crawled naked into bed beside her after throwing his clothes in all directions across the floor. She tried to offer comfort thinking this would help soothe his fractured disposition so she sought and found his penis and gently began caressing it into life. She half succeeded in this endeavour while he groped breasts and pinched nipples that only made her cry out in pain. A hand ploughed its way roughly between her legs and several fingers went on to penetrate and open her vagina. He clambered on to her and tried to push his still mainly flaccid member inside her expectant slot. But his contribution was not swelling sufficiently. Doubtless the amount of alcohol he had consumed that evening as he played the tables, along with his generous Scotch nightcap, had led to a classic case of erectile dysfunction and he rolled off her and promptly, fell asleep. Saskia turned over and sobbed quietly.

A few days later, Saskia met up with the one true friend she had made among the other wives and girlfriends. They had sat next to each other at a dinner given to honour the recipient of an award by the Professional Football Writer's Guild and became immediate friends. It was after a few glasses of wine, while the rest of the audience applauded the speeches and the presentation was made, that the two women slipped off to an adjoining small conference room. It was obvious to the second of them that Saskia needed a sympathetic ear. Ensuring they were not being overheard she began to unload the emotional baggage she had been carrying for far too many weeks.

"You certainly don't need that hassle," agreed her new friend. "No woman does. The first time they do it should be the last. Don't believe all that, 'I won't do it again', shit. They always do but each time it tends to get worse. Do you know how many women are killed as a result of domestic violence? I heard about it on television. Over one hundred and I'll bet most of them thought it would never happen to them. One victim is one too many!"

"What about, Jethro?" she asked. "I've seen him play. He scatters opposition players like skittles in a bowling alley."

"No, he's kind and considerate and good where it really matters," she winked but decided not to extol more of her boyfriend's virtues as Saskia already looked dispirited enough.

***

Three days later and the day after his team had won, a very repentant Kelvin, his contrition bordering on grovelling and having promised never again to raise his hand against her, took Saskia to a fashionable Italian restaurant in Soho. She had summoned up the courage during his outpouring of 'sorrys' to say that if he did break his word and hurt her again, she would indeed, 'piss off'.

Eating out on that particular evening but quite alone was Sefton Mather rewarding himself with his favourite food and drink, after a long week in the Commons.

Their evening was progressing quietly and satisfactorily. A few fellow diners had recognised Kelvin, asked for and received autographs and 'selfies' but he had behaved impeccably and had made no effort whatsoever to grab the limelight. He merely smiled, did as he was asked and sat down to enjoy his girlfriend's company He had even bought her a little bouquet from one of those aggravating itinerant flower sellers who somehow always manage to evade the waiters and skirt around the tables offering their wares.

An hour into the meal it all changed. Kelvin suddenly stood up and advanced menacingly on a diner sat at a nearby table with another male. The vexed footballer accused the unfortunate man of ogling his woman. It would in fairness to the man be reasonable to suggest that it would have been difficult not to notice Saskia. She was sitting opposite him wearing a very short, low cut dress. Thighs and breasts were only too visible and he surely thought he must be imagining other delights. Kelvin swung a fist at the 'offender'. The clenched fist connected with the man's chin and he fell back. The momentum of the delivery carried Kelvin forward and he fell upon his victim. Almost immediately, hands began to pull Kelvin away but not before a clutch of mobile phones had been in action recording the whole sorry scene for that ever-growing band of followers who believe reality television and the mobile phone are the height of cultural fashion. So there was a certain inevitability that in an age where a proportion of the population lives to worship at the altar of the false god, 'celebrity', that the second after the fracas had begun, those images would be appearing on various media sites. Kelvin had been recognised, so tomorrow would be a very happy day for the back sports' pages of the tabloids. Surprisingly, Sefton, no great fan of football, though he had followed England's progress in the 'Euros', like millions of others, knew who the pugilist was. Rugby, cricket and rowing were more his kind of sports. He had also taken an interest in unarmed combat and was wondering if things got out of hand here, whether he would need to rely on it to protect himself. This fascination had begun during his time as a soldier when like so many fit young men and women he had considered applying to join 22 SAS Regiment, who were famed, secretive but much admired across the world. After discussing the possibility with a friend he realised he would probably fall short and as failing anything did not suit him, he withdrew his application realising 'who doesn't dare can still achieve elsewhere'. He did continue to develop a curiosity about a system of self defence the Israeli Defense Forces were said to employ; an amalgam of the best of everything from wrestling to Akido and began to pursue an interest in this Krav Nada as it was called. Sefton, for a time had even subscribed to an 'unarmed combat' magazine. It certainly helped with his fitness for many other pursuits.

Even now after watching this football star's drunken antics, voices of opprobrium he had heard speaking in his boyhood a score and more years before, were coming back to him. When, as a small boy he had crept into the back of those Conservative Association meetings chaired by his father, to wait for him. As the meetings broke up and they shuffled past him usually bound for the bar he would hear their griping. Some of those old, reactionary Tories had by now been thinned out by death but doubtless the sentiments they habitually expressed had not changed much; 'too much money, too soon'; 'give 'em two years national service'; 'no respect for anything' were typical of those aged Tories' comments who saw nothing but chaos falling on the country unless flogging and hanging were re-introduced immediately and all foreigners banned from entering the country.

"It was a funny old world," Sefton thought, "when you can pay the likes of them, hundreds of thousands of pounds a week for just booting a bit of leather about when a nurse receives only a fraction of that, a year! Too many of them paid in a week more than the PM's salary but who helped us through the pandemic, footballers or nurses? Good grief, I'm even beginning to sound like a Labour Party Political Broadcast!"

Although one young footballer he could have also reflected, had taken the Government to task over ensuring children were properly fed. Receiving much well-deserved praise from across the country for his continuing campaign.

After all the excitement, Gianna Bianchi joined the seven or eight persons milling around the protagonist and the still dazed young man who had been pulled up and sat in a chair. Gianna brought an air of calm to proceedings. Sefton could not quite catch what was being said but after ten minutes, Kelvin returned to his seat and after a brief exchange of heated whispers with the men at the nearby table and then his now, almost certainly former girlfriend, left the restaurant, still in something of a rage, after paying not only his bill but that of his victim and his friend. His very attractive companion was left sobbing. This prompted Sefton to cross the dining room and ask her if he could be of any assistance.

"May I help?" he said.

She looked up imploringly while at the same time trying to dry her eyes and asked without thinking, if he a complete stranger, would take her home. Then realising Kelvin may have gone there first, she said:

"No, not there, I don't want a fight."

She then asked, realising the possible folly of her earlier impetuosity, if he would escort her to the nearest taxi rank. She would crash at a friend's.

"Come back to my place," he offered but unusually for him, with no ulterior motive in mind. "I'm not too far away."

"Aren't you the MP? Your picture was in the paper the other day."

"Guilty as charged," he replied, grinning and he sat down beside her. "How about a brandy to revive you. I could certainly do with one after all that excitement."

Drinks were duly ordered and poured but before they had time to sip them, she asked to be excused for a moment and headed for the 'Ladies'. Three minutes later she returned after spending that time attending to her make-up and sat down opposite him.

"What's it like being a Member of Parliament?" she asked.

"I suppose It's about five per cent boredom; sixty of hard work and the rest a mix of frustration, aggravation and irritation."

She looked a little puzzled but after carrying out the remedial work to her eyes they were now sparkling and she appeared much more relaxed than not many minutes before.

"It's an odd sort of way I suppose to earn a living but no two days are the same. There are even times when I think I may be doing some good but that's where the remaining thirty five goes. It's frustrating that at times we can't get things done quicker and there are so many rules and regulations. Having said that it's probably just as well, as it stops us from doing daft things. Anyway that's enough about me. How are you feeling?" he asked.

"I'm very much better. I think I've calmed down," she admitted.

She was warming to this man, a stranger but not really a stranger for now she felt at ease as though she had known him for years. He had been kind, had nice eyes and helped her overcome some of the embarrassment she had been feeling during the public show Kelvin had created from his jealously.

"If your offer's still on I'd like to come back with you," she said

Cheered by this he paid his bill, said goodnight to Gianna and led Saskia off towards Wellesley Mansions; an apartment block that had been renovated extensively at the turn of the 21st Century. Opposite his particular block was a row of mid-Victorian, three storey houses. Very desirable properties too from the updated original servants quarters with dormer windows at the top of each house to the very habitable cellars. Most, but not all of these properties had been converted to flats, accessible via a flight of steps up from the pavement to a solid front door. Access to the cellars was down a flight of steps. Most properties retained painted iron railings in front of the house. Standing on the steps leading down to number 24e opposite the Mansions was a figure. This man, binoculars at the ready appeared to be waiting for the arrival of the two people about to be dropped off from a cab only some sixty metres away, judging by the speed with which he raised the original Zeiss 'night vision' instrument to his eyes. This however was merely coincidence. He had arrived opposite the Mansions to check out the address with a very dark, ulterior motive in mind. The taxi pulled into the kerb. Another man, who had hailed a cab just after Sefton, asked the driver to wait while the couple in front almost fell out of their taxi. Sefton paid it off and he and Saskia headed up the steps of Wellesley Mansions.

***

Kelvin, after rushing from the restaurant had gone off in search of a cab but after finding a trio parked, waiting for fares was uncertain what to do. His first thought after exiting Gianna's was to take-out his anger at the roulette wheel. Then he thought he should go home but remembered he had left Saskia, looking abandoned in the restaurant. He made up his mind and took one of the waiting taxis back but found her leaving Gianna's, arm in arm with a tall, well-dressed man, perhaps eight or nine years older than his twenty-two year old girlfriend.

"Can you follow those two?" Kelvin asked the cab-driver.

"Don't need to. I know who he is and where he lives. I've driven him there with his other friends," was the response.

"Fifty, plus the fare if you can get me there before they do," Kelvin said, excitedly waving a fistful of crisp ten pound notes in the air.

"Ok mate, consider it done," and off they sped!

Just half a minute before the two turned into Sefton's road, Kelvin's cab came to rest.

As Sefton Mather tapped the key pad and the heavy front door sprang open, Kelvin hissed:

"I'll get you for this."

Then a thought struck him: He asked the driver:

"Who is he then?"

"Sefton Mather, Tory MP. Likes the ladies' that one."

Kelvin thanked his informant, paid him as promised and stepped from the cab and on to the pavement. He walked briskly to the front of the building and looked up at the first floor where a light had been switched on. He caught a glimpse of Saskia as the blinds were lowered.

***

Sefton and Saskia had walked up the steps of Wellesley Mansions with her 'Good Samaritan' slightly in front. This he did, so he could get them inside without attracting too much, if any attention. He was still thinking of security, prying eyes and a low profile. After that heavy door opened he steered her towards the lift. They moved silently to his front door and he quickly turned the key and ushered her in. A very relieved Saskia, fatigued by the restaurant scene was pleased to sit and take in the simple but tastefully decorated apartment. She accepted Sefton's offer of coffee as he moved across to the windows and quickly pulled down the blinds before moving into the kitchen. He stood keeping an eye on the coffee machine while ensuring as any good host should, that his guest felt at ease.

"You are more than welcome to stay the night; there's a spare bedroom through there," he said and surprisingly for him not even the slightest hint of an ulterior motive. "Or, I can call you a cab to take you home." He frowned, "though, in the circumstances perhaps best you go to a friend."

"No, if you are sure I'm not putting you to any great trouble I'd like to stay. I feel safe with you," she replied, glancing up at him somehow reassured by his clear blue eyes.

Sefton poured two cups of coffee, filled a jug with the hot milk he had been warming in a saucepan, spread a selection of biscuits, including his favourites, dark chocolate digestive, on a plate and placed them before his guest.

"I'll get some bedding and make up a bed for you. Turn in whenever you like," he said sitting opposite her.

He was trying desperately not to look at and beyond her slightly parted knees towards a patch of what he had first thought was the dark nylon of her underwear but when she had first crossed and uncrossed those long, slim legs had realised was a patch of perfectly groomed pubic hair. It was like a scene from 'Basic Instinct', for she was not wearing panties! They drank their coffee and ate several of the biscuits with Sefton glancing, unable to stop himself, from looking in the direction of the hem of her dress and beyond

He would, had it become necessary to do so, swear that it had not been his intention to seduce her. She was first and foremost a damsel in distress and he had convinced himself that he would have helped her at Gianna's even if she had been ninety years old. There was something about Saskia that made their ending up in bed together as inevitable as the sun rising the next morning and not only parted, teasing knees. Instead of him initiating the seduction it proved to be the other way round and Sefton was, if nothing else a great supporter of equality for women and unlikely to let such an opportunity pass. It had been Saskia's intention earlier in the evening to try and drive her boyfriend wild with desire by allowing him brief glimpses of her naked genitalia. Now she decided her saviour deserved that far more than Kelvin had ever done!

"Shall we go to bed?" she asked, finally opening her legs to give him full view of a dark framed slit.

To make the scene even more enticing she licked the tip of her right index finger and slowly drew it down the inside of her very swollen inner lips. This, something that she had never contemplated doing during her time with Kelvin. This man seemed to have unlocked all that pent-up desire. Kelvin had started little more than a girlish crush but with Sefton Mather she was discovering her sexuality as a woman.

He crossed to her, all thoughts of low profile and being careful about whom he associated with totally forgotten. He kissed her, his tongue finding hers. For the first time in many months she experienced a thrill, an almost electrifying moment before he led her into his bedroom. There followed more kissing but not restricted to mouth on mouth, there was also serious petting, the removal of clothes and caressing. Off came Sefton's shirt and trousers, his shoes had been kicked off as they had first entered the apartment as was his habit. That short, low cut dress took very little time for Saskia to vacate. As she stood there, his eyes totally seduced by her, Sefton was soon shaking with lust, all the more heightened, as at the start of the evening, sex had not been on the menu. He turned her completely around as he carried out a favourite sexual manoeuvre but first the thin half cup bra was removed. His hands began to knead her quite generous, very round breasts. His penis began to exude its usual involuntary droplets in anticipation of the stream to follow and on into the groove below the one that separated the cheeks of her backside. Her gently eased her onto all fours with both hands moving down to push the backs of her thighs apart. He looked down; two very willing holes were now facing him. The top one's muscles so relaxed that her anus looked to be a perfect circle over one centimetre in diameter. He licked a finger and ran it around the circumference of that anal ring and soon was hitting the spot with its very sensitive nerve endings. Below it was another hole, certainly not presenting itself as a perfect circle but soft, relaxed, pinky-red, glistening and waiting to be filled.

Sefton, using his left hand gently parted the swollen folds, her petals as some called them, on either side of the entrance to her love tunnel. His right hand began to tease the whole length of her slit by gently running the tip of his erection from clitoris to vagina. Once again using a technique that seemed ever popular with his lovers he pushed his helmet, the glans just as far in as its reddish-purple rim and then withdrew it. He repeated this action several times; just entering then withdrawing; teasing that sensitive female orifice. She was quivering, the anticipation of his entry each time sending waves of ecstasy through her from vulva to navel and beyond. She was aching for him to complete the entry and was breathing very heavily. Then he pushed his engorged, still oozing member deep inside her. His right hand now free from guiding his dick, moved forward to squeeze her full right breast from base to nipple. Once more he pulled right out and then thrust his hips forward. This was too much for Saskia who began to whimper with pleasure. He was near to ejaculation and withdrew once more. He rolled her over and she fell back her thighs wide apart and her vulva almost glowing with sexual warmth. His head moved forward, his lips and tongue seeking and finding clitoris, labia and the very wet, musky entrance to her vagina. Saskia's lower body responded in orgasmic joy as a stream of almost colourless liquid squirted over Sefton's face, throat and down to his breastbone. With a final lick to the length of her vulva, Sefton pulled out from between her legs. Saskia, still quivering with excitement had followed him as he had moved out from between her legs and now was half sitting up. Sefton eased himself forward and was soon astride her just above her waist. He pushed her shoulders down on the bed and moved up. His right hand grasped his penis and guided it up between her breasts. Saskia moved her hands either side of them and squeezed, providing Sefton with a firm valley to push into. He needed no second invitation and was soon moving up and down. It only took three entries to her warm, firm tunnel before a jet of semen streamed up, coating Saskia's chin, lips, nose and closed eyes before she recovered enough from the ejaculation to lick some of the sticky blobs from her face and swallow them. Sefton, in the meantime had fallen back and now lay quite exhausted by her side but congratulating himself for acting like a gentleman in the restaurant. He looked across at her thinking that if he hadn't already set his sights on Sophie then Saskia could very well fit the role of constant companion. The one suited particularly well to fill the gap in his life that Browne had suggested would promote respectability and one day perhaps complement his progress to very high office. It occurred to him that many prime ministers had not lived pure, celibate lives before turning the key in 10, Downing Street and several notable ones had begun affairs while holding that office. He already had some of the other necessary qualifications; he came from a good family, was well educated, a good military record, was highly articulate and even, he modestly decided, looked the part!

"You reap what you sow," he was thinking. For Saskia, who now lay back with her legs apart, totally relaxed, was thinking about what she had been missing all these months with Kelvin.

***

Very early the next morning, Sefton awoke with his customary erection. He had moved across to Saskia and turned her over on her back. Her legs opened and he caressed her breasts, then kissed her lips before moving his right hand in search of the gap between her thighs; she began to respond and before very long he was inside her and thrusting for the second time in a few hours. She was squealing with delight as her whole body trembled in an ecstasy of orgasmic pleasure. All before breakfast and like nothing she had experienced before with anyone. Sefton eventually sat up after rolling off her, before cuddling her and running his hands over her shoulders, breasts and stroking her gently between her legs in much the same way he did after intercourse with Serena. He found this after-play as indeed she did, very soothing and thought Saskia might find it satisfying and therapeutic too. Saskia was now certainly finding it so for she was almost purring with delight when he sat up and said:

"Saskia, why not shower while I fix breakfast. What would you like? Toast, cereal, an omelette, scrambled eggs, coffee, tea, orange juice?"

"Oh, I didn't expect that as well as bed," she said with a very appreciative look on her face. "Perhaps scrambled eggs on toast and some tea, please."

"Your every wish, is my command," he replied, only stopping to kiss her lips before getting out of bed. He dressed but not before Saskia had time to take in his quite firm muscular body, taut buttocks and his genitals, his penis now wrinkled but still adequate in its flaccid state and resting. It had certainly served her every need, not once but twice. She was no longer that same rather subservient female in awe of a footballer who would likely be an ex-boyfriend. She had certainly recovered from that earlier trauma and upset and had enjoyed not only the sex but the company of a real man. Kelvin was certainly fit but so was Sefton and she could certainly vouch for his stamina! He now completed the perfect time she had enjoyed by giving her his number.

"Call me any time," he said and seemed quite sincere.

Though deep down she thought that it would not be quite as simple as that; to go from one relationship so soon into another

After they had shared a leisurely breakfast together, he called her a cab; they kissed as they parted, before she was on her way back to Wimbledon.

***

It was with a great deal of reluctance that she had finally decided she must return to their shared house in Coburg Gardens, SW19 and have it out with Kelvin once and for all. She hoped as she turned the key in the front door that he would be out. This would give her time to pack a bag if matters reached a point of no return stage. She had been in the house for only a few minutes and was in their bedroom when she heard the front door slam shut. He had been sitting in his car parked at the other end of the short road where they lived, drinking from a vodka bottle when he saw Saskia going inside the house. The jealous rage he had been working himself into, enriched by the vodka was reaching its peak. He resolved to confront Saskia about the man he had watched accompanying her as the two of them had disappeared into Wellesley Mansions. He rushed unsteadily up the stairs just as she emerged from the bedroom clutching a handful of her clothing.

"I'm going to kill you, you cheap slut," he snarled in a slurred voice.

He reached the landing and pushed her back towards the bedroom but she fell to the floor. She somehow scrambled to her feet still clutching that clothing and managed to dodge past him. He grabbed at her and she dropped those items but struggling, perhaps for her life succeeded in fending him off. Kelvin, following closely behind tripped and fell heavily back down the stairs crashing against a solid, antique hat and umbrella stand. Saskia, shocked, ran down the stairs to see if he had hurt himself only to be met with a torrent of obscenities interspersed with loud cries of pain. Unable to provide any comfort or practical help she rushed into the sitting room to retrieve her mobile phone from her designer handbag, one of the first presents Kelvin had given her in happier times. She sat down desperately trying to control the shaking from nerves that seemed to numb her brain. At last calming down she called for an ambulance and seven minutes later a paramedic motor-cycle responder arrived. The medic quickly and expertly examined and assessed his injuries and contacted the Hospital. Then he turned to Saskia:

"He's in pretty bad shape. Every sign of concussion, breathing problems; every evidence too of a rib puncturing a lung and an ankle with a bad break. We need to get him to A & E as soon as," he said. "It's a job for the air ambulance. I'll wait for backup and we'll get him across to the Park and away to St George's A & E."

Within five minutes of his call the air ambulance was landing at the northern end of Wimbledon Park causing considerable interest. A second paramedic, accompanied by a doctor sprinted the short distance from the ambulance to the Gardens with the paramedic manoeuvring a lightweight, yellow trolley before them. On arrival, this was collapsed and the patient, already made as comfortable as possible by the first paramedic, was loaded on to it. Then the three, after the doctor had further examined him and provided additional pain relief and set-up a saline drip, rushed across the road, down a short stretch of Wimbledon Road then left and on into the Park. Seconds later Saskia saw the ambulance rise and head south-east in the direction of the Accident and Emergency Department of St George's Hospital, Tooting, where he was given a whole body CT (Computed Tomography) scan to assess the full extent of any damage to bones and internal organs and much more.

In spite of Kevin's avowed intent to cause her harm Saskia felt some modicum of guilt but this did not prevent her once the ambulance was out of sight of returning to the house and going back upstairs. She began to fill a case but abandoned that. She felt nervous and was trembling and went back downstairs, went to the fridge and clutching a gin bottle and a trendy aluminium can of tonic water, sat down to steady those nerves. She poured equal quantities of both beverages and touched Alysha's contact number on her mobile.

"Sorry, to call you, Alysha but I didn't know what to do or who else I can turn to," she said her voice struggling to be heard as it was broken by short breaths and sobs, as she went on to relay, still punctuated by those sobs, the details of the previous hour. "You were right all along about Kelvin," she added and then, "I don't want to stay here a moment longer than is necessary."

She had fleetingly considered calling Sefton Mather but even as vulnerable as she felt, did not want to inflict her problems on a man she barely knew; even though in terms of physical proximity they had been about as close as any man and woman could be. People often said give me a call but how often did they mean it? Furthermore she decided that she had no wish to compromise his position as a Member of Parliament. Besides, she and Alysha did go back some way.

"Good for you," was Alysha's immediate response. "I'll have a word with Serena; I'm sure she won't mind if you stay with us until you can sort something more permanent out. I'll have a word with her and call you back. In the meantime pack your bags."

Saskia thanked her and turned to another pressing matter. She must go and see Kelvin and tell him that they were finished. She rang the Hospital and asked how he was. They were reluctant to discuss a patient's condition with a non-relative but said that she could visit him later that afternoon. She did have some concern for him but was managing to convince herself partly after speaking with Alysha that he had brought his injuries upon himself. He had also threatened to kill her and although his subsequent behaviour was alcohol-induced she knew of too many instances as a result of Alysha telling her, where a domestic falling out had resulted in death, usually of the woman! It was with much trepidation that she ordered a cab to take her the twenty odd minute drive to St George's. She asked at the Reception Desk and as soon as she uttered the words, 'Kelvin Fenwick' then a woman sidled up to her and began asking questions. She recognised Emilia Granger, a tabloid journalist.

"No comment," she said brusquely and hurried off, following the Receptionist's instructions.

She reached Kelvin's small, private ward and was told on enquiring that he was still in discomfort and she should not stay too long but allow him to rest. The initial diagnosis was fortunately nowhere near as bad as it was first feared. His ribs were badly bruised but not broken; his headache was the consequence of a large intake of alcohol rather than the result of falling-down stairs which could also have led to him being concussed but he wasn't; but his ankle had suffered a very serious break. Saskia was still rather startled to see him with his lower right leg in traction and a very uncomfortable looking Kelvin with a pained expression staring at the ceiling. She walked purposefully to his bedside, having left the door open. She sat down thinking she had to confront him now or she may never have the courage to do so again.

"Hello," he began, as though nothing out of the ordinary had taken place. "It's really good to see you."

"Is it?" she said. "The last time you spoke to me you said you were going to kill me," Sakia replied, her voice loud but thick with a mix of anger and her reaction to their meeting after such a frightening confrontation earlier in the day.

"Keep your voice down," he said in a whisper.

"Why? Frightened they'll realise that Kelvin the famous Premiership and International football player is really, Kelvin the jealous bully?"

Saskia was a bit taken aback by her own confidence in speaking so directly but continued:

"I'm sorry, Kelvin, I thought there was a real vibe between us but not anymore. You attacked me and who knows what would have happened if you had not lost your balance and fallen down the stairs."

"Oh, come on," he replied, his voice descending into a whine. "You know it was only the drink talking. Won't happen again."

"I told you that if you raised your hand to me ever again then we would be over. I hope you get better soon but when you get back to Coburg Gardens you won't find me there."

"And what about that guy you left the restaurant with?" he countered, the tone of his voice becoming threatening.

"Yes, what about your jealousy and you're always belittling or ignoring me when we have been out for the evening?" Saskia replied. "Yes, a kind man, a very good man took pity on me and treated me like a real woman, after you stormed off as a result of that jealousy."

"Did you sleep with him?" he asked in hardly an understanding tone.

"Yes," she blurted out, "not that it's any of your concern now and just for the record, he was gentle and considerate. Not like you! I'm more like a football in bed to you, to be kicked around merely for your own gratification but no thought to my feelings. But no more!"

Before he could say anything else she rose from the chair and told him she was returning to the house to finish her packing and would drop her keys through the letterbox. Once again she wished him well, turned and walked away with expletives and the word 'slut' following her through the open doorway. She moved to go round the several staff who were standing there after being drawn to the exchange of harsh words in the room involving a well-known celebrity. At her approach they hurried away and back to their normal duties.

"Wonder what the papers will say about you sneaking off to shag an MP," he shouted.

"Show everyone what a miserable, jealous rat you are, I expect," she retorted in her new found, confident voice

"Go on then, piss off, see if I care," was his parting shot but it was lost on her as by then she was out of hearing range.

Saskia found a cab waiting at the rank by the Hospital and returned to the house she had been sharing with Kelvin. She asked the cabbie to wait while she poured her clothing into two suitcases but choosing to leave most of the presents her former partner had given her:

"I can't take presents given as a result of a guilt trip," she said out loud though she decided she had earned that very expensive handbag in payment for all the knocks and bitter disappointments she had suffered during her time with Kelvin.

Then her mobile trilled; it was Alysha:

"Hi, Saskia, if you're still up for it we are all set here. Shall I come and collect you?" Alysha asked.

"Hello, Alysha you are both so kind," Saskia replied, "but I'll come to you. I've just been to see Kelvin in Hospital to tell him we are finished and I've got a cab waiting outside so I can come over right away."

"How did it go?" Alysha inquired.

"Let's just say that I am not too popular," Saskia replied. "And just as you predicted, he promised once more, that he would never do it again, but I swear to you I mean it when I say it's over."

"Good for you, sweetie. We'll expect you soon; the bubbly's already chilling," her friend replied cheerfully.

Within the hour the two were embracing on the threshold of 21, Victoria Mews:

"Come in, love," welcomed Alysha, "and say hello to Serena and let's crack open the Bollinger," as she picked up one of the cases and steered her into the house.

"Hello, again Saskia. We have met," she said, "at one of those publicity bashes and you are more than welcome to stay as long as you like. We've sorted out a spare bedroom for you but let's have that drink my friend here promised you simply hours ago. Let's get the bubbly and just chill."

They laughed, enjoying the comment and at ease in each other's company. As they drank their way through a second bottle of 'Bolly', Serena playfully described their current sleeping arrangements, which merely drew a smile of understanding from their new house guest. Saskia, still barely believing her own previous evening's very satisfying 'sleeping' arrangement certainly was not going to judge or comment over or with whom Serena and Alysha shared their bed. Neither did she feel obliged to mention that her own sex life had been considerably boosted by her encounter with a member of parliament. Before other simple, mundane details connected with house-keeping and the like were outlined, Saskia placed a wad of twenty pound notes on the table.

"Please accept this as my contribution towards household expenses. It's little enough considering the favour you are doing for me," she said, "and this way I'm less likely to give in and crawl back to Kelvin though at the moment that's the last thing on my mind."

"No," Alysha said firmly, "I know too many women who fall over and over for the same old lies, but somehow I don't think you will and I don't see your name being read out in Parliament as a victim of male violence. We'll done, girl."

Saskia went on to say that if it was alright with both of them she would like to stay for only a week or two just to recuperate and before returning to her family home in Wymondham in Norfolk where her parents owned a prosperous 'High tec' business. Before she had met and fallen for Kelvin it had been assumed she would join the family firm in some capacity or other. She was at Carrow Road that afternoon when Kelvin's team, the visitors, held Norwich City to a draw. She was accompanying her father, a life-long season ticket holder and club sponsor and had stayed on for the post-game dinner where she had been introduced to Kelvin. The parents had not lost hope that her infatuation with the footballer would be short-lived. After the break at the Mews she intended returning to East Anglia. It was after midnight before an exhausted Saskia slipped into bed. It had a testing day certainly when she had visited Kelvin in hospital to end their relationship but it had been rescued by the kindness of Serena and Alysha.

A couple of days into her short holiday, it was Alysha who brought a news item on the sports pages of a Sunday newspaper to her attention thinking it best for her to find out from a friend rather than stumble across it or see it on television. The article stated that Kelvin Fenwick currently recovering in Hospital after a training accident may not it was feared play football at Premiership level again. There was even a suggestion that playing at any level was unlikely, as the damage to his ankle was too severe and could leave him with a permanent limp. Saskia, grateful for being forewarned in case reporters caught up with her, imagined how badly Kelvin would have received this news when the doctors had told him.

"He'll be looking for someone to blame, Alysha," she said gloomily, "and I know who that will be, me!"

"He's only got himself to blame," her friend added trying to console her.

"Kelvin won't see it that way. He's football mad and something he really is good at," she replied, if a little bitterly.

"Probably best you lie low for as long as possible then," suggested Alysha.

"Yes, stay here for as long as you like," added Serena who had wandered in to her lounge after returning from shopping in the West End and had caught part of the conversation.

"There's one thing that does bother me though and that's involving you two. What happens if he realises that as Alysha and I originally met at some football bash and remained friends he might just realise that I am staying here with you," Saskia said.

"Don't worry on our account. This place is quite secure and I know one or two people who could if necessary, warn him off," replied Serena reassuringly.

"You are so kind but I think I'll stick to my original plan and stay for that week or so then go back to Wymondham. He'll get very short shrift as my Granny used to say if he turns up there," Saskia added.

That seemed to settle matters and the three women returned to the wine that seemed to be a feature of everyday life at number 21. Then Serena offered to cook them supper having visited a well-known store's food hall earlier in the day.

Saskia was heartened by their support but one thing was still bugging her. What if Kelvin decided to try and cause trouble for Sefton Mather? She decided when she had the house to herself to give him a call and warn him of the possibility

This opportunity presented itself the following morning so Saskia called him on the number he had given her.

"Hello, Sefton Mather," a voice replied.

"Oh, hello Sefton," she replied but rather nervously. "Sorry if I've caught you at an awkward moment but I must speak to you."

Sefton was a little taken aback especially by those last six words. They usually meant trouble.

"What's the problem? Is it Kelvin, that well-known footballing bruiser?" he asked.

"Well, yes I'm afraid it is, or rather it could be. I don't know whether you read about it or heard it on the news, but when I broke with him he said he might contact the papers about us," she said but very pleased to get the matter off her chest.

"Thanks for the 'heads-up', love," he replied. This was hardly a new experience for him but he was surprised and grateful for Saskia's concern.

"I did tell him when he said it, that it would show the world what a miserable, jealous so and so he is but I'm still worried that if he did carry out his threat it would damage your reputation," she said.

"That really is so sweet of you but please don't worry. Just take care of yourself and perhaps when all the fuss over him dies down we can meet up again," he added with some relish as he recalled their very sexual encounter.

After the call, Saskia felt relieved. Sefton Mather certainly didn't seem to be overly worried and he had much to lose. Well, so had she if he did catch up with her. He had threatened to kill her but even so she wasn't planning on spending the foreseeable future looking over her shoulder. She had wasted enough time on Kelvin Fenwick!

Chapter Eight

Serena received a phone-call, early one morning.

"Hello," she responded, affably.

"Is that Serena?" a voice asked.

"Yes," she replied but with a little caution as she did not recognise the voice.

"You probably won't remember me and I have absolutely no wish to alarm or upset you but if I mentioned Exeter and Heavitree Road you probably will."

Serena's caller would have heard a sharp intake of breath and a look of shock tinged with fear spreading across the face of the owner of number 21, Victory Mews. The combination of those three words had re-awakened old, perhaps best forgotten memories.

The voice quickly added:

"Please don't be alarmed and I know my contacting you must be upsetting."

"Yes, it bloody well is," Serena thought at the same time resisting the urge to just slam the phone down. Curiosity was overcoming that desire and encouraging her to try and remain calm in order to elicit more information before dismissing it as one of the many calls offering all sorts of deals. These often included possible scammers of various kinds trying to part her from her savings. Consequently, she asked:

"Who are you and what do you want?"

"Well to cut a long story short, I always believed we let you down badly. However, there may be a way to at least give you something back. Some sort of justice after all these years."

Serena was intrigued but very wary. If something was too good to be true then it probably was. On the other hand there was something about 'mouth' and 'gift horses'. She was still surprised, or rather taken aback at receiving a call on her landline when most of her business was conducted on her two mobiles. One big question needed answering first. How did the caller know her name, number and who was she anyway?

"You know my name and have the advantage of me; who are you?" she asked but her tone firm.

"Sheila Andrews," responded the caller.

"Do I know you?" Serena asked.

"Yes, well it has been a long time but I was one of the detectives investigating your case in Exeter," Sheila replied.

"Yes, I do remember you and that you were very kind," Serena said, "but how can I help? What do you want?"

"Can we meet?" Sheila persisted. "I'm in London, attending a funeral in Kensal Green at 11 o'clock next Tuesday. Then it's back for the wake in Leigh Gardens. I was planning on doing a little shopping after that. Perhaps we could catch up, if it wouldn't be too much for you, Serena?"

"How about somewhere near Marble Arch?" suggested Serena.

"Yes, somewhere public because after your earlier experience you've no reason to trust anyone connected with Exeter Police," said Sheila.

"No, that's fine. What time do you think you will be free?" enquired Serena, her curiosity approaching fever pitch.

"Well the funeral's at eleven so shall we say 4pm?" Sheila asked.

"I'll look for you outside the entrance to Marble Arch Underground Station. Best give me your mobile number in case there's a problem. How will I recognise you, Sheila? It's been over ten years after all?"

"I don't think I've changed that much. A few pounds here and there and ten years holding back the crow's feet. I will be carrying a dark red holdall and hopefully a couple of Harrods' bags," she replied.

"Incidentally, just how did you find me; my numbers not listed," Serena asked.

"I am a detective," she replied simply.

"Till next week then," Serena added, though her mind was beginning to race. How on earth could a police officer say or do anything that could change events that occurred a decade ago?

***

The following week, Serena ensured she was at the rendezvous in good time. She stood, with a good view of the underground station's entrance. The area around Marble Arch was busy but Serena was not convinced that it had returned to it's pre-Covid level. Ten minutes after arriving, she caught sight of the woman she had not seen for over ten years. The very same woman who had been so kind to her and who had helped her through her ordeal. Sheila Andrews would also prove to be as good as her word.

"For a woman the wrong side of middle age she carries her years well," Serena thought.

Sheila was dressed in a dark trouser suit; no doubt selected by its wearer for train travel and funerals. In her right hand she carried the red holdall and in the other, two large shopping bags, one of which was a distinctive green colour.

She crossed to the entrance where Serena was standing clear of the commuters and shoppers either entering or leaving the station. They stood looking at each unsure what to do until Mrs Andrews broke the silence.

"Oh my God," she exclaimed, "you look bloody marvellous. No, absolutely beautiful. What's your secret?"

Sheila had let the red bag drop to the pavement partly as a result of seeing Serena looking so well-groomed and confident and partly because it was fairly heavy. Quite what she had expected Serena to look like after her ordeal and the passage of time, she had not really been sure. Too many other victims of male violence and abuse carried it with them for years. She was pleased for Serena that life seemed to be treating her so well. Serena by now had stretched out her right hand to greet Mrs Andrews formally but then changed her mind and threw both arms around Sheila, hugged her and kissed her cheek.

"I think I'm a little better than the sad creature you first interviewed in the Devon and Exeter Hospital," Serena said smiling and after releasing her from the hug. All at once she felt at ease in the presence of one of the women who had tried so much to help her back from the depths of despair. She continued:

"It did take a while though to straighten myself out and with some help too from a therapist. It was not only the trauma of the attack but the fact of that bastard getting away with it."

"Is there somewhere we can go to sit and talk?" Sheila asked.

"Yes, just a few minutes from here. I'll treat you to coffee and cake," responded Serena picking the holdall up in her right hand and threading her left arm between Sheila's right arm, now carrying both of the shopping bags and the side of her body.

The two women moved slowly off as though they had been friends for years. As they walked, they talked. Serena asked if it was Sheila's intention to return to Devon that evening. She was told it was. She had travelled to London yesterday morning and had stayed at a friend and former colleague's home in West Kilburn. It was her friend's husband whose funeral she had attended earlier that morning. Ingrid Saunders, the friend was the other female detective who had interviewed Serena back in Exeter. Now Serena and Sheila having reached the cafe, sat down and ordered; the waitress glided away and Sheila continued:

"Ingrid's husband, Vernon Saunders was promoted six months after your case went tits-up. There was a move to London and Ingrid couldn't wait to go. Yours wasn't the only case handled, or more accurately mishandled by the third member of the investigative team, Detective Sergeant Andrew Croft. Much to the surprise of many of us he is now Detective Inspector Croft. Though he's had his moments; apparently, almost singlehandedly he disarmed a gang holding up a bank a few years ago and somehow he has managed a high percentage of arrests which has no doubt diverted senior officers from taking too close a look at his more dodgy activities. Certainly as far as I know until recently no one has pursued his having a possible link with local drugs deals. Now it seems there is almost certainly a connection with him and a London-based drugs controller of 'county lines' involving our part of Devon."

Serena interrupted:

"Excuse my stupidity but I don't understand if he's in that deep why has he got away with it so long?"

"No, you're certainly not simple. Others have wondered the same but it may be he has friends in high places, or he's been undercover and gone native, or his activities are well-known but he's being allowed to run with it to land the bigger fish," Sheila said. "It does go back a long time though. I was told that his drugs contact is the very same as the guy in whose release after a drugs raid he had shown considerable interest. Evidence also 'disappeared' at about the same time too just as yours had."

"Certainly sounds as though he has been very lucky," commented Serena.

The coffee and the patisserie arrived. Both sipped their drinks and took a bite of their cakes almost in unison.

"Yes, it was poor Vernon's funeral I attended this morning. A lovely man who did no harm to anyone but was diagnosed with bowel cancer two years ago. Then he contracted Covid and never really recovered," Sheila said.

Serena had noticed a few tears in her eyes and let her ramble on. Sheila seemed relieved to have got this off her chest. Serena though was desperate to find out how and why Sheila felt she could help.

"Of course we had spoken on the phone about yours and other cases that we always believed Croft had deliberately mishandled. I told Ingrid that you and I were to meet and she agreed that it would be a good idea to give you the so-called lost evidence. We even discussed it after poor Vernon's funeral today."

"Ah," thought Serena, "we're getting there at last!" However, she also thought it good manners to offer her condolences.

"How very sad for Vernon and for poor Ingrid. Yes, I do remember her."

Sheila sensed that it was time at last to answer Serena's main question regarding the purpose of their meeting. She moved to retrieve the holdall and unzipped it. Serena watched as she lifted out a large brown paper folder with a white label, the name Serena MacDonald printed across it and several dates scrawled below.

"There's also this," she said, indicating a brown bag laying across her neatly folded clothes inside the holdall. She was very careful to keep the red bag between them and away from the casual gaze of the fifteen or twenty others enjoying afternoon refreshments.

"What are they?" Serena asked quite innocently.

"The original notes and transcripts of your case and the evidence bag that mysteriously disappeared. You must have them and use them," Sheila said, her face grim.

"Thanks, but surely the case is ten years old. Won't someone wonder where I got this stuff from? Wouldn't the lawyers call this inadmissible evidence if I suddenly produced It? And wouldn't it be better if you used it?" a puzzled Serena asked.

"No, I only wish I could but let's just say I came across it all under rather dubious circumstances. Yes, you're right about inadmissible evidence but not if you follow my suggestion."

"I must be very obtuse but I don't see what I can do. It's not as if I can walk into West End Central and demand a re-match, is it? And won't Croft realise that this stuff may have come from you?"

"No, that doesn't matter if my plan works. What you don't know but I mentioned it just now, is that as he is currently under investigation rather than merely being suspected of wrongdoing. This," she confirmed, emphasising the word, 'this' and pointing to the bag and file, "suddenly appearing will add to that growing uncertainty about him. Neither does it matter that it won't be used as evidence in the current case against him in the normal course of events. After all he has managed to wriggle out of similar scrapes but not if this crosses a particular desk."

Serena was growing more and more uncomfortable and could not stop blurting out:

"I still don't understand. Just how can I use It?"

"Sorry," she apologised. "Let me just say that currently he faces charges of accepting bribes and more importantly from your point of view, of perverting the course of justice by losing or destroying evidence. It all certainly appears to have started very soon after that raid on a key figure in the importation and distribution of drugs throughout the South-west. There is still growing evidence of an ongoing link with that same man and Croft. He could face a life sentence for what is called, 'Misconduct in Public Office'. What I suggest you do is send these packets to the Office of the Devon and Cornwall Police Commissioner. She's held in high regard and even though this material is as you say, officially inadmissible, what it will do is demonstrate that Croft's offences have a long history. It's another nail in his career coffin and he's going to find it difficult to refute all the charges. Mud sticks!" she added sagely.

Serena's face brightened but then added:

"Won't he come after you?"

"No, as soon as this shit and all the other stuff hits the fan he'll be arrested and in the circumstances denied bail. I'm confident the Police Commissioner will ask the right questions. Anything that will undermine his already shaky credibility. There are other cases very similar but later than yours that will be re-examined and in any case my husband and I are off to New Zealand to visit one of our sons and his children, our grandchildren. By the time we're back, hopefully his case will be over and him behind bars."

"Well, if you are absolutely sure you'll be safe, then I'll send it off with an appropriate covering letter," Serena said putting the two items in a supermarket bag that Sheila had thoughtfully brought with her for Serena to carry the material away with her.

"One other fact did creep out from under the rock occupied by your attacker, Webster. Croft kept very quiet about one of his sisters being married to him. You weren't the first student he'd assaulted. At least two other young women were raped but at the time we were unable to make it stick as Webster's wife colluded with her brother to tamper with the evidence and alibi him. She set fire to the clothes he was wearing at the time of one of the offences and in the second because the victim was drunk, swore her husband hadn't strayed from her side all evening through to the following morning."

"I don't understand how that could change," asked a bewildered Serena.

"In the normal course of events it wouldn't have done. Martha Webster, his wife, rather liked the lifestyle they enjoyed in Exeter. That is, until she found him in bed with her younger sister. Whatever was said between that unholy threesome did not stop or perhaps it accelerated her dash to change her statement."

"What happened?" Serena asked.

"Sadly, not too much. Webster's barrister laid into the wife, a woman scorned and all that, basically saying she had lied. She was discredited, other evidence had gone walkabout and the judge had little choice but throw the case out. His wife could have been done for perverting the course of justice but the Crown Prosecution Service decided more harm than good would be done if that line of enquiry was pursued, so it was dropped."

Sheila paused, for Serena again looked puzzled. Mrs Andrews returned to her tale but smiled encouragingly at Serena:

"What it did do however, was raise even more questions over Croft's role in events. He always did seem to be around when cases went wrong so there was an investigation. I was drafted in to assist in the search of his premises. As I was the smallest of the officers involved I was tasked with groping around the loft. During this, I slipped and dislodged a joist. In a hidden compartment I came across various papers, over two thousand pounds in assorted currency, US dollars, Euros and sterling. Then, wrapped in plastic, an evidence bag, this one here," she said pointing at the bag sat between them, "as well as this folder of notes; your case notes. Of course, I recognised your name."

"What did you do?" she asked now totally gripped by the unfolding drama.

"With some difficulty I managed to hide the bag and file beneath the very little I was wearing under my forensic suit. Not easy and with the mask I had on, the confined space, the stale air and particles of dust and insulation floating in the void I was not feeling my best and was glad to clamber down the folding steps. I was carrying in one hand the currency and a few other items not connected to your case. While holding the other one across my stomach as though I was feeling unwell but really stopping my other finds from falling out. I reported to the SIO waiting expectantly in the mobile incident room parked outside and handed the currency and a few other things over to him."

"You look hot and bothered, Sheila," 'he remarked', "anything useful?"

"I found this, sir. A pile of money and a few files. There's a secret hideaway concealed under some joists. May be there's a few more stashed up there," 'I said', "but kept quiet about the other material I'd found. I know it was wrong and I risked demotion and worse if found out but it was seeing your name Serena, that did it. Anyway, he realised that I must be suffering under my plastic 'all in one suit' and told me to go home,"

"All I can say is a very big thankyou, Sheila. Not only for taking such a risk but for coming to see me," Serena said.

"Perhaps when I'm back in the country we can meet up again and compare notes," Sheila added brightly.

"Yes, I'd like that," answered Serena.

Sheila smiled and said:

"It's been my pleasure and to meet you again but if I'm to catch the 17:22 back to Exeter St David's, then I had better make a move."

They stood up and embraced.

"Good luck," Sheila said quietly.

"Thankyou so much and a safe journey and enjoy New Zealand," responded Serena.

The two parted and Sheila turned into the Marble Arch underground entrance.

A very thoughtful Serena sat back down and ordered more coffee. There was so much for her to think about especially the opening of old sores but it could lead to settling old scores. She had also promised Sheila and fully intended sending the material to Devon. She was now in no particular hurry to return home. Apart from Jemima dropping in to discuss their mutual business interests and her friend's occasional use of number 21 for the odd escort appointment, Serena missed female company. For Alysha in accordance with her mother's wishes had accompanied her parents back to Antigua. Her mother, Amisha Joseph realising her life would soon be over wanted to be buried on the island of her birth. Alysha was unlikely to return to London for the foreseeable future as she had been offered and had accepted a job with the Antiguan Tourist Board. Fortunately for Serena, Alysha's 'Zoom' call advising her she would be away indefinitely had coincided with a visit from Sefton who made an Olympian sexual effort to compensate the near grieving Serena for the absence of her special lover.

The following day having looked up on the internet the name and address of the Devon and Cornwall Police Commissioner, Serena typed a very carefully worded letter on her computer and printed off a copy. Then she parcelled everything up. The evidence bag remained unopened but before sealing the parcel she had made copies of the contents of the file. These in due course would be lodged with other potentially important items at the office of her mother's solicitors in Holborn. A Royal Mail, 'Click and Go' label was duly produced and before mid-afternoon of that Wednesday, a tracked parcel was bound for the West Country.

Chapter Nine

China's Gross Domestic Product much boosted by the scramble to import Chinese goods by the multi-container load as well as Western lethargy has helped the Chinese not only to fund their 'arms' expansion but has given them a 'green light' across a broad swathe of the eastern Pacific. Hong Kong has been bludgeoned into submission though what really surprised Sefton Mather was China's apparent reluctance to prod North Korea into goading the United States into seeing just how far they could go before the President was forced to take action. He asserted during those first days in the Oval Office that he would take whatever steps were necessary to protect the freedoms of the United States and its allies and resist aggression. Russia has also been warned not to test American patience over Russian interference in the Ukraine. This appears to have prompted the Russian President to tell the West not to concern itself with the status of the Crimea. Mather could only think that another potential irritant and danger to stability in the region, the Korean, 'Rocket Man' was too distracted by internal issues to return to international muscle flexing and carry out China's bidding. China was also in belligerent mood. As if to celebrate the centenary since the founding of the Chinese Communist Party last year, the current General Secretary of the Party (and President of the country) had made it clear that any interference in China's affairs would be strongly resisted!

Sefton's interest in matters concerning China had already reached the ears of the Foreign Secretary. A note had been sent early on Monday to Sefton finding him soon after his return from Hampshire, inviting him to be a member of a Joint Parliamentary Delegation to Beijing. He was to attend a briefing at the Foreign Office in two days' time and depart from Heathrow the following afternoon.

At the morning briefing, the five Conservatives, two Labour, one Liberal Democrat, one Democratic Unionist Party and one Scottish Nationalist were given documents regarding etiquette, do's and don't's, questions to ask and questions not to ask. The SNP representative had been included, it had been cynically suggested, as their presence on the mission would suggest that independence was unnecessary as they were regarded as an integral member of a truly united, United Kingdom. A similar argument no doubt applying over the inclusion of a Northern Irish representative on the team after the sea border hiatus. Overall this was regarded as an example of the Government's promise to pool the resources of the four nations to fully defeat Covid and its economic consequences, maintain influence abroad and move forward together. The team's mission concerned human rights. It was hoped they would fare better than last year's delegation that had been refused entry following the very close questioning of China's Ambassador to the Court of St James over the vexed question of human rights and the belligerent activities of their naval forces in the East China Seas.

In Mather's and many others' view the Government of the so-called People's Republic of China must be made accountable and their feet held to the fire. Previous experience demonstrated the Chinese considered giving in to be a weakness and he wondered just how far the British Government was prepared to go. He remembered watching an old 50's movie, 'The Yangtse Incident' but at the time it had not meant much to him. Now it all seemed to be falling into place.

Sometimes the only course of action was to call the bully's bluff. As far as human rights is concerned the Chinese were hardly new kids on the block. His father had told him about the bloody aftermath of Tiananmen Square The briefing though had urged caution. Britain had after all shown they supported the United States in the latter's standing up to China. The Prime Minister had already on more than one occasion, ordered an aircraft carrier and support ships to the region. This was regarded overall as being less risky now the Americans are back on the international scene apart that is, from their giving up Afghanistan!

Much of the emphasis over foreign policy seemed focused now on China; having shifted from eastern Europe. It was believed, Sefton thought prematurely that dissent was spreading so rapidly across Russia that before long Putin's grasp on power would stop. A democratic regime more favourably disposed towards the West would at long last, replace him. Sefton dismissed this as wishful thinking and thought the West should glance occasionally at a world map to keep not only China in global perspective but Russia too!

Later that Thursday afternoon, as he prepared to return from the House to his flat, Mather was handed a note advising the Chinese had withdrawn their entry visas. This left him at rather a loose end so he phoned Serena.

"Hello, this is Serena. Sorry to miss you but if you leave a message then I will get back to you as soon as possible," was her recorded answer-phone's response.

"Hi, Serena. I'll call you later. Bye darling," Sefton responded.

**

As Serena recovered on top of her bed after fairly energetic sex, she heard Sefton's muffled voice and regretted her current situation had prevented her from answering but consoled herself with the thought that her present companion rarely stayed beyond 5pm.

A very disappointed Mather decided he would make up for it by pouring himself a comforting gin and an equal measure of a very fashionable brand of tonic advertised almost daily on television. He scrabbled inside a pine drinks cabinet in the corner of the small office he shared with Marcus Browne and poured his drink. Then he turned without much conviction to a file left for his attention by Alicia but he was unable to settle after his double disappointment. Firstly, the trip to China was off and secondly, he hadn't been able to console himself almost immediately in Serena's warm embrace. Something he had been looking forward to considerably after receiving that 'no – go' note. Even the sound of her recorded voice had been enough to stir him and he could barely wait for 7pm to come. To kill some time he decided to leave the confines of the Palace of Westminster and stroll back to Wentworth Street from where he would call Serena again.

Serena since the middle of the afternoon had been entertaining Ranulf Faulkner. He, earlier in the day had set in motion a train of events that would eventually overwhelm many people including both Serena MacDonald and Sefton Mather. Other than the promise of a very satisfying shag, Faulkner had an ulterior motive for that visit. He used it to reconnoitre the presence or otherwise of security cameras around the entrance to the house. Blissfully unaware of the storm soon to crash all around him, Sefton at 6-30pm left his own flat and set off with purpose towards Victory Mews, arriving a few seconds before a church clock began to strike the hour. He followed Serena into the bedroom, which showed no evidence at all of her previous visitor. She after Faulkner's departure had showered thoroughly which she always did after sex; but particularly in Ranulf Faulkner's case it was to wash every physical trace of him having shared her body and bed. She had always found him disturbing company. His continued to feature on Serena's special list only because she thought he could prove useful to her in the event of ever finding herself compromised in some way.

***

Ranulf Faulkner was not a man who cared too much about what people thought of him; neither did he feel the need to cultivate a wide circle of friends. He knew a lot of people; a few he liked, most he tolerated for expediency's sake or, just did not. His first concern was to carry out his duties and responsibilities as a senior department head in MI6. In practical terms this involved protecting the United Kingdom from its enemies. To achieve this he more often than not found himself at odds with the new protocols that governed how the Security Services should be run in modern Britain. He clung to the old view that these Secret Services should be 'secret'. To achieve results he interpreted the rules very liberally. He had a job to do; that is what drew him to prosecute what he regarded as the war against terrorism with particular fervour. To that end and to confound any enemies of the State, he would simply employ whatever methods were necessary or whatever he could get away with to secure those ends. Of course, his superiors and even the appropriate Government Ministers were not always made aware of how he managed to foil Her Majesty's enemies. Or, if they did know, thought it expedient to overlook his unorthodox methods if the results meant that the citizens of the United Kingdom could go about their lawful daily business without fear of terrorist bullet, bomb or chemical/biological outrage. His successes and persistence in the gathering and acting on intelligence from his network of contacts at home and beyond the Channel had been largely instrumental in securing more Government funding for the Security Services. This in turn consequently contributing to achieving victories in the on-going war on terrorism! He was currently under consideration in recognition of his diligence for the award of Knight Commander of the Most Excellent Order of the British Empire in the next New Year's Honours list

At Balliol College over twenty five years before, the prospective Sir Ranulf Faulkner had read PPE (Philosophy, Politics and Economics) and had been considering the Civil Service or the Bar as possible career routes. What was very evident was that he was a young man with an excellent memory for facts, a keen eye for detail and an incisive mind. It was following a session with his Politics tutor discussing his essay on the 'Politics of Terrorism' when he was approached and subsequently recruited by the British Security Services. In his written response and subsequent discussion with his tutor, he had argued cogently and persuasively. He had posited that after the collapse of the Soviet Empire, the consequent re-shaping of Europe and the more belligerent stirrings of self-determination in the Middle East and with the United States re-examining its role in World Politics as the end of the 20th Century approached made the rise in terrorism inevitable. He based part of his analysis on the terrorist attack on New York's World Center in February, 1993 when Faulkner had been a seventeen year-old halfway through his A-levels. At Oxford, four years later, completing his degree he had remarked how difficult it would be for even the strongest nation on Earth to stop a determined terrorist let alone destroy him or her! Faulkner supported the view that the Cold War would be replaced by a new kind of war in the Age of the Computer. Whoever had access to information and communication could undermine an enemy's infrastructure and bring down any government. Future wars would be fought by 'thinking' machines so knowledge was power!

Almost unobtrusively but steadily he gained promotion and then experience in the field. Serving in Hong King just weeks before handover, then Turkey and Cuba before a one year secondment to Langley, Fairfax County, Virginia, the headquarters of the Central Intelligence Agency where he made some very useful, like-minded personal contacts.

Some of his acquaintances were soon speaking of Ranulf Faulkner as being like a spider in the centre of his web. The slightest tremor at the extreme edges caused spider-Ranulf to react. Had he known they referred to him in that way it would have pleased him. That's if he would have bothered to even consider others' view of him. He controlled; he manipulated. He was at the centre of sexual extremes, secrets and intrigues. He decided people's fate and woe betide anyone who dared to antagonize him. Mather, who much later he would regard as having crossed the line would pay a very high price. He might concede that one has to consort with sewer rats in order to carry out one's role in protecting Society. Terrorists were sewer rats so it was reasonable and too bad if some of the shit rubbed off and resulted in him retaliating using especially nasty ways.

The four co-ordinated terrorist attacks by Al-Qaeda on 11th September, 2001, or 9/11, as it would long be remembered had rather proved his original argument. Subsequent outrages demonstrated that those targets could only react to terrorist action rather than effectively prevent the bomber and the assassin from carrying them out in the first place. Using one particular contact he had made, he was waging his own anti-terrorism campaign. This arrangement suited Faulkner and the U.K.'s cause well. Terrorists were rounded up, often before they had had a chance to carry out their missions. There was a cost however. For years, Ranulf with the connivance of at least two police officers had given the Iranian free-lancer, Bahram Asghar, who operated using a variety of aliases, some latitude. This in exchange for providing inside information on terrorist activity. Asghar certainly by the end of the second decade of the 21st Century, owes no allegiance other than to himself. Any show of religious zeal is a front to fool those religious bigots into doing his bidding. In his latest 'sting' operation he was easily passing himself off as an Islamic State supporter. He had even chosen the targets and once the terrorist cells were in position, would warn Faulkner accordingly. The British Security Officer had argued with his MI5 counterparts that by allowing Asghar access to the 'county lines' drugs supply chain they could better control it and when the dedicated police units formed to counter those 'lines' were ready to strike they could seize all suppliers. In the meantime his agents in co-operation with the U.S. Drug Enforcement Agency and the C.I.A. would continue to track and destroy the growers and manufacturers of a wide range of drugs. It had proved a very easy task for Bahram Asghar with Faulkner's unseen support to recruit Croft. Much of Faulkner's work involved the calling in of favours so when Croft asked Asghar if he might do him a favour, it suited the Security man to approve it. Croft, aware the net was finally closing in even though his and the Iranian's activities had long been shielded by Faulkner, wanted an irritant and a former colleague who knew too much, both removed. Asghar would oblige later near Dunsford and on Haldon Hill but Faulkner wanted something in return. The task Asghar was to be set soon after his return from Devon would be to implicate a Member of Parliament in scandal and murder. It would also suit a number of people if part of the collateral damage surrounding the downfall of Mather turned out to be Sophie Fortune. Over the years she had been a constant thorn in so many sides. The removal of Serena MacDonald would likewise tick some retribution target boxes, particularly Croft's for it was she who had posted that old file to the Police Commissioner. As for Faulkner, she had proved useful to him and not merely for her performance under the duvet. There would be no physical link to him once incriminating evidence was removed. Jemima had become Faulkner's cuckoo in Serena's Victory Mews' nest as punishment for her failed attempt to blackmail him as to his rampant activities in Serena's bed. It would be Jemima who would switch off the security camera above the front door of Serena's house and ensure the door itself be left unlocked one particularly fateful evening. He had also forced her to keep an eye open for any damaging evidence concerning another of Serena's 'visitors', Bertie Jameson. It was Jemima who had given him ammunition on Bertie's sexual antics that had made it an easy task to bring pressure to bear on the Television man on various occasions. He had also persuaded her to check the material passed to Serena's solicitors in Holborn before it reached them. Faulkner insisted Jemima remove any film, pictures, discs, indeed anything that showed himself having sex with Serena before putting his own plan to discredit Mather into action. He kept all other material on the other men, 'recorded in action', for a rainy day. When Faulkner discovered that one of these other star performers was Sefton Mather this normally dour, 'po-faced' man was almost incandescent with joy.

"Dropping him from a great height into the shit is going to be easier than I thought and a real pleasure," he exclaimed.

***

After Jemima's clumsy and failed attempt at blackmailing him when he had judged Serena culpable too, he had continued to make the occasional visit for vigorous sex but the time was nigh to tie off all the loose ends. He regretted that his wife, Athena knew about these liaisons with Serena MacDonald. It was not so much the fact of her knowing that he sought and enjoyed the services of an escort but he did not like it when anyone held such intelligence about him even if it was only his wife. He was confident that neither Serena nor Jemima would dare speak out about him. Ultimately that didn't matter anyway as both would soon be silenced. What made it worse was how and why Athena knew. This was simply the result of a singular, uncontrolled moment. He had called out Serena's name during a very restless night. She had thrown her name back in her husband's face soon after a very crucial moment with a rampant Sefton poised to plunge deep inside her. In the first years of their marriage all had been well; they were in love and sex between them satisfactory but soon settling into a regular, predictable mode. More and more the predictability of their union reducing the quality and frequency. Then as Faulkner's work began to encroach on the time they were able to spend together, Athena grew more and more bored and became increasingly more frustrated. When other men began to take an interest in her she responded and soon they were regularly finding their way into her bed. There she readily opened her legs to receive what her husband seemed reluctant or was often absent or too distracted to give her. Losing her to other men was one of the costs Faulkner's dedication to his duty had to endure. Seeing Serena he convinced himself, was part of his work; his wife was never at home, too busy attending charity events. Abstinence from each other became the norm but Serena with her sexual skills added the missing dimension to his narrow life. Now though it was time to move on and leave this all behind. He would be a little peeved when one of his targets, Jemima would manage to move very quickly and leave the country before appropriate steps could be taken. She would indeed carry out the tasks of removing all recordings and ensure the front door was unlocked as requested but then the seriousness of events happening around her had an effect. She would realise how much danger she was in and that she could be implicated in someway with Faulkner's plans for dealing with Serena. Faulkner however would decide that she posed little threat to him so retribution could wait. It was a pity as events turned out and something he would reflect on much later that the liquid harvest she would soon be gathering would not be feature in her own undoing. It could though if it was made available still be used to discredit the original sower of the seed! If the charges against him didn't stick then the DNA trail Mather had blazed across many a duvet would certainly discredit him and destroy his career.

***

Faulkner's very first acquaintance with them had been when the two women had worked for Exclusive Escort Services. All the two of them knew or needed to know at that time was they had been booked to provide sexual favours for a visiting foreign business man. The whole affair though had been part of a 'sting' operation organised by undercover reporters of a leading tabloid assisted but controlled by the Security Services in the person of Ranulf Faulkner. One of Faulkner's rather dubious operatives, Jamail Hallet was to act as the deal's facilitator. He would bring an executive of a weapons manufacturer to meet two government ministers of a Middle Eastern country. As an inducement to sign the arms contract a large sum of cash as well as those sexual favours would be available for those foreign guests. There was an unfortunate, incriminating link between a British Government minister who had until recently owned stock in the same Company who were forever lobbying it. The attempted deal was exposed but the newspapers denied the opportunity of splashing the sordid details over its front page; in the interests of national security! Once the major players in the performance left; the two foreigners claiming diplomatic immunity; or were escorted by armed response police officers, Faulkner and a police office, Detective Inspector Valentine were left in the hotel room opposite two very attractive young women. Faulkner suggested the women forget everything they had witnessed, which wasn't much as they had been ushered into another room and told to keep silent, when officers had stormed in. Nor did they know much for they had been paid to provide sex and it was part of their business to be discreet. Who of the four left at a loose end in the room had first suggested it, seemed to have been quickly forgotten. Though regardless of whoever it had been, the offer was enthusiastically taken up. Serena paired off with Valentine and led him to an adjoining room leaving Jemima with Faulkner. Some time later Faulkner thought he would try out the other escort's favours and soon found Serena very much more to his liking and booked her for future sessions. This time neither of them needed a second bidding, after all everything was bought and paid for courtesy of the British Government and the newspaper. So it was that over the years the two men would occasionally visit the two women but it would be the latter who would have cause to regret them meeting at all. Jamail Hallet three weeks after the 'sting' operation, liking the attributes of one of the women he had caught a brief glimpse of at that time, purchased her escort services, As Jemima later confided in Serena he had liked it a bit too rough for her liking.

***

Detective Superintendent Gareth Valentine as he now was, still managed the occasional very discreet liaison with Serena. Several times they had sex at Victory Mews where his performances were duly recorded though unknown to him. For some reason he began to feel rather uncomfortable at that address and she agreed to meet at a small hotel in Croydon where his sexual capacity returned to his earlier gold standard. Serena found it difficult not to compare him with Sefton Mather. She attempted to always remain in control; on top of each of them during their session and allow them when it was their time to suck, lick and gently nibble the most intimate parts of her body. She gave both of them oral satisfaction too but if she had to choose just one, the pole position, the analogy somehow appropriate, would be given to Sefton. He was also more readily available than the Police Officer and unlike the latter, unmarried. It was of concern to Serena that Gareth's marriage was failing and whereas she had been assured by him that the failure was largely down to the pressures of the job and his high rank, she felt that she was coming between the two of them. Consequently, although she liked his penis deep inside her he should be screwing his wife and pleasuring Mrs Valentine and not her. As for having a useful contact in the Metropolitan Police so far there had been no advantage. Serena did not want to be regarded as the 'other woman' if, to quote a favourite phrase, things went 'tits up'. She reflected on her original sextet of what she had hoped would also be useful contacts, Faroud Nassad was rarely in the country and therefore rarely in her, so she discounted his usefulness. Something about Ranulf Faulkner still bothered her; she certainly felt threatened when he was in the same room as her but she thought he could be helpful if the occasion warranted it. As for Queen's Counsel, Vivian Sage-Bedford so far, she had never needed to resort to law but who knows, one day in the future, perhaps! The barrister had first come into contact with the escort world when he had defended the joint owners, Barney Anderson and Millie Savage of Exclusive Escort Services on various charges under Sections 47 and 52 of the Sexual Offences Act, 2003. Vivian argued that the defendants were not living off immoral earnings by causing, inciting or controlling prostitutes as all escorts acted independently. Other charges accused them of gaining advantage by exploiting for sexual services, person or persons under eighteen years of age, or of trafficking people for the purposes of sex. He argued that all documents identifying each young woman showed them to be at least eighteen years of age and freely able to come and go as they pleased. Escorts merely paid a proportion of the fee for the companionship they provided, be it for the theatre, dinner or other such activity. What they arranged to do after this was between them as individual and client and totally independent of the agency. Mr Sage-Bedford convinced the jury of the pair's innocence and as well as his generous fee the aspiring young barrister was invited to share Millie's services for no payment. Not quite free as in the legal expression, 'pro bono publico' but if not for the public good, Millie's contribution certainly did Vivian some good. Years later, acquiring a wife and children and appointed Queen's Counsel his visits to Exclusive Escort Services became rarer. They revived for a time when Aurora (Serena) replaced Millie and when Serena set up on her own he continued to enjoy the occasional 'work-out' as he liked to call them, with Serena who in turn was pleased to include him as one of her more exclusive clients.

***

Sefton, oblivious to the machination and plotting of others, would soon be appreciating the cool, minty fresh scent of his lover's skin with overtones of musky cinnamon. Serena too was also unaware of the scheming of others!

Chapter Ten

They sat down and savoured their post-coital coffee and slice each of Battenberg cake. Sefton, had as usual showered after his exertions but now felt fully mentally and physically refreshed; completely relaxed and at ease with the world. The particular holistic energy that sex provides washing the stresses and cares away. He was ready but not necessarily willing to go home to his flat and return to the paperwork he had abandoned during the previous afternoon, a Thursday. The Hansard volume in which he wanted to check some details, and other Parliamentary business were very poor company when compared to Serena's assets. He still planned on using some of the rest of Friday to catch up before returning to Durford. There was little in parliamentary terms happening most Fridays so sessions finished early to allow members from far flung constituencies time to get home for the weekend. He arranged to meet with Serena in five days time but as the day ahead unfolded in a different way to that expected, he would be returning very soon to seek the warm, comforting refuge he always found with her. Now though before he ventured beyond the front door of Number 21, he sprinted back up the stairs and glanced through the blinds of the front window. Little was stirring so he skipped jauntily back down the stairs, grabbed Serena affectionately around the waist and kissed her with some passion. Then he made a final check of tie, trouser zip and other items of clothing, including a trilby hat he had taken to wearing when walking in London Yes, everything was tidy and all correctly in their place, as he let himself out of the house.

He walked at a brisk but comfortable pace and in a change to his usual route, headed over the Thames on the Millennium Bridge towards St Paul's Cathedral. His rough plan, sub-consciously trying to put off wrestling with paperwork was to take the Central Line from St Paul's to Oxford Circus, then on the Bakerloo Line to Baker Street and the short walk to his London home. He reached the Cathedral and spent a reflective moment looking up at Wren's incredible edifice. Mather was just about to head off through Paternoster Square in the direction of the underground station when he was surprised to see a very familiar figure. Even with her face partially obscured by a head covering and her body shrouded in plain, dark grey clothing, there was no mistaking her. For walking towards the Cathedral down Ludgate Hill was the woman he knew very intimately as Bahira Abadi. She was not alone but was deep in conversation with a tall, well-dressed and carefully groomed bearded man. His dark eyes seemed to be constantly on the move. Sefton pulled his hat down a little more and turned sharply to the right to avoid them walking straight into him although they seemed totally unaware of his presence. They hurried past. Now full of curiosity, not necessarily tinged with jealousy for he was sure her companion was not a rival but, according to Mr Grey's description of him, likely to be her twin brother, Bahram. Sefton decided he must follow them. Yet, was it really that murderous individual? Blatantly walking the streets of London in broad daylight? On the other hand, if he was risking his life and liberty then there was a strong possibility that something serious was about to happen.

The two walked into St Martin's Le Grand and then turned left towards London Wall before moving on into Thomas Street. Mather ducked behind an 'Open Reach' van, as his quarry reached a house with a dull, dirty yellow door above a short flight of stone steps from pavement level, some sixty or so metres down the street. They disappeared from his view down the cellar steps of that house with the neglected door. Mather moved back to the shelter of the van having decided to wait for a while to check if they were merely delivering something and consequently likely to soon re-appear. Ten minutes passed and he decided to walk away as fast as his legs could take him. By the time he had reached the street corner he had checked his pockets thoroughly but could find no sign of his mobile phone.

"How stupid is that!" he growled, realising he had left the offending instrument at Serena's.

He smiled, wondering if too much sex with Serena was making him smug and forgetful.

"No,' he exclaimed, "you can never have too much sex with Serena so I'll settle for a little forgetfulness."

This statement much to the consternation of a young woman he passed pushing a sleeping infant in a buggy.

He reached the underground and caught a westbound Tube train to Oxford Circus and a second one to Baker Street. He almost ran the rest of the way home. Sefton rushed into his flat and grabbed his landline; with haste he punched in the numbers of a Parliamentary colleague and waited impatiently for a response.

"Hello, Genene, is Marcus about?" he asked.

Yes, is that you, Sefton? I'll give him a shout," she replied.

Sefton heard a shrill voice call:

"Marcus, phone!" before she resumed speaking to the mildly agitated caller.

"How are you? You must come over for drinks. Ah, here he is. It's Sefton Mather."

"Hi, Sefton, what can I do for you?" he asked.

"Well, this may be nothing at all but I swear that not an hour ago I was standing about thirty metres from the Asghars, brother and sister," Sefton declared, having barely paused for breath.

"Where? Are you sure? He's managed to stay under the radar for quite a while," Browne replied.

"Near St Paul's; I followed them to an address near London Wall. Don't know the exact number in Thomas Street but it's on the northern side of the road and has a very dirty, yellow door," Sefton said.

"Near London Wall you say? Isn't that where you thought Derifa Asghar lived. You'll doubtless recall our chat in the Italian restaurant with Mr Grey?" he added.

Sefton thought:

"Not likely to forget it!"

The two men exchanged pleasantries including an offer of drinks before Marcus Browne rang off. Sefton, went to his fridge and pulled out a chilled bottle of lager. He spent the next few minutes speculating on what Brown's next move would be. He assumed that even as he drank his beer, Marcus Browne would be contacting Mr Grey and the Security Services including both MI5 and MI6 would soon be bustling with activity. Indeed this was so but when Ranulf Faulkner received an 'alert' call his immediate action was to make a call of his own before alerting all local field agents and the duty officers at Thames House and 'Legoland'.

***

The Asghar twins had grown up during a time of great change in Iran. They were born in 1992, Bahram first, followed five minutes later by his sister, Derifa. As they grew up they became enthusiastic supporters of the on going Islamic Revolution but during conversations with their grandfather, Bahram began to have a few nagging doubts that the promise of the Revolution would never and could never be fulfilled. He began to ask questions though he was always very careful who he approached to provide him with answers. His sister, however seemed to display more revolutionary zeal. Change for her was happening far too slowly and needed help even if that meant violent action against those who were growing increasingly more antagonistic towards the Islamic Republic of Iran. Her country, as far as foreigners were concerned deserved its lowly place in the world and sanctions over Iran's nuclear policy were legitimate. She totally rejected the West's negative view of the country she loved and was prepared if necessary to take the fight to the West and die for the cause to show that Iran must not be ignored.

The Revolution had begun in February, 1979 when their parents had been around nine years of age. They discovered that their grandmother had been a schoolteacher and a great supporter of the exiled, Ayatollah Khomeini. From exile in Paris he had encouraged women to take an active part in preparing the way for the Islamic Revolution. In return for their support the women of Iran assumed this would be the first step in a series of measures to reward that support by giving them equality with men at every level of society. It was true that under, king Mohammed Reza Pahlavi, the Shah of Iran, some steps along that road to women's equality had already been taken; government employees, like the Shah himself adopted and were encouraged to wear Western dress and the wearing of the 'hijab' in public was banned. During the early 1970s however there were increasingly more protests, particularly in Tehran, the capital, over corruption and the spread of Western influence and culture which seemed to permeate every echelon of the state to the detriment of Iranian life. Causing even more rancour were the very repressive measures taken against those who protested.

Fearing for his life, the Shah left Tehran, bringing to an end his thirty eight year reign. It was his replacement, Ayatollah Khomeini who announced the Iranian Revolution. He had declared that only a Government, given legitimacy by God can implement a radical,(Islamic) rebuilding of a fragmented society.

Derifa and particularly Bahram, grew increasingly more confused as their grandfather talked of the Revolution and how, although he had flourished during the Shah's corrupt and narrow, regime hoped for a better one with the promise of its replacement. These hopes were short-lived as he realised one repressive ruler had been replaced by another! The new leader immediately declaring he wanted a country whose religion promoted basic Islamic values and swept away Western ones. Women hitherto had some limited rights; in 1963 they had been given the vote and could be elected to Parliament but now instead of increasing them the Ayatollah swept them away. Working women were ordered back to their homes to serve their husbands and children. Adulterous women faced death by stoning. Numbers of officials who had held their position during the Shah's regime were shot; there were rumours too of the beheading of many hundreds who criticised the new government. Female bus passengers were restricted to the back seats while men sat at the front. A metaphor if ever there was one for the condition of women for a time, in post-1979, Iran. The twins were told these reactionary changes did not go unchallenged. One hundred thousand women gathered in Tehran to protest about their loss of freedom and the right to vote as well as the enforcing of the wearing of the hijab in public. This gathering was suppressed with much violence by the 'Revolutionary Guard'. One of the fatalities was their grandmother and it was bitterly ironic and not lost on the Asghars, that she had supported the Ayatollah, felt women would gain from regime change but had now been killed in trying to secure what they believed had been promised to them.

Even a family, brought up and subjected to only one version of news and truth could see for themselves a rise in poverty, unemployment and the suspicion that the country was run inefficiently. If the Revolution had been aimed at including the 'Mostazafin' – the downtrodden, who the Shah had done little or nothing to help, then it had yet to succeed. Though after Khomeini's death, a change has begun under his successor as Supreme Leader of Iran, Ayatollah Khamenei and certainly literacy has more than doubled since the Revolution and women's place in Society is improving but its record on human rights is poor and Iran executes more people including minors, than any other country except China. The Iranian Economy, certainly harmed by Western sanctions though, was still being held back by mismanagement and corruption; unemployment among the young remains a continuing problem. Protest and dissent is also continuing while Iran remains the pariah of the Middle East.

The Asghars', in common with most young Iranians were caught up, if at differing levels of commitment in the Revolutionary cause; some believing that in order to rid the country of outside influence particularly that of the United States any means was and is acceptable from extreme terrorist measures to the development of a nuclear programme.

Bahram emerged from university as a very intelligent, charismatic and very capable young man but one who when looking back at the Revolutionary struggle realised it had achieved very little. What he could do was to use whatever measures were necessary to continue the fight and to cover whatever he needed to do, to fund and further his own financial cause. His sister, Derifa unaware of his personal agenda and rather in awe of her brother's strong personality resolved to do anything that would promote the cause of the Revolution. Which she believed would ultimately lead to an Islamic State where equality was everyone's right. Sefton Mather, a young soldier had been her first target for subversion and so, for the cause, she had slept with him. Later, when they discovered he had been elected to Parliament, that seat of bitter hostility towards her own country, what had been merely a hopeful, random choice for future blackmail and manipulation now had real possibilities in their broader scheme to subvert the disenchanted and dissatisfied people of Britain. Their plan to bomb key points in London and the big cities along with a programme of radicalisation from the capital through to the Midlands and the North would certainly Derifa believed, trigger dissent across a Britain whose morale had been sent reeling by the Pandemic. Derifa reflected on what a relatively small number of Jihadists in Syria had achieved and how supporters had flocked to help. Although that Islamic State had been short-lived the next one wouldn't be! Her brother agreed with her that Mather, whose Party was in Government would be playing a role in future events but did not tell her that his involvement would be quite different if his own part in a plan went ahead; Bahram would emerge considerably richer!

***

In the converted cellar, now a rather featureless, undecorated apartment, Bahram Asghar put into words a concern, for his sister's benefit, that he had been brooding over since they had crossed Paternoster Square. Still troubling him was the presence in that area of a particular, well-dressed man wearing a hat. His sister agreed that at least one of the businessmen hurrying from their offices did indeed resemble Sefton Mather. A man they had targeted for subversion years before in Afghanistan as a possible mark for blackmail, but who she assured her brother was unaware of her true identity. If it was him then what would he be doing there anyway? His territory was more Bond Street than London Wall. He rarely ventured north or east of Oxford Street. In any case she had convinced her brother what could they have done? Spent hours giving him the slip or confronting him with the possible consequence of drawing unnecessary attention to themselves? At one point near St Paul's, she noticed her brother had been reaching under his coat and she had half-expected to see a Glock-17 in his fist. That would have been a rash move and caused them a very sudden and possibly fatal change of plan. As it was, she had whispered to him that it was far too late to change their arrangements and deal with him which of course for those different reasons suited them both. Unaware of his true reason for not taking any immediate action against Mather he had succeeded in giving his sister the impression he had been thinking about killing the MP. This to forestall any rash act she might have attempted to stop Mather in his tracks and spoil plans his contact had for him.

The central part of their mission involved an attack on the Prime Minister's car as it travelled the short distance from Downing Street to the Palace of Westminster for next Wednesday's 'Prime Minister's Questions'. Other attacks were planned, including suicide bombs on Government buildings, New Scotland Yard and Trafalgar Square and in the City centres of Birmingham, York, Newcastle and Liverpool.

Bahram Asghar was shortly to depart, ostensibly to give final briefings to the leaders of the other missions before they dispersed including the group of two men and two women who would launch themselves from opposite sides of the road at the PM's car. The Asghars' role was to co-ordinate rather than personally participate in the action and at 12 mid-day on the following Wednesday, inform radio and television and claim responsibility on behalf of the new Islamic Revolutionary State.

***

Nearly an hour passed before Bahram Asghar, after receiving a call on one of his mobile phones actually left the house for although the attacks were still days away there was still much to do. He dare not risk waiting around in case other events moved rather quicker than anticipated or not as arranged. An example of such a change in plans occurred almost immediately. He had assumed his sister would be accompanying him but he was unable to persuade her to leave the cellar where she was going over the planned attacks with an accomplice, checking every detail. This particular man's role next week would be to plant a bomb outside the National Gallery. Asghar moved quickly back up the cellar steps and walked east and north towards the first of several destinations; this one was a safe house near Liverpool Street Station occupied for all appearances by an 'ordinary' immigrant family who had been in the country for years but radicalized during the time of the establishment of the Islamic State, known variously as Daesh, ISIS, or ISIL during Syria's civil war. As Bahram turned right, and out of the end of Thomas Street, two white vans entered it from the other end. Had they turned up two minutes earlier they would have spotted him heading east. Only later did it emerge that anti-terrorist officers had been ordered to let him go but keep him under surveillance. They were also not told that he would be deliberately leading them to terrorist locations. During the briefing the team had been ordered to arrest Derifa and detain her but avoid, unless their own lives were under serious threat, from discharging their weapon or weapons. At no time was he to be apprehended. One of the vans parked ten metres to the left of the yellow door and the other ten metres to the right of it. Seconds later two more vans appeared at the far end of that same street and two more at the western side. Police officers spilled out from their vans at either end of the street and began to cordon it off. Armed officers filed out from the two vans parked either side of the target house and ran to the two houses on either side; quickly, efficiently groups of very startled residents were soon being evacuated and escorted to the cordon at the western end. At a given signal armed officers bounded up the steps from the pavement to the yellow door of that suspect house, so desperate for fresh paint. Others descended the cellar steps. Out of sight and to the rear of the Thomas Street properties, were even more armed officers covering the exits having gained access through the houses of the street running parallel to Thomas Street. At a given signal by the officer in charge of the operation the cellar door was battered open at the same time as the yellow door was about to be smashed open too. Then just as that second officer raised his battering ram, the door was flung open by the householder who happened to have glanced out of his window at the same time the vans had drawn up. The very startled resident found himself staring down the barrel of an MP5SFA3, semi-automatic carbine. The 'cellar flat, anti-terrorist team' began a fast, thorough but careful search of the property, room by room. In the kitchen and a small bedroom off the hall where the police were fast approaching, two people were reaching for weapons, alerted by the collective noise of breaking locks, glass and splintering wood and the sudden pounding of boots on bare floorboards.

An officer appeared at the open kitchen door, Glock-17M in hand, having shouldered his carbine. He shouted:

"Armed Police! Drop your weapon."

But Derifa, fully prepared to die a martyr for the cause, ignored the order, grabbed a pistol and loosed off a shot which hit the top of the door frame.

The officer shouted the order once again and seeing the pistol being aimed once again in his direction and believing his own life to be at risk had no other choice but to fire one shot.

The woman fell dead at his feet!

In the small bedroom, a man known as Farouk, moved towards the bed.

"Armed police. Stay where you are or I will fire!"

Farouk continued towards the bed and fell to his knees and began to frantically reach underneath it.

The officer who had ventured a few paces into the room saw that the man was touching wires connected to what appeared to be a blue denim vest. The man was within a milli-second of detonating a homemade bomb! The policeman yelled again and fired a shot but just too late! He did have the presence of mind after discharging his weapon to throw himself back and out of the room. That split-second decision saved his life. There was a loud explosion and soon he was covered in fragments of wall plaster, blood and what an instant before had been a living, breathing, human being. Fortunately, although concussed it could have been far worse for the officer, had the mattress not absorbed most of the blast.

That evening, television news bulletins reported an explosion in EC2 and two fatalities. One individual died after detonating an explosive device and another shot by a member of the Metropolitan Police Anti-Terrorism squad. Police officers had fired one shot only after being fired on by a suspect believed to be a member of an extremist Islamic terrorist cell, possibly Al-Qaeda. No terrorist organisation has yet claimed responsibility. One officer sustained minor injuries from the bomb but was expected to be discharged from hospital within forty eight hours.

The newsreader ended the news broadcast with:

"It is believed this was part of a concerted terrorist plot and the security level has been raised from, 'Substantial' to 'Severe' and the public are warned to be vigilant and report anything suspicious to the police."

There were further reports mainly consisting of complaints levelled at the police over their handling of the operation. That residents had been given no notice to evacuate, that the lives of innocent citizens had been put at risk and damage had been sustained by nearby property.

Sefton's comment on this was:

"The Police are damned if they do and damned if they don't!"

A very senior Metropolitan Police spokesperson issued a statement at 11pm declaring that acting on information received and with the full co-operation of the City of London Police, Officers had acted with speed and with the public's safety uppermost in their response to a palpable threat to the safety of the citizens of London. Prompt action was taken as security forces did not want the incident to escalate into a siege or allow the terrorists time to seize the initiative and create more martyrs for their cause. Delay could have given them the opportunity to detonate more bombs and cause a substantial threat to life and property. Loss of life was deeply regretted.

The Thomas Street incident was the last topic of that evening's BBC 2's 'News Night.' Appearing on the show was a familiar figure, answering the host of the programme's very incisive and probing questions. He rounded off the interview with a statement:

"The Police acted with minimal force in breaking up a very dangerous terrorist criminal operation. Other raids on suspected terrorists took place simultaneously and numerous arrests have taken place. During these operations two other suspects resisted arrest. Police acted in accordance with protocol where they sincerely believed their own lives to be at risk and after due warnings fired two shots," declared Marcus Browne. "The Government wishes to assure the country and the citizens of London that their safety is paramount. I commend the combined actions of the City of London and Metropolitan Police in protecting our freedoms at great risk to themselves."

Just before the close of the programme, the next day's newspaper headlines were quickly reviewed; they generally endorsed the work of all the Security Services involved.

Sefton Mather, to whom thanks for the success of it all was due in no small part, turned off the television at 11-20pm. He was pleased that Police stock had risen. They did not always receive the credit they deserved and their's was a potentially dangerous job and he was ever pleased to congratulate them at every opportunity! He also reflected on the death of Derifa. He was in the main sorry, reflecting they had shared intimate moments then realised he could have put himself in danger as she was potentially a very dangerous individual; it was she though who had chosen the path resulting in her early death.

Some of the evening's events would soon be forgotten. Sefton had made two calls late that afternoon. The first one, the catalyst for that small victory of democracy over the forces of evil and hate. That second one in the early evening, to Serena whose television he had just switched off while she was in her bathroom preparing for the coupling to come with an invigorating shower; a body shampoo of very cool mint with just a hint of cinnamon to get the pulses racing.

***

In that earlier call to Serena he had been barely able to contain his excitement. This was unusual for him as from the time of his experiences as a soldier he had deliberately cultivated that state of 'cool' that only the very young and self-centred thought was their preserve alone. Very necessary too for a politician to remain level-headed and in control. On arrival at Serena's he realised just how hungry he was, particularly as the day's key events were being relayed on television in front of them. Thirty minutes later they were enjoying a take-away and the wine to wash it down. Although he had calmed down after taking a cab from Baker Street to York Road near Waterloo Station then walking the rest of the way to Number 21, what hadn't gone away was the enormity of the day's events. He felt burdened by a huge feeling of responsibility and not for the first time was trying to absolve himself from guilt. Partly as a result of his intervention at least two people had died; one of whom he had enjoyed incredible sex on various occasions. Not helpful in trying to keep a low profile if that hit the headlines:

'Member of Parliament in sex tryst with terrorist!' He could, in his mind's eye see the headlines that would not be good for him and certainly not for the Government

He had killed in Afghanistan but this was different, more personal.

While walking that last part of the journey to Serena's he reminded himself of his obligations to the Government. As a direct consequence he must only share with Serena what was already in the public domain. He was also supposed to be maintaining that low profile not that he and she engaged in much pillow talk. Their horizontal activities generally involved very few words.

After flossing, teeth-brushing and peeing, the two of them wandered into the bedroom where Serena had already pulled down the duvet. Sefton removed all of his clothes, most of which were then folded neatly on the dressing table's chair. Neither felt it necessary anymore to rip each other's clothes off like desperate teenagers. For Sefton and Serena, the sexual act was an experience to enjoy together. Serena stripped down to bra and panties. She knew one of her lover's foibles was to remove these garments for her at the appropriate time. They stood at the foot of the bed and kissed; there was an almost immediate stirring in his loins. They fell back together on the bed with their bodies, from their hips down overhanging the mattress. Soon fingers, hands, lips and tongues were exploring kissing, licking and caressing. For once Serena allowed Sefton to enter her while he was on top; his feet for the moment planted firmly on the floor while she, with her back flat to the mattress opened her legs wide and bent them in a position she found both comfortable and which from experience she knew would offer deeper access. Sefton grasped a kneecap in each palm and began a steady rhythm of thrusting. Then he withdrew as she moved up the bed so her thighs were in contact with the duvet-covered mattress. Then he turned her on her left side with her her back to him. Then he lifted her right leg and eased up behind her and slid his shaft into its waiting wet quiver and continued thrusting. He ejaculated on the upward stroke and then withdrew, rolling her fully onto her back before bending to lick her clitoris. He continued until her whole body began to tremble as she climaxed. Then her body went limp and she felt totally relaxed and satisfied.

***

Serena woke first. Sefton lay on his back in a deep, self-satisfied sleep. She turned onto her left side and cuddled into him; her right hand playfully tweaking his pubic hair. He stirred and uttered a low groan of contentment. Yesterday had ended particularly well for him though not for a former lover but that particular detail would he concluded, be best forgotten.

There had been one other very interested party watching the news on television from his safe house in E14, during that evening. He also very much regretted the death of his sister. Whatever level of remorse remained though was tempered with the thought that Derifa had played a dangerous game and was collateral damage in his overall scheme. Had she accompanied him when he had left the Thomas Street cellar she would have survived though she may have been suspicious of his ability to evade lines of armed police with ease and would have asked some awkward questions. Bahram swore revenge on the man he held responsible for her death.

Sefton would have felt less at ease with the world had he known that his ex-lover's brother was already planning to revenge her death. Matters had not gone quite as Bahram Asghar and a significant other had planned. Mather had already been targeted for special 'treatment' but now Asghar had a personal reason for revenge. He, like his sister had of course known that it had been Mather they had seen near St Paul's and had set matters in motion before the time agreed. That was history for now he planned to use a contact; that significant other he had deep within British Intelligence for his own ends regardless of what he was being directed to do. Once but briefly, ideology, a belief in the Islamic State had been his inspiration and a cause for which he had once been prepared for martyrdom but now it was mostly money. He had seen and tasted Western culture and liked the benefits it offered. There had been a time when he thought about working towards replacing the Islamic State with an alternative. Numbers of young, contemporary Iranians hoped for something different too. For some it was a Western-style democracy but he thought that would never work but could not think of an alternative so he decided to continue as he was. He easily sacrificed others who still believed that the West, the infidels, must be bombed into submission. Believed to be sympathetic to the cause he was entrusted with organising attacks but then betrayed terrorist groups to his British contact with the where, the whom and the when. This blood money a welcome addition to his income from drugs and other activities. His one regret after the events of the day was the death of his sister although unlike him, she had remained committed to the cause and was completely unaware of his double-dealings. He had failed in his attempt to persuade her to leave the cellar below that yellow door and held Sefton Mather wholly responsible for her death.

***

Sefton's current companion in bed pulled the duvet back to first look at and then explore his manhood which for a short while remained limp and shrivelled under her amused gaze. Then she reached under it and began to pull his foreskin back. Then a little further on to cup his balls in her palm and marvel at how heavy the content of his sac was. She circled his purple rim with the tips of her finger and thumb. This prompted a reaction as blood began to swell his limp member into the response for which she was hoping. She slipped the encouraging hand to the base of his almost completely stiffened penis and massaged it from that base to the tip. Then the tip of her index finger and thumb returned to that base again and she slowly began to run the two digits back to the top; the fingertip tracing the shaft's sperm tube, the urethra back to its opening at the very end of his helmet-shaped glans. She could see and feel that clear pre-cum liquid that was dribbling from the helmet's eye to serve as lubrication once again for entry into that special place; that too was also moistening again. She bent forward and took the glans in her mouth, letting her tongue sweep across that still dribbling slit; she licked off all his pre-cum and prepared to receive his rod of skin, blood and gristle for the third time in two days. She placed two of her fingers inside her very wet vagina and began to slide them in and out as thrills began to sweep through her lower body. This action produced even more natural lubricant. The she sat up, removed her fingers, grasped Sefton's erection and slowly eased herself down on it and inside her. She gasped as she felt first the rim slip in then cried out as the rest of the gently tapering member followed; her vagina stretching to accommodate most of its length.

Sefton, other than providing a substantial amount of the apparatus for these sexual athletics was content to remain passive as she continued to rise and fall on him. She felt in complete control even as his seed spurted up and inside her.

"Just as it should be," she thought.

Sefton, in complete contrast was losing control as waves of orgiastic thrills spread through him.

Serena too, was soon experiencing ripples of ecstasy as she rolled off him. She squeezed her thighs together, continuing to feel shivers from thighs to navel. She leaned forward, kissed the tip of his now wilting dick but inhaling strong scents of their union. She rolled out of bed and was probably imagining a dribbling sensation between the soft valley made by the folds of her labia and the tops of her thighs. She stood in front of the mirror and ran a hand through that same wet region then clenched her vital internal muscles and her legs together in a repeat, though of less intensity, of those earlier thrills.

***

Later that day Sefton spoke to Marcus Browne. There was one point he wanted to clear up and that was how the Thomas Street incident had mushroomed into a larger anti-terrorist operation.

"Simple," cooed Marcus, "you will know from security briefings that 'Prevent Team Officers' spend a lot of time attempting to deter the vulnerable from being drawn into terrorism. Acting on information, addresses, suspects and so on from their covert operations as well as MI5 surveillance, the City of London Police were able to liaise with the Metropolitan Police Service Counter Terrorism Command move in on suspected addresses. At the same time, units of armed response teams in the Midlands and the North were doing the same; all within minutes of your initial intelligence."

Sefton expressed surprise at the speed of the response.

"Just as well though Sefton, for they had some really nasty plans that had you not set the whole thing in motion could have caused one hell of a mess. Assassination of the PM, attacks in public places and all manner of mayhem. The one regret is that one of their principals, Bahram Asghar slipped through the net," Marcus said.

***

While Sefton and Serena were engaging in the second leg of their Olympian standard copulation, Sophie was involved in a less frenetic but very absorbing cause. She had been named after her great, great,

great aunt Sophie Fortune who had campaigned for votes for women as a Suffragist and women's rights generally. Conditions for the poor overall and women's issues specifically were dire in the closing years of the 19th and at the start of the 20th centuries and conscious of her very privileged background she had worked for change. She travelled to South Africa as part of mission enquiring into the welfare of Boer women and children incarcerated in British 'concentration camps' during the 2nd Boer War. Sophie had been killed caught up in a fire fight between Boers and a British Army patrol. The latter under the command of her brother, an officer in the Rifle Brigade.

As Sophie Fortune stood at the entrance to the police station preparing to act on behalf of yet more of life's casualties she despaired at how little distance along the rocky road to equality, peace, freedom and justice, women had progressed. Earlier that evening, a well-known actor on behalf of a charity had appealed to the public for their support and money to prevent the exploitation of girls and women in certain Asian countries. A recurring theme among her portfolio of rights' abuse was the Chinese Government's attitude towards Uighurs. Even to the extent of their sending agents to neighbouring States to kidnap and return those Uighurs who had fled China to avoid rape and torture. Sophie had vociferously campaigned for Britain's Overseas Aid to be restored to even more than its pre-Covid level and for the British Government to keep up denouncing the Chinese for their serial abuse of human rights. Just how far had large sections of the human race progressed since her namesake's time?

Sophie had been called to West End Central Police Station following police raids on the homes of suspected terrorists who were about to launch attacks on various targets across London. One of the women accused and arrested for being in possession of bomb-making equipment was also charged with entering the country illegally; a rubber boat across the Straits of Dover had brought her to England after managing to escape detention from a camp in Turkey. There, she had been identified as a former British citizen who had originally travelled to Syria in support of 'Daesh' and married one of the so-called, Islamic State's freedom fighters who had been involved in beheadings. Her 'husband' had been killed and she left abandoned and stateless. In a carefully planned undercover operation by Security Services a bogus charity worker had been identified as helping the woman still regarded as a threat to Britain and continuing to be sympathetic to Daesh. In exchange for money and other favours she had been helped to escape from the camp, cross Europe and secure passage on the rubber craft. From the very moment of her arrest she had long and loudly denied any such lingering support for any terrorist organisation. She claimed to have been manipulated by members of Daesh. This story did not quite tally with the accounts of those members of the Security Services who had been tracking her from Turkey. The British Government was not particularly sympathetic to Jihadists reformed or not and a medieval treason law had been updated to make their arrest, punishment and /or deportation the more easier!

This police station was almost like a second home to Sophie as she seemed to be spending more and more of her professional time there but where she herself had also been detained more than once. She had attended various demonstrations during Covid-19 and represented others who had been arrested. On one particular occasion many women had been caught up in violent scuffles with police; the latter accused of aggravating a sensitive situation by their use of heavy-handed tactics at a peaceful protest! Scuffles broke out as women were outraged in what had started as a peaceful demonstration against the curtailing of personal freedoms. The irony was not lost in the headlines of the following day's newspapers. The police attended the event to ensure social-distancing was being observed in order to stop the spread of coronavirus but attendees interpreted their presence as the thin end of the wedge that would all the more quickly usher in a police state and a further assault on freedom. Already, 'big brother' if not in residence was omni-present as Britain's reputation for its citizens being the most filmed on CCTV was growing across Europe.

Although, 'lock-down' was in force, protesters turned out in droves on Clapham Common and Hyde Park and elsewhere in London as well as cities across Britain. The man-handling and handcuffing began of those who were technically in breach of the very rules aimed at protecting them from the ravages of Covid. Sophie, following her own arrest was very quick to point out that if ordinary citizens were subject to such rules then why weren't the same restrictions being applied to everyone. She had then cited several Government advisers and Ministers who had flouted the rules but no action had been taken by the Government.

"Little wonder there is violence in such an unfair Society," Sophie had thought at the time. "It's everywhere displayed on film and television."

That evening she spent rather miserably deliberating on the rise in the violence quotient, much increased against women, in several television dramas. If only she and Bertie Jameson could return to an earlier project and bring this subject to the fore. She also wondered what is the point of advertising on television if as programme makers maintain, television does not influence its viewers. Why then bother with advertisements? Each production company seems to be in competition with the last one in their efforts to capture the viewing public. Up goes the violence and the overuse of weapons including knives. This sad statistic reflected in the rise in real life of knife crime among the young in the streets of London. This, irrespective of a variety of initiatives aimed at reducing it and reclaiming the streets. It was not only knives being used but too often gangs resorted to pistols and even rapid firing semi-automatic guns to gain control of those same streets. Sophie considered that social media and the internet which have so much potential to improve the human condition too often falls short. Even video games repeatedly portray violence and in such a way that the body count is surreal and meaningless. For children and those incapable of discriminating between reality and fiction, or between right and wrong such acts of violence no longer shock!

Sophie Fortune, a caring, concerned individual then considered the growing lack of tolerance in society. Was any single person to blame? At university, politics lecturers had discussed the rise of the selfish, 'me' society from the 1980's onwards when instead of the country growing more united it seemed to be becoming more and more divided. The wealthy are growing wealthier and the poor even poorer. If the politicians had been the mid-wife of a fractured society could they not now change direction and care for the growing child's overall well-being by redressing the balance and have a Welfare State that did not dole out the welfare but cared for the welfare in all of its facets, for all? The Labour Party seems to be struggling, the minority parties are just that and no more and the Conservatives have been forced to intervene on what pre-Covid would have been regarded as too much reliance on the 'Nanny State' and certainly not their concern. The Covid-19 outbreak had tested the NHS to near breaking point but it had emerged, more specifically, its workforce had emerged with flying colours though the 2020 'clapping mania' was a poor substitute for the increased salary they deserved but did not receive! What had also fallen short under the pressures of the pandemic was the 'Care system'; it had been shown up to be underfunded, understaffed and still waiting for Government pledges to be fulfilled. Had 'Education' been failing too? Education once regarded as the panacea of all post-war shortcomings had probably suffered too much from political interference rather than allowing teachers just to get on with teaching. What Sophie did know was that her work constantly brought her into close contact with the casualties of failure, the consequences of poor decisions, greed, violence and inequality not only towards women but ethnic minorities and the disenchanted as well. It also made her influential enemies. In recent years, in this 'social media age' another cancerous phenomenon had been growing and 'education' desperately required to assist in cutting it out. This trend is aimed at teenaged schoolgirls. Sophie had been appalled to discover many girls reported being constantly harassed, exploited and pressured by their male peers into sending revealing pictures of themselves or receiving shots of boys' genitalia often accompanied by crude and vile messages on their mobiles. Her ancestor however, would have been so proud of her but wait until she saw Sefton Mather, MP next!

Chapter Eleven

His video door bell rang and Sefton, slice of toast in hand slipped off his kitchen stool and ambled towards the door. After Browne's warning him to be careful he had installed the latest 'Ring Doorbell Security Camera'. He glanced at the security camera monitor. He was surprised to see the slightly contorted image of Jemima Wilkins smiling up at the camera. She was holding a thin, brown, A4 official looking envelope. He 'buzzed' her in and moved towards the door when it opened then ushered her towards his kitchen. He offered a swift, chaste kiss on her right cheek as she passed.

"Hello, Jems," he said cheerfully, "go right on in and make yourself comfortable. To what do I owe the pleasure of your visit?"

"Hi, Sefton. Serena asked me to drop these in to you. Thought you could make use of them," she replied, offering him the envelope.

"Thanks," he said intrigued to see the contents.

He tore open the envelope and was delighted to find two very expensive theatre tickets. This was particularly gratifying as it had been a long time, thanks to Covid that he had been able to attend live concerts of any kind. Now most of the restrictions had been lifted and cinemas, theatres and other 'live' entertainments were gradually beginning to return to something approaching normality but tickets for any show were soon snapped up such was the demand after those many months of suspension. It was thanks in large measure to

Government support that any venue as well as theatre and concert performers had survived at all.

"Serena said she was double booked but hoped you'd be able to take her place. You and a friend," she added, frowning slightly.

"I'll call later and thank her," Sefton said, "but I'm forgetting my manners. Haven't even offered you a drink. What will it be? Coffee, tea or something stronger."

She settled for coffee and sat on the second of the four kitchen stools that generally resided under the breakfast bar.

"Excuse my dishabille," he said pulling his dressing gown over his naked top half and covering his pyjama bottoms.

"No, please don't worry about me. I was brought up with two brothers! Anything goes with them!"

"Most days I'm up and in my suit before the sparrows have stopped coughing but I've been promising myself a lazy day for weeks. Haven't been up long. The plan is to catch up on correspondence, answer a few e-mails, make a few calls and placate a few constituents."

"Have you constituents that need placating?" she asked.

"It's a funny old job," he replied. "Whatever one does, one cannot always win. Or put another way, you can't please all the people all the time."

A naughty thought crossed her mind.

"I bet you could please me!" she mused, under her breath.

While he had been apologising she had caught more than a glimpse of a hairy chest and two perfectly formed erect nipples. There was also his muscular and very creditable six-pack and she smothered a giggle at an alternative meaning of six pack and began to long for him applying it to her. She could almost feel his thumb and two fingers finding their way into her vagina and anus respectively. Sefton, in his turn was feasting his eyes on her long, slim, nylon clad, crossed legs as the skirt she was wearing was steadily riding up. One of her high heeled shoes was dangling only half on, exposing a nylon-clad heel that somehow, Sefton found arousing.

"Sefton," she said, after finishing her coffee then looking him directly in the eye, "will you take me to bed? I need a good shagging."

"What about Serena?" he asked lamely.

"Well, she isn't here, but I am," she said, in a sly, provocative voice.

With that, she moved off her seat, took a small silver object from her handbag then reached up under her skirt and pulled down her tights before unzipping her skirt and letting that drop to the floor. Then she removed her red sweater and stood before him in white bra and high legged panties. She leaned forward and pulled open his dressing gown which he dropped to the floor near her discarded skirt and jumper. They faced each other and as he moved forward to lift her up in his arms he could feel an erection rising under his grey underpants. He kissed her lips tenderly then swept her up and carried her into his bedroom. There, he placed her carefully on the bed he had risen from not that long before. He threw back the duvet most of which already lay open and crumpled at the bottom of the bed. At least the bottom sheet was fairly smooth as it came into contact with the very ample curves of her back, buttocks and thighs. Sefton edged forward to remove her bra releasing her two very voluptuous breasts. Impressed by them he bent over and kissed their tips and rolled them in his hands then eased down to let his chest come into contact with them. She was warm and they were so comforting. He lifted himself up and returned to kissing those firm points before moving his lips gently from breast to throat and then to her ear lobes. His hands pulled down her panties but not before thumbs and fingers dallied along the warm, moistening furrow between her thighs. Then a thumb moved back to seek and find a wet orifice while first one then a second finger rubbed slowly over her anal ring whose muscles clenched, then released in anticipation of further investigation. Which there soon was as a single finger wet with the love juice from her furrow pushed into her anus, followed by its companion. As fingers found their mark the thumb was pushing into and exploring that other, very wet hole.

Jemima mumbled:

"You read my mind about my six-pack," she sighed with contentment, before her body began to shake as she moved closer to that orgasmic moment.

She just managed to remember in time the condom in its silver packet and reached for it. Holding in it her right hand as Sefton continued to explore her, she reached up and over his back and carefully tore it open being even more careful not to let the lubricated, very slippery contents slip through her fingers and so allow it to fall beyond her reach. She pushed Sefton a little to his right and into a more accessible position for dressing his erection with a condom. This she achieved while his cock moved from pressing against her belly as he continue to toy with her holes She reached down to that special very stiff column of flesh and blood and somehow but with difficulty, managed to put the rubber accessory, its lubrication mixing with the other liquid dribbling out from the glans, in place. Then she began to roll it down. Sefton, now took up the challenge and removing his right hand from its 'six-pack' position grasped the head of his penis and completed the rolling of the gossamer thin rubber, down the length of his own member.

As he thrust forward he could feel her very ample body moving up and down and from side to side to exaggerate his penetration. Then it was all nearly over and Jemima called out:

"Oh yes, oh ye…ssss," and thrust both hands with some force down on his very firmly, clenched buttocks.

He released his load with an appreciative groan and seconds later rolled off her. As he did so he felt her run her hands down his dick before carefully removing and rolling the condom up. He was a little amused to see her dealing so attentively to this piece of discarded rubber. She carefully rolled it out to its full length squeezing it so that every drop of his seed was collected in the elongated nipple shape at its end. Then she tied a knot just below the open end of the condom and let it drop to the floor.

In contrast to Serena, her business partner, Jemima seemed unconcerned about winding-down after their vigorous exertions through after-play but said merely:

"Wow, Sefton!" before turning her attention to safely harvesting his output of semen from where it had landed. Very soon after, she turned to him and said:

"Sorry, Sefton, but I really must go."

She dressed quickly and ten minutes after rising from his bed was walking back out through the door that she had entered only forty five minutes before. Now though she was wearing a very self-satisfied smile. The sex must have been good or was there another reason for that smug look?

After her rather abrupt departure Sefton got up pulled the bed into reasonably good order, tidied up the kitchen and then after a sudden thought, returned to the bedroom. For five minutes he groped around the floor and even looked under chests of drawers but could find no trace of the condom, the late container of the recent manifestation of the fruits of his loins.

"Perhaps she's taken it as a souvenir," he said out loud to his reflection in the hall mirror. "Oh well, some men like to keep their lover's knickers so perhaps she's got a collection of used condoms rather than notches on her bedpost. Must be a desperate smell though, that combination of rubber, lubricant and sperm. Still each to their own," he chuckled.

He showered, dressed and returned to the kitchen where he made an omelette, a particular speciality of his. He dismissed the events of the morning from his mind, merely retaining a warm feeling in his loins then spent the afternoon and evening on constituency business. Around 8pm he remembered he had promised Jemima he would ring and thank Serena for the tickets. This he did and was told Jemima had insisted she bring them round in person that very day.

"Would you thank her for dropping them off?" he asked.

"Yes, I certainly will but she's going back to her own flat this evening and not staying over," Serena replied.

Sefton decided against mentioning to Serena that he had bedded Jemima that very morning!

Then Serena wished him a pleasant evening at the theatre in a few weeks time, arranged to meet him during the coming week and rang off.

***

Sefton would have been surprised had he been a fly on Jemima's kitchen wall when she returned to her flat in Kentish Town and watched the fate of that condom. For once inside her door, she moved quickly to the kitchen and opened the freezer. She sought and found an almost empty packet of 'petits pois'. She discarded the edible contents and very carefully placed the condom she had recovered from Sefton's spent penis, inside the green zip-up container and placed it beside the more conventional items in one of the freezer compartments. As she had made her way back to her flat after that unusual harvesting session she turned to thinking about the reason for it. Surely, sperm could only survive for a very limited time after ejaculation unless it was very deeply frozen. She had been told to keep it until 'required' in the freezer compartment but where else could you keep it and the 'why', was still nagging her. She came to the conclusion that as it could not be used for inseminisation then it must be involved in some mischief. Why else hold on to a used condom with a supply of semen? Sefton, whom she knew, partly from recent experience, was both a womaniser and an MP and had probably upset someone; this however was beyond a practical joke. Ranulf Faulkner, a man she had known since her days as a young 'escort' had asked for other favours before this strange one. Jemima had made a mistake a couple of years ago and that was attempting to blackmail him. She had found his performance with Serena on DVD and his apparent penchant for quite vigorous but rough sex. His response to her demands for cash in exchange for her silence had led to him threatening her with severe harm that might lead to permanent silence. He was dangerous and she believed him! In exchange for a promise that no further action would be taken against her, she agreed to carry out 'small favours' as he called them, for him. According to rumours, spread by another of her's and Serena's old clients, Bertie Jameson, Ranulf's wife was known for her serial indiscretions. Perhaps she and Sefton Mather had shagged and Ranulf now planned some bizarre revenge in order not only to demonstrate the MP's weakness for women but at the same time destroy his career. Though if what Bertie had said was true quite a percentage of the male population of London could be at risk! The latest favour done and before she too showered and changed and using a 'pay as you go' mobile phone, she called and spoke briefly:

"It's done, everything's cool," perhaps alluding to the packet in the freezer.

A voice almost as brief said:

"Good. Say nothing!"

Then, singing contentedly, Jemima headed for the bathroom removing the same clothes that had been discarded once before that day. Only later as she prepared for bed did she begin to think about the consequences of her own recent action. She concluded that perhaps she knew a little too much about Ranulf Faulkner and even Sefton Mather. After staring at the ceiling unable to sleep until long past a distant church clock had struck a muffled one o'clock did sleep overtake her. But this respite was short-lived as too soon after, she was tossing and turning. Several times she woke with a start. The man's shirt she favoured as night attire wet with perspiration; so much so that the second time she had felt uncomfortable, she pulled it off and threw it in the direction of a wicker basket she kept for most of her dirty washing. She padded into the bathroom grabbed a towel and wiped the moisture from the skin of her neck, shoulders, breasts and legs before returning to her bed. There she threw back the duvet punched two pillows into submission and flopped down determined to sleep. Minutes turned into a couple of hours. That church clock sounded 5 o'clock before restless sleep claimed her again. The 'sweats' returned but now accompanied by psychedelic-like images of tormented, mangled and broken figures, including her own writhing in pain as blood issued from every orifice. Across the 'technicolor' screen of her nightmare was a familiar figure, Ranulf Faulkner. Finally, she sat upright in bed screaming before jumping out of the bed and running to the bathroom where she vomited. She snatched at tissues to wipe the mix of stomach contents, saliva and 'snot' from her lips, flushed the w.c. bowl and stuck her head under the cold tap. This shocked her into regaining an element of control and rationality. She sat on the toilet seat to consider the options. Yes, it had been a nightmare or a series of them but she could not ignore their likely portent of danger. She must leave and as quickly as possible. What if Faulkner was tidying up a few loose ends? If he was attempting to implicate and discredit Sefton by utilising his semen sample and questions were asked, then she might be asked some of them and let slip how and for whom his sperm had been collected. Bertie had said he was a devious man with friends and influence in some extraordinary places. Worryingly, he had also more than hinted Faulkner was capable of anything. She must have a quick shower, breakfast, grab her passport, milk an atm (automated telling machine) of her daily cash limit and go. South Africa was beckoning as one of her cousins lived there and was forever asking her to visit. Perhaps a quick call and go.

***

Her fears and concerns were well-founded for Ranulf Faulkner was taking stock. Several projects were well under way but there were still i's to dot and t's to cross. One of whom was Jemima Wilkins. She had served his purpose well but it was now time to cancel her contract; he savoured the irony that she had contributed to her own demise. The contents of the freezer specimen would be spread strategically across her mattress, bedding and items of clothing as proof of Mather's presence and sexual performance alongside her body as yet another example of his jealous rage. Even if subsequent murder charges failed, not to mention having sensitive Government papers in his unauthorised possession then he would find it difficult to escape accusations of sexual promiscuity. This, once the tabloids latched on to his flitting irresponsibly from woman to woman would demonstrate was so unbecoming to a man in public office!

Chapter Twelve

Sefton and Sophie had arranged to meet up earlier in the day and after several hours of idle chatter the two of them began to drift back to his flat. On a whim and thinking about her somewhat depressing review of the country's situation she had decided that rather than waiting to see Sefton Mather when they happened to be back home in Durford she would call him, arrange to meet and compare notes. He was surprised and thrilled to receive a call from her. Sefton suggested that in addition to a more serious discussion of national and international politics they mix business with pleasure and take advantage of the two complementary theatre tickets Serena had given him. She had worked almost without a break for many days and said she would leave her Leman Street, Whitechapel office early, around 1pm. They agreed to meet at King's Cross at 2 o'clock; roughly the half way point between her office and where Sefton lived. Then a stroll into Chester Road and Regent's Park and around the edge of Queen Mary's Gardens, past the tennis courts and on to Baker Street and then Wellesley Mansions.

They were in no particular rush and enjoyed ambling through the Park but Sefton just could not shake off the feeling of being followed and several times looked cautiously round. Each time though he could see nothing to really trouble him. But that surely is the point! Stalkers be they security, terrorist or sexual predator probably choose not to advertise their presence to their intended victims. He would have been very concerned if he had known that as he and Sophie reached

Regent's Park, Sophie's London home was being entered by one of Asghar's operatives. This man was drawn immediately to a small, antique writing bureau and within seconds had taped a large envelope to the back of it.

Meanwhile, a second man was keeping an eye on the pair strolling arm in arm to ensure the flat would remain empty.

At 4pm, Sefton and Sophie stopped for coffee before resuming what had been a very pleasant walk through the park; for Sefton, arm in arm with Sophie it was a long hoped for wish coming true. Here, in London neither of them was constrained by the interference of parents. Both were adults and free to do as they pleased and Sefton certainly hoped very soon to do something that would please him!

They reached the front door of the apartment block entered the foyer and the key to his own door was inserted but Sefton hesitated and wondered if the faint scratches he was seeing on the barrel of the lock had been there earlier.

Sophie noticed his vacillation:

"What's wrong, Sefton?"

"Nothing. Just my imagination," he replied, shrugging his initial fears off.

In they went and just as Sophie stepped into his living room, Sefton placed his hands gently around her waist.

"It's been a long time, Sophie. You know I've always wanted you. Perhaps we could even take it further. What twist of fortune has brought us together?"

"Sefton, you say that to all the girls. And," she added, "have you forgotten that 'knee-trembler', a decade ago during 'Freshers Week'?"

No, he had not forgotten; indeed every detail remained in sharp focus; every time he drove past Durford Hall he thought back to that night during those early days at Exeter University. Did it really matter that their first and so far only time so far, that she had dismissed so casually had indeed been rather a rushed affair. He would certainly settle for a more permanent relationship if they could move on from that teenage fumble to regular shagging as a married couple.

***

It had been the final night, the traditional ball, of that introductory and quite frenetic week. Both of them were caught up in the excitement of the occasion and the intake of booze. Sophie finally succumbed to his persistent pleas and he managed as they danced, to move them both towards an exit and stagger out into the warm autumn air. Sefton had steered Sophie towards an oak tree and within seconds his hands were fondling breasts and caressing buttocks through her dress and finding the way inside the back of her very flimsy panties and probing down and round towards her lush pubic mound. She gave in and eased her legs open and started pushing his body against hers with one hand while the other was pulling his head down so his lips could meet hers. Shaking with anticipation he withdrew his own hand from inside her knickers where it had been sandwiched between vulva and gusset to make his approach more comfortable. Then lifting up the front of her dress he moved his hand back inside her panties and on between her legs in search of the fast moistening mouth of her pussy. Many times during the years that followed he had reviewed and relived his performance. He had been so desperate to consummate the union that he had not taken time to fully arouse her. At the time he had feared she might suddenly change her mind and pull herself away from his thrusting or the drink he had consumed might hamper his own performance. Then he was thrusting up and away and climaxing as she groaned, more from discomfort than pleasure. Then it was over. Sefton prepared to withdraw but still had the foresight to run his thumb and forefinger down the length of his penis to ensure that every drop of sperm was in Sophie rather than dribbling down the front of his trousers and her dress. Then he replaced the shrinking member into his boxers while Sophie with much difficulty reached down and put the leg that had stepped out of one half of her panties to allow Sefton easier access to her promised land, back in them. She then pulled the garment up and over her sopping vulva. The ample contents of her bra were returned to their proper place. With underwear, more or less restored, Sophie adjusted her shoulder straps and straightened her dress. Sefton kissed her, almost as an apology, Then they moved off without looking back at each other, in separate directions to their lodgings. Sefton to wash away, if a little reluctantly Sophie's smell, while Sophie removed her panties after sensing blobs of semen dripping into her gusset. Sophie also for the first time carefully feeling her back; the bark of the oak tree that Sefton had propped her against had been very rough.

Over the weeks that followed, their encounter became just a hazy memory. Certainly for one of them it had not been a memorable example of copulation. For Sefton it had been over and done with all too soon but for Sophie it was perhaps best forgotten. As the academic year rolled on, their paths rarely crossed and Sophie threw herself wholeheartedly into one cause or another. Her view that sex was a messy, smelly business certainly not changed by that oak tree incident and little different to that underwhelming evening months before when one of the Walpole twins had been the first to penetrate her. Sophie's work in pursuing women's rights particularly, seemed to confirm that for too many men, sex was for their satisfaction only.

Pants down, straight in and piss off! Little or no foreplay and had any of them ever seen, touched, licked or knew what or where the clitoris was? Women, she had once heard her grandmother say liked to be romanced. The feminist in her might rail against the submissive edge to that sentiment but why should it be the man who thought he should always be in the sexual driving seat? Attitudes need to change.

***

Sefton looked again at Sophie. Yes, she would suit the role of a rising parliamentary star's wife, perfectly for she was certainly beautiful, intelligent if a little too headstrong but an ideal foil for him. Marriage would not be popular with their respective parents but it was not their parents' futures that mattered but Sophie's and his. Apart from which he could almost taste the sex to come. She was an independent, determined woman and he, well he was a man with strong desires.

"Put us together," he thought "and you've an explosive mixture." He could feel a hard coming on just thinking about it. True, that first time had been little more than a drink-fuelled fumble but if he could bed her formally as his wife then the shagging would be formidable.

Sophie returned him to that time in Exeter:

"I think that answers your question. Not to mention that you do have something of a reputation for 'bonking anything with a pulse'. Your horizontal shuffle is fast becoming the talk of Hampshire. So is it my turn to be an entry on Mather's Menu of sexual delights?"

"We haven't seen too much of each other because we've been moving in very different circles. Why can't we give it a go. No, not just a repeat of that fumble but a real relationship. Even marriage?" he said brightly.

***

Perhaps all these years later it was curiosity, perhaps on this occasion she just wanted sex; it had after all been a month or more since her last shag and she had been feeling quite low. Her most recent sexual encounter had certainly not been anything special but even before then she had been meticulous over taking her pill! Now she finished the drink Sefton had offered her as well as 'coke' soon after they had arrived in his flat, The wine poured from a Chianti bottle never far from his reach when he was in his flat. He drained his glass too. Sophie had shown little surprise at the presence of a little Class A drug. Both, like so many of their generation experimented with it to cope with the stresses, real or imagined, of life. Their respective jobs at times persuading them to look for an extra 'lift' but in their cases nothing to excess. She looked at Sefton; perhaps he would live up to his reputation but then she thought:

"Why the fuck am I here? I spend most of my life trying to help women who have been screwed in every way by men. Still, what the hell!"

Suddenly she turned towards him and kissed him passionately.

If Sefton was taken aback by this he didn't show it. He seemed ready, he was always ready, and the blood began immediately its customary journey to stiffen not only his resolve to win Sophie over but his ever-ready dick as well. In something of a frenzy, clothes were removed as both of them, oblivious to everything but themselves, rushed into the bedroom. Sophie was on her back, her legs opening slowly at first but so enticingly but then her knees were wide apart. Sefton got his first and long anticipated view of the dark folds of her intimate skin on either side of the waiting pink gash as she waited for him to plunge his erection deep inside her. That thrust was delayed for

Sefton lowered his head instead and licked the whole length of her slit from below the carefully trimmed pubic mound to the darker tones of her anal ring wishing to savour every moment of their coming together after so long a delay! Then his lips were back to encircle her clitoris. His tongue curling around it before his teeth very carefully nibbled it. Her body began to tremble, her mouth opened and her breathing quickened. Then Sefton moved preparing to plunge in and up. A hand caressed first one breast then the other before squeezing her hard nipples in turn. Then he moved up kissing first her lips before working his way down her neck then on to both those erect buds. His right hand moved down to gently squeeze her swollen labia between finger and thumb, then push them apart as he imagined the wet groove his penis was about to enter. Sophie was more than ready. Yes, that very wet slit was ready. He eased his erection down and felt his moist glans make contact with the entrance to her magic circle. He slowly, deliberately eased the head of his dick back out, then back in again so the rim of his 'helmet' was in warm, rapturous contact with the first few centimetres of her tight ring. Then he pushed deep inside Sophie Fortune and she gasped then squealed, not with pain but with sheer pleasure as the walls of her vagina stretched to accommodate his massive erection as he slowly and methodically twisted his hips to exploit the growing sensations they were both feeling. His balls were slapping rhythmically against the clenched area below her stuffed slit and anus. He groaned as he shot his load deep inside her while her squeals became louder as she felt his warm stickiness. His member was gripped as all his juices were squeezed from him.

After that explosive exchange of bodily fluids they lay back on the bed. Sefton's left hand found and softly tweaked the swollen nipple of her right breast. She turned into him, her left breast squashing into his chest. She sent an exploring hand down past his hip, through his pubic hair over a slippery dick and under his balls. She began to gently knead them. Several times as she moved her fingers across his sac he moved involuntarily as a fingernail inadvertently caught a ball awkwardly. Then she sat up, grasped his penis, rolled back his foreskin and kissed the glistening end of it before returning to laying flat on her back. This Sefton took to be a signal to continue to manipulate nipples and breasts. After a few minutes of this he turned on his right side and began to run the fingers of his left hand across her pubic mound before slipping down to tweak her clitoris again. He looked across at her to see a look, an almost beatific expression on her face, before he withdrew his hand and folded both arms across his chest. He had a sudden thought about the theatre tickets. Nothing on the West End stage that evening could possibly compare with their own performance.

It took some minutes for them to recover from the full sexual act and five minutes of after play and just as they were enjoying that whole post-coital moment, Sefton's landline sounded to shatter that special post-sexual interlude. Very reluctantly, Sefton as the ring-tone continued, rose from the bed, bent down and kissed the tips of Sophie's breasts, then her lips before answering his phone's persistent shrilling. To say he was irritated would be to understate how he was feeling. As he grabbed at the receiver he glanced at the clock on his bedside table. It was 8-20pm as he managed to utter a very restrained, considering the circumstances:

"Yes?"

A desperate voice on the other end begged him to drop whatever he was doing and come at once to Victory Mews.

"Oh, damn," he said, replacing the instrument on its cradle. "Sorry, Darling. Stay where you are and I'll be back as soon as I can."

A puzzled, aggravated and very annoyed Sophie looked up from the warmth and snugness of the bed where she had enjoyed the best sex of her life.

"What is it? What's the panic?" she demanded.

"It's a friend. Sounds in a hell of a state. Wouldn't have called unless there's a real problem. I'd better go."

"What friend? What's so fucking important that after getting me into bed and shagging me as though there's no tomorrow, you're just going to rush off. Hardly flattering for a prospective wife to be ditched, is it?" she yelled at him.

"It's Serena MacDonald. You've met her, haven't you?" he replied feeing embarrassed.

"We have," she agreed but the tone in her voice was thick with annoyance. In the present circumstances the empathy she had long felt towards Serena evaporating. "Why you? You've made me feel like some cheap tart."

"Sophie, I can't tell you how bad I feel but it does sound like life or death."

"What about one of her other men friends," she almost spat out the words and there was particular emphasis on the word 'friends'. "Shall I come with you?"

"No, but thanks all the same. You stay here. I promise I'll be in and out." Sefton said, rather lamely as he limped towards the door. This, after tripping over in his haste to hurriedly pull on his trousers.

Then he was gone; out of his flat, through the foyer of the Mansions and out of the heavy front door and into the street where he set off urgently to find a cab. In his haste he did not notice a parked, plain blue van. Neither did he notice a tall man in the shadows opposite, signal the two occupants of the van. The evening was going even better than the tall man had planned. He had originally been informed the two in the flat would be at the theatre and his men would have to enter the apartment and just wait for their return. Now they had made alternative arrangements to entertain themselves that phone call from Serena could be brought forward a few hours. The whole operation could be over and done with before midnight. Just as Mather disappeared from view those two men rushed quickly up the steps of the building Mather had just left, noiselessly entered and then vanished from sight.

That last remark almost amused Sophie but seeing his mind was made up and the clothes he had so quickly shed were now back on, she resolved to stay calm, remain where she was a for a little longer before getting up, finishing the Chianti and going; but not before leaving him a very terse note. If he wanted to make up for his abrupt exit he would have a lot of grovelling to do.

"Marriage indeed," she snorted though she might consider another meeting if only for a good shag but only when it suited her.

She lay on top of the bed, completely naked but just touching her breasts with one hand and feeling between her thighs with the other to relive some of those heightened moments of pleasure she had experienced twenty or so minutes before. She heard a sound like a door opening somewhere close by but dismissed it as one of the other tenants. Then she pulled the duvet over her head and for a moment her nose was almost overcome by a mixture of scents; a reminder of the very recent, brisk lovemaking. She felt warm and very comfortable and had to stop herself from falling asleep. She was just collecting her wits with a view to throwing the duvet back, taking another drink, before showering and then going home, when she was conscious of movement in the room.

Surely not Sefton back; it had only been a matter of minutes since his departure. Perhaps he had changed his mind? No, not either of those! For just as she threw the cover off her shoulders, a hooded figure wearing some form of white overall, rushed across the room and fell across her chest expelling the air from her lungs making any chance of her screaming impossible. An arm was pushed across her throat choking her. As she looked into cold, dark brown, almost black eyes she struggled to remain conscious. Then the man rolled off the bed quickly pulling her onto its side. Her legs, hips and waist remained in contact and across the bed but with head and shoulders bending back down towards the floor. Then two hands gripped her ankles and began to force her legs apart. She was desperately trying to scream but no sound came. A hand, wearing a surgical glove, its fingers outstretched and intent on cruel abuse moved towards that still very wet, love orifice. The pain was intense and keeping her conscious but she was unable to scream. Then the hand began to pinch, squeeze and twist the tender skin of the inside of her thighs. Arms, other white plastic covered arms pulled the top of her body upright against the legs of her assailant. One arm moved across from her left shoulder to grip her near her right temple; a second arm grabbed her lower jaw. Then a sickening crack as her neck was twisted and broken. Her murderer released his grip and the top half of her broken body fell limp and quite dead back across the bed. Sophie's head lay at an awkward angle; her lifeless eyes staring at the wall opposite. Her naked, lower body still remaining warm for a little longer from those earlier sexual gymnastics but now her genitalia and those thighs showing evidence of bruising and abuse and not the loving and tender care and attention of earlier.

By 8-50pm their horrific task completed the two men having

removed their white protective clothing were back in the blue van and driving hurriedly away. Very soon after, they would be rushing over Westminster Bridge and heading for 21, Victory Mews where they would join a third man who had forced Serena into making that call to Sefton Mather. The 'signaller' from earlier, as the van sped away was approaching his own home grimly aware that another piece of his devious jigsaw was now in place. Using a much favoured tool of the intelligence, criminal and other classes who sought anonymity, the pay-as-you-go mobile, he made a heavily disguised call posing as a neighbour, to West End Central Police Station, that someone's life was under threat:

"Sounds like there are screams coming from Mr Mather's apartment," he said.

***

Sefton had walked resolutely into Baker Street but no cabs so he decided to go by Tube instead and reached Baker Street Underground Station. Chalked on a board was a simple message apologising for the delay caused by a points failure on trains travelling east. He caught sight of himself in the glass of a ticket and enquiries window. He had dressed quickly and it showed. He looked tired and felt tired and was certainly dishevelled. The wine and 'coke' had not helped overall. It was now either a fast walk or find a cab but much time had passed. Serena sounded frantic so he decided to give her a quick call on his mobile but there was no tone. He began to feel concern and thankfully managed after waiting an unusually long time, to hail a cab as it approached from Park Road and within sixty five minutes of the original 8-20pm call was turning the key in the lock of 21, Victoria Mews.

He rushed up the stairs and barely had time to process the state of the bedroom and the sight of a battered and bloody Serena. She was stretched across the bed looking up at him in a pained, desperate, frightened, wide-eyed appeal for help. Suddenly, he was gripped from behind and a cotton pad placed brutally over his nose and mouth. Something sharp stabbed his arm and a blunt object caught him on the side of his head. He felt himself falling and then everything went black!

No sooner was Mather on the floor then the three men were leaving the Mews as quickly and as silently as they had entered. They made a quick call to the tall man. He, in turn made a second call using a second mobile to West End Central Police Station saying there was a disturbance at number 21, Victory Mews.

***

A second piece of Ranulf Faulkner's jigsaw was now in place! As he entered his house situated not too far from his office on the Embankment, he met his wife just returning or so she said from one of her charity evenings. She was taken aback by his good humour and wondered which poor soul would be suffering. She would find that out from the media before long and remember an interrupted, potentially very intense sexual encounter with the same, intense young man whose image would soon be splashed across the tabloids. After supper, Ranulf retired to his study and poured himself a Scotch then sat back in the black leather chair behind his desk, a self-satisfied look on his ordinarily rather dour countenance. His overall plan was working out very well but there were still loose ends to tie. There was a direct link between Croft and Hallet, also known as Bahram Asghar. Croft could wait. The deaths of the two women could be laid squarely at the door of Asghar. That's if Mather managed to wriggle free. Asghar was now regarded by Faulkner as another loose end that required tying. A quick call to his American opposite numbers concerning the whereabouts of a known terrorist they were seeking could solve that problem. Then Faulkner remembered there was the Devon connection. Asghar owed a favour which if not paid in full could lead to a certain police detective revealing the tie that bound Asghar to Croft and the two to himself. Once Asghar had carried out his mission in the West then he would supply his Poplar address and suggest they approach with caution as he should be regarded as armed and dangerous. Not known for their subtlety in such a situation the CIA, with any luck, would bring Asghar out from his unobtrusive location in a body bag. Or, if necessary British Security Services would look the other way if Asghar survived the encounter and the CIA spirited him away to the American Air Force Base at Lakenheath, then across the Atlantic to stand trial for terrorism and murder unless of course he was 'lost' on the journey across the 'Pond'.

***

Only very slowly did Sefton begin to be conscious of his surroundings but his head was still swimming, his mouth was dry and his body felt as though it had been given a good kicking. Was he imagining it but were there aliens in white spacesuits all around him? Had he imagined too Serena naked and beaten on the bed. Had they had sex? Then there was the sound of a pistol shot and of a ringing in his ears. Why did his arm at the elbow itch so much? He began to feel frightened and very much alone.

Then he had felt himself floating, being born aloft by those white creatures then pushed forward. He was aware of cameras, of voices, some angry but others soft and coaxing. Then he remembered travelling, of bright lights, surely not a flying saucer but he definitely remembered traffic of some sort. His brain ached as he tried to think rationally. He had always argued that sightings of aliens was incorrect. Any alien, so technologically advanced as to reach planet Earth from distant galaxies surely wouldn't bother with primitives as human beings who seem to delight in hurting each other. But who were these ethereal beings? He heard another voice, his voice:

"Where am I? Where's Sophie? Where is Serena?" he heard himself saying.

***

Following that first anonymous call to West End Central Police Station, a uniformed police constable accompanied by a Community Support Officer (CSO) were diverted from investigating a group of youths using insulting language not far from Baker Street to call on an address in Wentworth Street. The two officers rang the door bell to the left of the digital push button key pad on the left hand side of the heavy front door of Wellesley Mansions; Apartment One was the London home of Sefton Mather, MP. After two minutes continuous ringing but receiving no response, they rang the bell of Apartment Two.

"Yes," a voice answered.

"Police Officers. We've had a call regarding a possible disturbance in flat one," Constable Whitehead replied.

"Yes, I did hear a woman's excited voice but nothing unusual about that," she said drily. "I had better buzz you in then," the tenant of Apartment Two added.

They reached the door of Mather's residence where they found an elderly woman, the neighbour, waiting for them.

The policeman tried pushing the door open but finding it shut fast, rang the bell but still no response and the officer was about to use some force when the neighbour intervened.

"I have a key," she said and offered it to him. "When the House rises I go in a few times a week, check all is well and drop any post into the apartment."

"You wait here, madam and we'll go in and make sure everything is all right," Whitehead suggested.

In the two men went; Whitehead towards the kitchen and Sadler, the CSO, towards the bedrooms. There was a horrified shriek followed by a cry for assistance as Sadler walked into the master bedroom and was confronted by the wretched, abused and quite naked dead body of a woman sprawled across the bed.

"In here. Quick! For God's sake, look," the CSO yelled.

Constable Whitehead did not require a second glance; the poor woman was dead, brutally murdered.

"Everything all right in there?" a thin, anxious voice called.

"Take her back to her own flat and stay with her. We don't want her nosing around outside. Just tell her there's been an accident. I'll secure the front door of the flat and secure the immediate scene and call this in and wait for the team," Whitehead instructed.

Within the half-hour, Detective Sergeant Keaton assigned as the specialist leader of the HAT (Homicide Assessment Team) arrived and ensured the scene of the crime was fully secured. The team included two detective constables, the Police Surgeon and a photographer all wearing protective suits in order to avoid contamination. The Surgeon formally pronounced the victim dead! Although identification documents including a driving licence were found in a handbag near a small pile of women's clothes near the bed, the detectives recognised her immediately.

"She's Sophie Fortune. Poor woman; what a way to go," one said in a sympathetic tone.

Sadly, some of their work did bring them into close contact with the worst abuses the human race was capable of inflicting on its fellows. What was before them was as bad if not worse as anything the three detectives had seen before. Sophie had been a constant irritation to the police and to those in authority generally but she had been subjected to the vilest of attacks. No woman or any human being deserved that.

The seriousness and brutality of the crime compelled Keaton to contact his superiors immediately. This was a frenzied assault and the perpetrator must be caught as soon as possible. While SOCO(Scenes of Crimes Officers) began their work collecting forensic evidence from the bed, clothing and the immediate area around the body and after blood and body fluid samples, fingerprints and photographs were taken, the body was removed to the mortuary for post mortem.

"Looks a bad one, sir. The victim's Sophie Fortune. Yes, that Sophie Fortune, the rights for all, except us, do gooder. Poor woman's been left in a hell of a mess."

"First impressions?" the voice back at West End Central asked.

"Well, it looks like a wild sex session got a bit out of hand. Traces of 'Charlie' on the dressing table and the duvet and a large stash tucked away on top of the wardrobe. Killed in a frenzy after sex judging by the body's position on the bed. Broken neck. It all seems to point in the direction of the flat's occupant, Sefton Mather, MP. One of the neighbour's saw them arrive together earlier this evening and Mather I've just been told left in a rush about 8-30pm. I've got 'uniform' checking the cab stand near Baker Street."

"Thanks for that. I'll be with you in about thirty minutes," replied the case's SIO (Senior Investigating Officer).

***

By the time Detective Superintendent Valentine drew up outside Wellesley Mansions, a second anonymous call had been made to West End Central. Following up the call and urged on by the concerns of neighbours who were convinced they had heard a shot, the first police officers on the scene decided to break down the front door of 21, Victory Mews. There they found a woman shot dead and near her body, an unconscious man, a Glock pistol in his right hand. Later this would show gunpowder residue to be present. Both persons appeared to be or have been under the influence of Class A drugs. Small quantities of which were found in with her underwear in a drawer. The victim was soon revealed as the house-owner, Serena MacDonald and the alleged perpetrator, Sefton Mather, MP who, a further anonymous caller claimed, was a regular visitor to that address. Even more damning for Sefton was the fact that the constable who had been tasked with finding out where he had gone following his hurried departure from his flat discovered he had eventually caught a cab not far from Baker Street Underground Station. This had dropped him at the door of number 21, Victory Mews, not long after.

Unsurprisingly, Valentine linked the two murders but had a nasty shock when the name and address of the second victim was relayed to him. He hoped Serena had been sincere when she had assured him that no trace of him ever being in the Mews address could or would be found. He then considered asking his superiors to be relieved of heading up the case. He came to the reluctant conclusion this may just create more questions than he had answers. In an oblique way his being appointed CIO was his own fault. The result of his success in leading numerous murder enquiries. He was very relieved when no other male DNA, other than Mather's was found at Serena's address. Reluctantly he arranged to see the one man who would know of his earlier relationship with one of the victims. That man was Ranulf Faulkner who had supervised that 'sting' involving two escorts. And who, certainly unknown to the police on the afternoon of the murders had been busy. He had handed Asghar that brown envelope that was awaiting discovery by the murder team in Sophie's flat. Valentine did think and the deeper he thought about it was that somewhere, somehow Faulkner for whatever reason had engineered the whole sorry business. Motive however would be difficult and even if it could be proved that an MI6 senior officer was responsible for pulling all of the strings, then almost inevitably his own link with Serena MacDonald would be revealed.

***

The first few hours of any crime investigation are important; in a murder enquiry they are vital. Time is the vital ingredient as suspects can't be held indefinitely. Especially, as in recent years under PACE (Police and Criminal Evidence Act) suspects may only be detained for a short time before charges are brought. Everything in this case appeared to show that the two murders had been carried out by one man, Sefton Mather. He was the common denominator in the two murders with links to the two victims and the two scenes of crime. On the face of it charges would not be long before they were brought against him. Drugs had been found at both addresses. Both victims and the possible perpetrator had probably taken drugs; later confirmed. An initial search of Mather's flat had already revealed a file of Government papers that should have been in the safekeeping of senior officials in the Foreign Office. Marked 'Top Secret' and for the eyes of the Prime Minister, Foreign Secretary, the Cabinet Secretary and two other named senior civil servants only, it should not have been hidden behind a bookcase in Mather's sitting room. This file was sensitive and potentially dangerous and certainly embarrassing. It outlined the West's likely response to China's seizure of Taiwan. Mather was certainly a student of the Indo-Pacific region but it was not meant to be in the possession of a mere backbencher no matter how interested he was in such matters. All of this did look a little too obvious and convenient though! A dead woman's body in the apartment of a man who shortly after was found, gun in hand next to the body of another woman as well as drugs and a secret file! Valentine had been involved as CIO in enough murder cases already to remain cautious and not jump too quickly to conclusions. The correct protocols would be observed, answers sought to a variety of probing questions, motives established and other suspects, if they existed eliminated from their enquiries. Once again he appointed Detective Inspector Eilish Kennedy, as co-ordinator, a role that combined all the skills of an office manager, to take charge of the Incident Room. It was her job to oversee and ensure that every scrap of evidence as it came in from a comprehensive range of sources was sifted and used effectively. In practical terms this meant the right detectives in the murder investigation team were tasked with ensuring the right questions were asked and everything necessary done to ensure the right suspect was charged with the crime.

    What of the victims and their respective families? The decision was taken to delay contacting the victims next of kin until the following day. It was always a daunting task informing a parent that their child, no matter how old, was dead. Bad enough following an accident but where murder was suspected that made it particularly poignant. Hampshire Police in Winchester were duly informed of the circumstances surrounding the death of Sophie Fortune. Two officers called at the Hall at 9am and were directed to where Verity, Lady Durford was just completing a very leisurely breakfast. Her husband, Lord Robert, an inveterate early riser was somewhere on the estate. The sad news was imparted to Sophie's mother who took it, looking stoically at a family group portrait on the opposite wall of the small dining room where she habitually ate breakfast. Precise details of the circumstances of her daughter's death were kept to a minimum. There would need to be a formal identification of the body and 'Family Liaison Officer' appointed to assist Sophie's parents with the media. The next weeks would be unrelenting as details of the murder and likely suspect were revealed. Verity came from a long line of dour, strong-willed Scots, brought up to control their feelings. Tears and grieving would come later in the privacy of the bedroom but not before she had gently informed her husband who had always doted on his bright and beautiful daughter. When Serena's mother, Rachel was similarly informed at her Hampstead address, she broke down and a neighbour, who seeing the police arrive and sensing a problem just called in to see if there was anything she could do. Rachel, as she slowly recovered from the initial shock confided in the neighbour that she had been expecting something like this ever since that incident in Exeter, a decade ago. When Serena had told her that a kindly detective had brought her some lost evidence from that case she had said:

"Don't look back, Darling. No good will come of it. You're settled. You've a nice house and money in the bank."

Rachel had been worrying from the day Serena had returned from Exeter after the case against Webster had folded. She had wanted her daughter to use her language skills to take her to Brussels or Strasbourg and the European Union's Parliament or to the United Nations in New York to work as a translator. But no, she had gone her separate way and Rachel after accidentally discovering her involvement in the escort world had tried in vain to dissuade her from it.

A very bitter Serena had coldly responded to her mother when asked if it was true concerning her broader escorting duties:

"Yes, it is. If those sorry bastards want it they are going to pay for it!"

The venom in her daughter's voice had quite taken her aback and for a time they had fallen out and the two had not spoken or met up. Then one of Serena's brother Gareth's twins had been taken ill. The child recovered as did relations between Serena and her mother. Life was too short they both decided and they resumed the occasional joint outings and coffee mornings. Her mother taken aback once more but this time by how well her daughter looked and how confident she was. Now she was dead; her life had indeed been too short but someone must be held accountable!

***

Detective Superintendent Valentine looked out from his office into the Incident Room as various officers hurried about their business. At one end of the room Detective Inspector Kennedy was already adding details of victims, suspect, times, motives and a variety of other information to a large, clear screen as she began the laborious but necessary task of evidence collation. Cases are usually constructed on the smallest detail which singly may appear insignificant but collectively arrive at the truth. In one of the cells, their only suspect was still unfit, according to the Medical Examiner to be interviewed. In each of the neighbourhoods of the two addresses where the incidents had taken place a team of officers, uniformed and plain clothes would begin as the sun rose another tedious but necessary task.

That of questioning the people living nearby if they had any information that might help with the enquiry. By then however, Valentine notwithstanding his training which urged caution concluded the evidence already on Kennedy's board pointed in only one direction, directly at Sefton Mather. Naturally his fingerprints were omnipresent in his own flat. DNA matches too were present in semen deposits in and on samples taken from Sophie Fortune. The presence of traces of a white powder strongly suggested the two had indulged in taking cocaine. Confirmed in the post-mortem of the two women. Sefton Mather's blood showed the presence of the drug too.

***

Time passed. He was fighting to regain some sort of control. His head was still ringing but slowly, dimly, he began to focus. He was in a small, tiled but otherwise bare room. Very little expense had been given over to its decoration or furnishing. He was sat upon a dark blue, plastic covered mattress. In one corner was a plain, lidless w.c. bowl. Beyond the foot of his bed was a very heavy, steel-grey painted door with a rectangular panel near the top of it. He could hear footsteps a little way off. They appeared to stop on the other side of the door. There was a scraping of metal on metal and half the panel slid across to reveal a pair of eyes looking in his direction. Then the eyes disappeared, the flap returned with a metallic click and the door resumed its earlier condition. Slowly, painfully, it dawned on him.

"I'm in a police cell," he muttered with more than a note of desperation creeping into a rather plaintiff voice, "what's happened to me?"

He was finally declared fit for interview by the Medical Examiner and Custody Officer. Then followed many hours of questioning during which he resolutely protested his evidence. He had been informed that charges relating to his possession of sensitive documents were not being pursued. It was only June of last year when some very sensitive papers from a Defence Ministry file had been found scattered around a phone-box in Kent. Many passers-by now aware of UK plans to consider continuing a presence in Afghanistan and what the likely Russian reaction would be to our warships doing in the Black Sea what Russian ships did in the North Sea. That same month had witnessed the Russians dropping bombs very close to a British warship as it sailed close to the Crimea. Some very red faces deep in Whitehall must have decided pursuing Mather would do them more harm than good. There had been embarrassment enough over other mislaid documents in the very recent past as it was. Disclosure of more leaks would not help! The CPS (Crown Prosecution Service) was still considering whether or not to pursue the possession and supply of Class A drugs. Two murders were serious enough!

Sefton admitted using cocaine during his late teenage, early twenties' years and beyond. The death of a friend had convinced him of the folly of excessive drug use. He did admit to occasionally resorting to a cocaine booster during times of stress. 'Yes' he knew both Serena and Sophie had experimented with drug use too and the two of them had indulged more recently. Mather emphasised that Serena was by no means addicted; surely tests would prove that. Mather contended that she would never permit herself to become a regular user anyway as she liked to remain in control especially in the bedroom. He agreed they met quite regularly for energetic and mutually fulfilling sex but he certainly had not and had no reason to kill her.

No, Sophie had not tried to blackmail him in exchange for political favours. The police after a search of Sophie's flat had discovered very explicit photographs of Sefton and Serena enjoying sex. The pictures had been found taped behind an antique, late 19th Century, Davenport Ladies' Writing Bureau. This was a treasured possession of Sophie's given to her by her father. It had originally belonged to Sophie's Suffragist ancestor. The police concluded that Sophie with that material could have used it to blackmail him. Consequently their questioning pursued the line that Sophie, a well-known and feared agitator for a range of issues, would have then been able to manipulate Sefton in all sorts of advantageous ways. Was this the reason he had killed her in a drug-fuelled rage using his knowledge of self-defence and offence to stop blackmail demands? It emerged that no other DNA evidence could be found in his bedroom, the scene of Sophie's brutal murder, other than traces of other women. No one asked why Sefton had not shot Sophie instead.

He denied rushing in response to a call from Serena intent on murdering her. The police suggestion the photographs of him and Serena had prompted him to silence her too as she knew too much. Judging by the presence of his DNA in Serena's business partner's flat he had had sex with her very recently as well. No doubt he would have got round to her too before long had he not mistakenly overdosed on drugs. Or Serena, fighting for her life and stricken with fear had grabbed the only thing close at hand in an attempt to defend herself. A heavy glass ornament with fragments of Sefton's skin, hair and blood on its side matched exactly the wound on his head. He steadfastly refuted police claims he was jealous of Serena's other lovers. 'Yes' he knew there were several other men but he and Serena enjoyed an open relationship. They were both free agents and he was not jealous. Why should he be? He was not bitter or believed that Serena was only using him to satisfy her own insatiable sexual appetite. What if she was? If he was being exploited then thousands of men out there whose sex lives were unadventurous or non existent would be the jealous ones. He tried to point out to the officers that sex was not just a one-way physical exchange. He also asked them if they believed him to be careless or just plain stupid to have killed Sophie and not cover his tracks.

This dismissed by one of his questioners with a simple:

"People do silly things in the heat of the moment."

What was proving damaging was that even after extensive enquiries the police were unable to find witnesses, evidence, or any other suspects that could point to Mather's innocence. Instead, all the evidence was aimed irrefutably in his direction He was, after all was said and done, a politician and the common skill most of them shared was the ability to sidestep questions. The investigative teams had diligently sifted through every scrap of material and followed all possible leads, of which there were few. It still pointed to one man. Sefton Mather was duly charged with the two murders but sat there just shaking his head. Not only disbelief that anyone could think him capable of such crimes but in the realisation that someone out there had gone to such extraordinary trouble to utterly discredit him. He felt quite alone and began to sob in silent despair. Not only for himself but for two special women. Sophie, a beautiful, independent, sincere human being who would never be his or anyone else's wife! Then Serena, another beautiful, independent woman and one he had in his own way loved. Now she too was no more. As for Sefton he felt desolate and could find no answer to the two questions he kept asking himself, why and who had done this evil deed? Yes, he had been threatened by Ranulf Faulkner and even by a former footballer but could not believe either of them would be bothered to go to such lengths. Though he had given both names to the police, just in case! But officers had drawn a blank with Fenwick and Superintendent

Valentine had personally gone to see Faulkner. Little wonder, considering Faulkner and Valentine's intimate connection with Serena MacDonald that this senior detective found anything to support Mather's naming Ranulf Faulkner as the man ultimately responsible for the murders.

Chapter Thirteen

Sefton shuffled wearily into the visitors' room of the prison where he was remanded, awaiting trial. Sitting at a simple table divided into two halves by a large screen across its middle, at the far end near the door leading to the outside world, was his mother. She looked and felt extremely uncomfortable! She was certainly overdressed considering the surroundings but was oblivious to the other people in the room. Olivia Mather, barely looked up from her staring at the table top as her son sat down opposite her. There was little or no warmth in her greeting and her voice was shaking with emotion when she fired a question at him.

"Why, Sefton, why?" she asked.

"How can you even think that of me? Do you really believe me capable of harming anyone in that way?" he demanded, as he recalled those haunting images the police had placed before him of the two women he was accused of killing. His voice too was thick with emotion, a confused mix of strain, anger and disbelief.

"No," she replied in despair. "Not murder, not you. No, I am talking about your sleeping with Sophie Fortune. Haven't we always warned you off her? So what do you do? You always were obstinate even as a child."

"Yes, you did say," Sefton replied, unable to shake off a combination of annoyance and bewilderment, "but you never gave me a reason. What is there about the Fortunes? Why do you hate them?"

His mother continued to look uncomfortable not solely with the surroundings but with the subject of her son's questioning.

"No, I don't hate them," she answered.

He persisted:

"There can't be a better connected family in most of Hampshire, if not the whole of the South of England!"

Olivia's discomfort had turned to steady sobbing and the generous flow of tears was turning her carefully mascaraed eyes into twin, dark rivulets. She was fighting to control herself in order to speak. Hysteria was not too far away. Finally, shaking with embarrassment and still avoiding eye contact with her son, she spoke.

"Why?" she said, her voice rising to a point very little short of that hysteria, "because she was your half-sister!"

This revelation crashed over him. He was stunned and it was a full half minute before his brain was able to process but not accept the information.

Sefton, rocked back in his chair and he had to force his hands forward to grip the sides of the table to prevent his falling back. His brain was still finding it difficult to deal with the news and formulate a response. He was numb and only gradually did that give way to frenzy.

"How could this be true? No, this was all wrong," he was shouting.

Then he began to feel faint and then sick and was retching, desperately trying to keep the institutional breakfast he had eaten earlier, down.

"Why," he yelled at his mother, "didn't you tell me this, years ago?"

This and other questions reverberated around his skull and it felt as though the top of his head was lifting off.

Sefton was now struggling to hold back the tears but there was one question that he needed to ask.

"What happened then?" he asked simply but still bewildered yet hoping for some answers concerning his conception and early childhood and why he had been kept ignorant of such earth-shattering information.

Olivia, still looking at the table top and fidgeting with discomfort answered.

"It all started with a party at Durford Hall around Guy Fawkes Night and almost nine months to the day before you were born. Robert Fortune and I had known each other since childhood. Our families, as time passed expected us to marry. But for some reason that was not to be and not long after, we split-up and I met and soon married Gerald, probably on the rebound."

"Did Dad," Sefton began but corrected himself, "did Gerald know he was not my father?"

Inwardly he was struggling to adjust to this revelation regarding his conception and parentage. The man he had for three decades considered was his father, wasn't! His recent lover, that he was accused of brutally murdering was his half-sister with whom he had had an incestuous union. His mother was an adulterer too. Could matters get any worse?

"No, I don't think so," Olivia said attempting to answer her son's question, "though there were times in those early days when I thought he might have suspected something. Julian behaved so much like his father, same mannerisms etc but you didn't really take after either of us, though not surprising of course in respect of Gerald. You did though have the same shape and colour eyes as Robert."

"Did Robert realise he had fathered a bastard, me?" asked Sefton, bitterly.

"No, there seemed no reason to tell him and when we occasionally met up for charity functions neither of us felt the need to relive that drunken, November evening. As for Gerald, if he knew, there was little he could say about my one-night stand as he had been having sex with his secretary, Louise Goodyear, in the Winchester office for years. That had started when I was pregnant with your brother, Julian."

At the mention of Julian who was now revealed as his half-brother, Sefton slumped down even further into his chair. He was awash with so many emotions and was struggling but desperate to ask another question.

"Wouldn't it have been kinder to have come clean and just told me?"

"We can all have 'twenty/twenty' vision in hindsight but once you were away at school and preparing to go to university it no longer seemed necessary. You were loved, well educated and lacked for nothing. What extra could the Fortunes do that we weren't doing already?'"

"You've denied me my birth right, that's what. You've lied to me. Your action or rather inaction has been despicable," Sefton said but almost spitting each word out like snake venom.

Olivia Mather now felt utterly wretched. She tried to offer some sort of explanation.

"I don't think I was ever brave enough. Just hoped it would all go away. You were set for Cambridge to follow Gerald to King's and we heard that Sophie was heading to Exeter."

That had indeed been his plan. Originally his intention was to follow Gerald Mather to King's College where he had sung tenor in King's College Chapel Choir. This included the world famous, Christmas Eve's, 'A Festival of Nine Lessons and Carols'. Sefton too, though he rarely bothered to use it, also possessed a fine singing voice and it had been assumed he would follow in his father's 'vocal chords'. Had it been mere coincidence that encouraged Sefton to go west to Exeter and follow Sophie, rather than east to Cambridge?

"So that's it! That's why there was such a hell of fuss when I said I wanted to go to Exeter instead. That would have been an appropriate time to have warned me off and to have given the reason too."

***

His mind had been racing but for a few moments he seized on a subject that removed him immediately from the horrible revelations of his mother and the even deeper hole he now found himself in. He needed a strategy if he was to survive and perhaps recalling happier days would keep him sane. What though if he had gone to Cambridge instead of Exeter? How different might his life have been? Perhaps a chorister but certainly he would have challenged for seat 3 in the Cambridge University boat. He was not as big as the rest of a typical crew. His weight was still a constant 83.5 kilograms and he was a little over 182.5 centimetres but he was strong and had plenty of stamina. Numerous women would endorse that claim. Rowing was an excellent sport for developing and maintaining the top and lower body and for beathing. An excellent sport too for the sexual athlete. At Exeter he had rowed and competed for the University and trained on the River Exe. Later he had bought a single scull and rowed on the River Hamble. Now Sefton was awaiting trial and sitting opposite him was his own personal Jonah, his mother who had brought only bad news and little comfort. Now he searched his mind for abstraction and thought back with envy to last year's boat race that had taken place not on the Thames but on the River Ouse. This, partly as a consequence of social distancing which would have been a problem at the London venue but also because of fears of Hammersmith Bridge being declared unsafe. In the event, the light blues won both the men's and women's races!

***

Mrs Mather, for the first time since she had sat down was looking him in the eye and feeling very contrite.

"I'm so, so very sorry, Darling. It's all my fault. I should have told you but I felt so ashamed."

"It's a bit fucking late now, mother. I suppose you really are my mother?" his voice dripping with vitriol and sarcasm and swearing in the presence of his mother for only the second time in his life. The first time was in the middle of an evening meal during one long summer holiday. His brother, Julian had deliberately kicked his chair. Sefton's response was to call him a silly cunt. The temperature at the table suddenly dropped and the room went quiet before his mother seized his hand and told him that such a word was not to be used.

"Where did you hear it?" his mother had asked.

"Austin Chalmers in my class, called me it," Sefton had replied so completely innocently. Always possessing an enquiring mind he had then go on to ask what it meant.

A very red-faced mother had, at the time repeated:

"It's a word we do not use."

There was strong emphasis on the word 'not'.

Intrigued and curious, it was one of the first words some time later that Sefton surreptitiously looked up in a dictionary; a very large volume in the Winchester Public Library. There he discovered that it was a 'coarse word meaning the female genitalia, particularly the vagina or a common, abusive term to describe a stupid person'.

Sefton's mother continued to pour out her heart.

"I feel so wretched. Not only for you but for poor Sophie too!"

"Yes, what about poor Sophie? Who else knows about your bonking the local lord. If this all comes out in court, I stand even less chance than I did before."

"I don't know what to do. Tell me how I can help," she had stopped feeling sorry for herself and was looking imploringly at her son.

"Even if I could prove I was framed for both murders and the missing papers, oh, at least they've dropped the documents charge, I've still got a problem. The prosecution will say, if it comes out, that I killed Sophie to shut her up over the incest. That alone would be enough to destroy my career even without the rest of the inevitable mud slinging."

Considering the surroundings, a very polite bell rang to inform the visitors and detainees, some of whom within earshot of the Mather table had heard much to animate them. For some, unscrupulous individual there could be a financial reward for informing the tabloids. 'Incest' a 'disgraced mp', what a headline, what an informer's fee? This, a week later proved to be the case for a headline with a story provided by an 'informed source' declared, 'Disgraced MP in love-tryst with his half-sister'. Sefton, when eventually apprised of this revelation via the newspapers asked his solicitor a question:

"How the hell am I going to get a fair trial after this!"

His solicitor informed him that the judge would instruct all jurors to ignore anything they had read, heard or seen on the media.

***

Olivia Mather stood up, deserving to feel quite desolate. She blew her wretched son a kiss, turned and without looking back, left the room as quickly as her legs could take her. The news she had passed on to her son gave him absolutely no comfort. If ever a man looked 'broken' then he did. His situation was desperate. In the words of those who knew and the person or persons unknown who had arranged it, he had been 'framed' like one of van Gogh's finest. He faced multi-charges, from possessing and supplying Class A drugs and carrying out the vicious and cold-blooded murders of two women both of whom had been his lovers. The charge of stealing State Papers and passing them to an enemy, had been dropped but for all he knew might only be temporary.

As his mother disappeared from view he remained rooted to the spot.

"Move!" a voice said behind him.

He walked slowly back to his cell, his limbs heavy and his breathing quite laboured. Even before his mother's visit his case was lost before it had begun. Now the sky had fallen in on him. His future, one that had been so full of promise just months before was over. Ahead lay many, many years of confinement and too much time to think!

Unknown to him he was already under fifteen minute, 'obs', observations as a likely suicide risk.

***

Sefton's situation was hopeless! The evidence was overwhelming. Should he plead guilty on the grounds of diminished responsibility? His Defence Counsel had tried to cover every likely line of defence but having reviewed every possible argument realised he was less pursuing a 'not guilty' verdict but more looking at damage limitation. As Defence Counsel sat in Court, the case brief in front of him he wished he was elsewhere not only because this was one impossible case but because he and the Defendant had something in common. There was, fortunately for him he was sure, nothing that could link him to the second victim.

Robert, Lord Durford, saw something in Sefton Mather as the latter was brought up between two officers from the holding cells below the court. Robert shrugged it off as a consequence of the lighting, the surroundings and the seriousness of the case. Mather looked lost, beaten even before the trial got under way! There was little remaining of the confident, well-groomed, worldly wise womaniser who only a few months before had the world at his feet and usually a woman in his bed. The Jury were duly sworn in and instructed on their duty.

***

Sophie's parents, Robert and Lady Durford attended the first three days of the trial at the Old Bailey seated not too far from the accused's father, Gerald and his mother, Olivia. But well before the week was out three of the four attendee parents found they were unable to cope any longer as the whole sordid affair of Sefton's alleged crimes was revealed in detail by the Prosecution.

The accused, sitting in the dock stared down; he looked to be in shock and seemed to have aged ten years. His face was thin, grey and gaunt; those eyes usually so blue and penetrating had lost their lustre.

It was on that third day when Lord Robert noticed something 'odd' even startling about Sefton Mather. He gasped involuntarily:

"Oh, my God. It's me!"

He looked across at Olivia who at the sound of his voice had turned to look in his direction. He pointed at Sefton and then at himself. Robert mouthed:

"Me?"

His face took on a look of anguish and he rose unsteadily to his feet and somehow managed to blunder his way to the exit. His wife joined him. Olivia too had followed but retreated as she saw Lady Verity trying to put a comforting arm around her distraught husband's shoulders.

"He's my son! It's my son in there isn't it, on trial for murdering our own, beautiful, Sophie. Did you know anything about this?" he demanded his voice hoarse with emotion.

His wife meekly said, "I suspected it but I suppose I just wanted to ignore it. I am so sorry my Darling. Olivia was always a little 'off' with me, almost to the point of embarrassment soon after one particular Christmas and then years later whenever Sefton was around. I'd also suspected that at that Christmas Party at the Hall you'd had sex with her but I thought it best to ignore that as well. As I remember we had all had far too much to drink and I remember Gerald's hands up my skirt more than once during the evening. Fortunately, someone came into the Library where I'd tried to take refuge but he had followed me and interrupted him. I could have easily allowed it to go further so how can I condemn you for something I could have done too?

Besides, I was soon pregnant with Sophie and Hamish was such a happy little boy. I couldn't risk destroying that."

While she had been speaking, Robert had remained silent; his face contorting into a mix of fear, guilt and realisation. His blue eyes wet with tears.

"If only you had but it's not entirely your fault, though I did wonder why you were so set against Sophie and Sefton seeing each other. Oh, God," he said, "you realise they were closely related and had sex. Oh, God," he repeated, burying his face in his hands and sobbing.

He looked very close to a complete breakdown and with difficulty but pride preventing her from accepting the offer of help from court officials and to save them both the embarrassment of being a public spectacle, led him outside into the noise of the traffic and the hustle and bustle of passers by. They returned to Winchester by the next available train. Arnold Gibson, their chaffeur/handyman drove them from the Station back to Durford Hall. For the first time during many such journeys, Robert Fortune did not bother or was still too dazed to notice the entrance to Peninsular Barracks and just inside, the former Guardroom now a Cafe and small museum. The site very much a location with particular resonance for generations of Fortunes. Though no longer containing soldiers, for the barracks have been converted to apartments, it still houses other excellent museums including ones dedicated to the Gurkhas and the Rifles. During both the train and car journeys he had stared at the floor shaking his head in disbelief

***

Over the days that followed Robert Fortune slowly deteriorated even after the intervention and wise counsel of highly respected medical and other friends and the strenuous efforts of his wife. A stroke was suspected no doubt brought on by the stress of revelations concerning Sefton Mather as well as the murder of Sophie. A stroke was confirmed by Doctor Fraser Roche, a personal friend and family doctor. Robert did recover speech, although it was slow, slurred and hesitant. Most of the time he looked close to tears as the words failed to come. He regained some mobility though he looked when walking, to be like a man twenty years his senior. From being a solid, highly respected pillar, indeed leader of the local community he was reduced to a mere shell of that former self. He barely touched his meals. His wife so used to his strong, unflappable personality was shocked and deeply distressed by the change in him. Even Hamish their son, summoned home on compassionate grounds could do little or nothing to break down the barrier that he seemed to have constructed to keep himself from the world outside. The murder of his daughter had been bad enough but there had been those bitter truths about an illegitimate son that had combined to destroy his spirit.

***

It was a surprise to many present throughout the trial of Sefton Fortune, MP, in Court One of the Old Bailey how long proceedings did last. This was probably down to the salacious way in which the Prosecution set out its case. There was little the often stunned Jury did not know about Mather's life after Claire Morton, QC completed her demolition of the Defendant. The Defence Counsel, Vivian Sage-Bedford, QC's task was an impossible one as the evidence against Mather was so damning. The barrister wondered too that if he probed too much, would his own relationship with Serena MacDonald be revealed? A similar concern having crossed Bertie Jameson's mind prompted him to consider taking himself off to the United States for the duration of the trial. Links could be made between himself and both murdered women. He needn't have worried though, at least for the time being as, unknown to Bertie, Faulkner had confiscated for his own reasons much revealing material; nor had any such link been made by the investigative teams.

Mather, before the trial had consistently and resolutely refused to plead 'Guilty' to crimes he claimed he had certainly not committed. Throughout, he maintained his innocence. As this next instalment of his ordeal opened formally he did manage to rally with a little of his old confidence.

"Not guilty," he replied firmly.

As the days passed it became obvious that on the balance of the evidence presented by the Prosecution, the Jury's task would be easy. The result was a forgone conclusion. The Defence had done its best but could not refute that damning evidence; made all the more damning by the apparently 'cavalier' way in which Mather treated his women. The public perception of him soon become one of him as a selfish womaniser who in a fit of drug-induced jealousy had brutally killed two women who shared his guilty secrets and had threatened to expose him.

The Judge was advised the Jury had reached a verdict. Soon after, the jury keeper ushered the twelve men and women back to their places in the courtroom. Each of them having signed their name on the verdict form confirming their endorsement of the verdict about to be announced by the Jury forewoman. She sat holding the verdict form firmly in her right hand. Then, In response to the Clerk of the Court's questions and glancing down at the document she responded to both murder charges, in a clear, assured voice:

"Guilty."

Although the verdict was not really a surprise the mention of the word 'Guilty' relating to a Member of Parliament, still triggered a gasp of shock around the room. Then there was a buzz of conversation in the public gallery before the Judge quickly brought the room back to order. It was not unusual for sentence to be delayed for reports but the Judge decided that in the light of the seriousness and the nature of the crimes he would pass sentence immediately. He also made it clear that such violent acts against women could not and would not be tolerated. The Judge expressed a wish too that action be taken by the appropriate authority that would allow all women to conduct their lives without the fear or threat of violence.

Sefton Mather stood up and for the first time for many weeks seemed to have gained a little of the self-assurance that had abandoned him weeks before. He looked directly at the Jury and shook his head, then when asked by the Judge if he had anything to say looked him squarely in the eye and said:

"Your Honour, this is all wrong. As Defence Counsel said at the beginning I have been 'framed'. This is a miscarriage of justice. I did not kill Sophie Fortune. I did not kill Serena MacDonald."

Mr Sage-Bedford had of course attempted to pursue Mather's being set-up for the two murders but in the absence of evidence to the contrary and no witnesses or other suspects he had been unable to follow that alternative scenario too far. Other than being a success with women and a Member of Parliament, politicians not everyone's favourite after Covid, lockdown and other restrictions, why would he have been framed?

The Judge solemnly announced that after being found guilty of carrying out two heinous crimes against two defenceless young women he had no other option but to impose a 'whole life order' on Mather.

If there was a small consolation that could be drawn from this tragedy it was from the media's clamouring for the Government after this and other recent cases to take serious action to allow women and girls to feel safe.

***

In a final twist of fate or fortune and ten minutes after the trial verdict was reported on television, Lord Robert Durford rose from his chair in the Dining Room and shuffled to his Study. He very slowly but quite deliberately, if with some difficulty unlocked his desk and took out a Browning pistol, a souvenir of his Army Service with the Royal Green Jackets. He wandered through the Hall to the outside, his grey, thinning hair ruffled by the early evening breeze. He continued unsteadily to a favourite, quiet stretch of the river where it flows over rocks and drops into a large pond below, before continuing as it has done since time immemorial to the sea.

Seconds after his arrival and with a final glance at a place that had seen the presence of centuries of Fortunes, he removed the Browning from his pocket and raised it. A single shot broke the silence disturbing the birds and simultaneously putting an end to one man's anguish but through his final, desperate action would soon be bringing torment to others.

The news of the sentence had caused a tremor elsewhere. Not only throughout the rest of Hampshire but deep inside the Westminster 'bubble'. Deep within the Party organisation, plans had soon got underway as the Mather case started, to damp down the effects of yet another scandal in their ranks. Mather's sentence now meant he was no longer a Member of Parliament. His safe Conservative seat in rural Hampshire would be up for grabs in a by-election. There were fears that the Liberal-Democrat success last year might be repeated. It had unnerved many Conservatives that their seats might also be under threat. In the north, the red wall had been demolished; was the blue wall in the south about to be cracked from a yellow demolition ball in that by-election to be followed by collapse and disaster in the General Election now only two years away?

***

While legal events had unfolded in London and an even sadder one occurring in Hampshire, Bahram Asghar was preparing to execute an obligation to his old partner in drugs-crime, Andrew Croft. This involved the tying of a yet another of those loose ends much as he had done for Ranulf Faulkner which had resulted in Mother's imprisonment! He began by driving a large 4 X 4 from a lock-up garage near his Poplar retreat, west and towards South Devon.

Chapter Fourteen

The Andrews', Edward and Sheila had been planning the trip to see their son, Tobias, his wife Angela and the children in Queenstown, in New Zealand's South Island, for several years. Now, the start of it was only hours away and they would soon be leaving their small cottage in Devon and driving up to London, Heathrow. Both were very excited over the prospect of seeing their son and his young family again after they had emigrated five years before. Other than seeing them all quite regularly thanks to modern technology, they had yet to physically meet the latest addition to the family, their granddaughter, Sophia, born just before the outbreak of the Coronavirus. Edward, after a heart attack scare had opted for early retirement and an earlier opportunity to visit his son than originally planned. Sheila too, after many frustrations at work managed to secure extended leave and could not wait to begin their long anticipated, four month special holiday. As the departure date crept ever nearer she began to entertain some doubts as to whether she would ever return to the role that once she had found so satisfying and rewarding. That feeling of a job well done even at the end of a challenging shift was rarely experienced these days. This growing, negative belief all because of the presence of two or three 'rotten apples' who did not only bend a few rules in the pursuit of justice but deliberately broke them in what was beginning to emerge as a long established agenda for their own profit and gain. She did have another nagging worry over her own misappropriation of evidence.

Which, if she did return to work could cause her some difficulty. After the event she had consoled herself with the thought that while technically she had broken the rules, it had not been for her own gain. It was Sheila's strong belief that the material she had taken concerned an historic injustice. In all sincerity she had acted as a legitimate, 'whistle-blower' in order to put things right.

It was still very little consolation that at long last it seemed the net was finally closing in on two of those 'apples', Detective Inspector Croft and Sergeant McCormack. Croft, on many earlier occasions had managed to deflect accusations against him of corruption and other inappropriate behaviour while in public office. His, admittedly very good track record regarding the number of arrests he had made over the years persuading some senior officers that although his approach was somewhat unorthodox, his successes meant he could not be corrupt. For rumours to stick and translate into hard fact there must be evidence and there never seemed to be enough of that to take it any further.

A loyal McCormack proved to be a very willing confederate in their nefarious activities. He certainly colluded with Croft when evidence needed to disappear and witnesses 'leaned-on' to change their statements or withdraw from giving evidence in court. It had not been many months since suspicion had fallen squarely in Croft's direction, initiating a full scale investigation. Sheila herself had been involved in an operation to search for evidence but had been sworn to secrecy as enquiries concerning the two men had begun. Fortunately for Sheila, although she had been part of a team that included Croft and McCormack she had not been tainted or implicated as far as senior officers were concerned in the duo's criminal extra-curricular activities.

***

Sheila, like everyone else was hoping that the post-Covid recovery would soon return the country to some sort of normality. Indeed, that was slowly happening but any feeling of business as usual had been sent reeling by what had happened to Serena. This coming so soon after the two women had met up again. In many ways this tragedy had been the last straw, for the whole case as it unfolded had reeked of corruption and deceit. But whose? She was not personally acquainted with Sefton Mather. Yet the more she heard and read about the case against him and his protestations of innocence; even though the evidence against him appeared so overwhelming, then the more she had begun to wonder if somehow, somewhere the manipulative hands of Andrew Croft were helping to stir the mix. Among the accusations levelled at Mather was one concerning some very heavy drug dealing with a London-based drugs gang. They in turn had links with members of a terrorist faction. Had anyone managed to scratch the surface they would have revealed a name that would have come as no surprise to Sheila, namely Croft's. His relationship with a particular drug-dealer with terrorist connections in the Middle East went back over a decade. There were drugs in the Serena case and Mather was accused of attacking her while under the influence of cocaine. This would come as no surprise when it was revealed that a long term friend of his, Arthur Walpole had died from a drugs' overdose. It was alleged too that Mather enjoyed some very dubious foreign connections. A terrorist fatality, the result of recent police action had been one of his numerous lovers. It was not to great a leap of imagination to link murder, that foreign association including terrorist activity, to drugs. The incentive being high stakes in the form of very large sums of money.

Or was it, Sheila reflected, that because police work can all too easily become a breeding ground for cynicism or specifically disenchantment in her case in its view of the human race, was she only looking for alternative answers? This because she wanted Croft to be involved in some way in Serena's tragic story So could Mather have been judged for expediency's sake rather than truth and justice or not? Was it simply that drugs, greed, jealousy and carelessness had turned one very human and fickle member of parliament into a frenzied killer? Too many times she had seen examples of the very worst manifestation of mankind's darkest side. In twenty years service she had been involved in dealing with the aftermath of brutal murder, rape, drug abuse, child cruelty and much, much more! It was later that evening her growing pessimism was confirmed. Her colleague, Detective Inspector Stanley phoned her to say that she thought Sheila ought to know that somehow Croft had managed to shake off the surveillance team that was supposedly tracking his every move.

"He seems to have vanished. Happened about a week ago," she said, "but we've only just been told officially."

"Thanks, Tamzin," a stunned Sheila managed to say.

She barely had the presence of mind to ask if McCormack had been rounded up to as part of the ongoing investigation. She was informed that he was already assigned to desk duties pending further enquiries but was likely to be suspended within days.

"Perfect," Sheila thought, "no doubt still with access to 'crimint' (criminal intelligence) and able to warn Croft to scarper as well!"

Taking a very deep breath, she yelled:

"No, no, no!"

Then she threw her mobile phone across the room in disgust at this piece of unwanted news. The unfortunate instrument hit a silver framed photograph of the Andrews' twenty fifth wedding anniversary hanging on the far wall. Both items were sent crashing to the floor in a shower of glass.

A very worried Edward suddenly appeared at the side door of their cottage where he had been passing some time cleaning off the smears left by suicidal midges from their hired car's windscreen. This, days after a drive across Dartmoor; that much lived place of mystery which they often explored on foot or four wheels. Their most recent excursion had been to provide them with a fond reminder of their favourite landscape to take with them to New Zealand.

"What's happened?" he called anxiously. "I heard a crash. Are you alright?"

"I'm fine," she replied.

Edward had covered the short space separating them in an instant and gave his wife still quivering with rage, a comforting hug.

Then, barely a moment had passed before she added:

"No, I'm bloody well not fine. That conniving, lying, bare-faced swine, Croft has cleared off," she said but spitting out each word in a very menacing tone and so unlike her more usual, calm, soft and measured Devon accent.

"He's left a trail of misery and betrayal behind him," she added before collapsing onto one of the matching Shaker-style kitchen chairs. Suddenly she was feeling sick, tired and thoroughly wretched.

"Nothing you can do about it now, love. Just leave it all behind you," her husband said soothingly.

"That's easy for you to say and that's been the trouble. No one's doing anything!" she replied. The annoyance in her voice edged with bitterness.

She looked up at him a feeling of helplessness spreading over her as she rested her elbows on the table; her chin on top of tightly clenched hands.

"He's hurt a lot of people. Do you remember me telling you about Serena McDonald's case? He managed to bury the evidence but at the time no one could prove anything against him."

"That wouldn't be anything to do with the stuff that you took with you up to the funeral in London, would It?" Edward asked.

"Yes, what with that and Croft helping to fabricate an alibi for Webster back in the day. It all left poor Serena quite distraught. That was over ten years ago but she had managed to pull her life together. You remember me telling you how stunning she looked when we met up," Sheila said but her throat tightening as she recalled the sight of that poised, beautiful young woman.

"Now she's dead and surely that's no coincidence either," she reflected her face creased in a dark frown. Then she added:

"The biggest shame, no scandal of it all is that he's contrived and conspired to get away with it for so long and he's still getting away with it. Talk about, 'teflon man'.

Then suddenly her expression changed.

"You've cheered up all of a sudden," her husband remarked.

From somewhere buried deep in the recesses of her mind she was recalling a night spent on 'obbo', that she had shared with the then, Detective Sergeant Croft and Detective Constable McCormack.

"I wonder if he's hunkered down somewhere in Crete," she said, as her face, radiating pent-up irritation half a minute before, was now looking softer, more relaxed and even happier.

"Why Crete?" her husband felt duty-bound to ask.

"Must be at least twelve years ago. Not too long after I had joined Detective Inspector Walton's team. We were keeping watch on a suspected drugs den. It was a horrible, cold, wet November night. Pouring with rain and little to do but sit and wait for the dealers to show. My only consolation that I had not drunk very much before the stake-out had begun. Much easier for the men and their lemonade bottles."

For a brief moment her face relaxed into a faint smile as an image of the men putting those bottle to good use that evening and during many other similar missions came into sharp focus. Then she continued:

"I remember McCormack saying that he would rather be at home with a few beers and on a promise with his girlfriend than stuck inside a cramped, non-descript looking van, cold and hungry and having to keep tabs on the 'drug dealing dregs of Devon society'."

"What was you preference?" Edward asked.

"I think I suggested the Caribbean. You know, where we spent our honeymoon and certainly warmer than a late autumnal evening in rainy, downtown Exeter," Sheila replied.

"Then how does Crete come into the equation?" a rather puzzled Edward persisted.

"Well, the more I think about it, there was something in the way that Croft had mentioned Crete. 'Can't beat it,' he said. 'It's got the weather, the food's great, the booze is cheap and the people are friendly. Yes, me in the local taverns, glass of Metaxa in my fist. What could be better than that?' is exactly how he described it. He was so enthusiastic," Sheila explained.

She looked across at her husband, pleased that not only had she remembered an ostensibly insignificant incident from years before but at the same time realising that even such a tiny snippet of information as 'Crete' could have a positive repercussion. Especially if it contributed towards Croft's ultimate undoing. Police work relied on the pooling of fragments of information.

"Think I'll mention it to Ingrid when we see her tomorrow. See what she thinks."

This contributed to her slowly cheering up as deep down she still blamed herself for what had happened to Serena. Had she not passed on that file and evidence bag to her a short time ago, then perhaps that beautiful woman might still be alive. It was also the reason that she believed Croft's hand was in it somewhere. When she returned home from New Zealand she would make it her business to have a poke around. Sheila intended too to suggest that Crete be considered as a possible bolt-hole for Croft. Unless of course he was found in the meantime. Even when she reached New Zealand she would try and keep in touch with events via her friend Ingrid and if Andrew Croft was still evading justice she would ask her to pass on her thoughts regarding his possible whereabouts to the appropriate authority. She was consequently looking forward to meeting up with her friend. Sheila did not want to appear too vindictive or look foolish if her conclusion regarding the island of Crete proved to be wrong.

✳✳✳

Eventually, she calmed down and they both enjoyed a light supper. Sheila now couldn't wait to go and slipped an arm across her husband's shoulders. She quickly washed the plates and other utensils before setting out the crockery for the very early morning breakfast they would share before departing. That done they prepared to snatch a few hours sleep. Something Sheila had grown accustomed to doing over the years in her work.

"I've set the clock alarm for 1am. Is everything packed?" She asked her husband but not for the first time that day.

"Yes, and I've turned everything off apart from the main lights, cleaned out the fridge; just enough milk for breakfast and a last cup of tea, then I'll leave the fridge door ajar. So everything's all set and Janine'll be in after we've gone tomorrow. Remind me to leave this set of keys under the doormat. She'll hand them over to the estate agent in the afternoon."

"Are we doing the right thing?" Sheila asked suddenly, a note of concern back in her voice.

"What? It's a bit late now to change your, mind about going to the other side of the world, isn't It?" Edward responded, looking somewhat puzzled.

Then he answered his own question:

"Yes, of course we are. The break will do us both good. You've said often enough that you need to get away from your work and what could be better than seeing our son and his family. Well, other than Ehlana and her family coming with us."

Ehlana Stephenson, their married daughter, currently living in Portsmouth not too far from Fratton Park, the home of, 'Pompey', Portsmouth Football Club.

"No," his wife replied, "not about going away but it's renting out our home to strangers as a holiday let. It's just that it has always been our escape, our refuge from the outside world."

This hesitation was merely last minute nerves but it was certainly true their cottage had always provided them with a comfortable refuge to return to at the end of their respective stressful days at work. Edward, until recently as a Mathematics teacher in a large Exeter comprehensive school and Sheila, in the frontline of police detective work. As for holiday letting, that was not really a problem. Those holiday tenants had already been carefully vetted by one o the estate agents, Burton Reeves, a personal friend of the Andrews'. Their cottage, is situated in the charming village of Chagford. The latter is, according to a Sunday newspaper colour supplement, 'the best rural location to live', in England. It was also one of Devon's four stannary towns; a district with a court authorised to regulate tin miners and mining. The town (or village) is situated on the north-eastern fringes of Dartmoor and is a pleasant mix of stone and thatched cottages. There are many excellent public houses, including a 16th Century coaching inn as well as a range of restaurants catering for all tastes and wallet sizes.

Sheila, a local girl had met her husband during his time as a student at Exeter University. Come the moment for departure there would naturally be more than the slightest hint of regret at leaving their idyllic home and the small town of Chagford, albeit temporarily. Only a slight regret though, for they were off to see their grandchildren.

***

The UK part of their travel plan, which had evolved over many weeks of preparation was set to begin with their departing Chagford at 3am in their hired, compact Suzuki Jimny 4 X 4, off-road car. They were endeavouring to travel very lightly considering the distance and time away. It was their intention instead to buy clothes and other essentials in New Zealand as necessary. Even so there was little room to spare after loading their luggage into their small vehicle.

From the short spur of the B3206, join the A30 but only briefly before turning on to the winding B3212 at Moretonhampstead. Then cross the River Teign near Dunsford and on through Longdown before re-joining the A30 and pressing on to Honiton and then Basingstoke. From there for the final stretch that would bring them to Heathrow. There they would remove their luggage and park the Suzuki for collection by its airport-based representative of the nationwide hire company from whose Exeter branch it had been hired. It was part of the plan, just before reaching the airport that Sheila would phone her friend Ingrid Saunders and arrange to meet her for lunch. Then the Andrews' later that afternoon would depart, bound for the southern hemisphere. Sheila had spoken to Ingrid on various occasions including soon after her friend's husband's funeral. They shared the unease and distaste that surrounded not only Croft's devious behaviour but Serena's murder as well.

"Did you move the travel documents folder, Sheila? I'm sure I put them back a lot nearer to the fruit bowl than this after looking at them the other evening," Edward asked.

"No, sweetheart haven't touched them. I wouldn't dare," she laughed.

Again, Edward had the same feeling he had experienced several days before; a slight tremor of uncertainty. He was sure that the documents, including their itinerary showing roads and timings were in a different order to the one in which he was quite certain he had left them. He wondered too if his computer had been opened as he found the mouse on the right hand side of the mat. This was odd because being left-handed he always placed it on the other side. Sheila had her own machine and had no need to touch his. Not wishing to cause any fuss at this very late stage, he decided to put the whole thing down to his imagination or to an accidental overdose of his statins and beta-blockers.

***

Chagford in high season can be busy but hardly frenetic; at three in the morning it is very quiet. So it was that at 3am precisely, the Andrews' in their hired vehicle pulled out from their driveway and joined the B3206 before turning right, then left and on through the still sleeping little town of Moretonhampstead, four miles from their cottage. There was an early morning chill outside the Suzuki but inside they were warm, comfortable and almost glowing with anticipation as they looked forward, in spite of the ridiculous hour of the day, to their great adventure. They crossed the River Teign and moved quite alone on the road through Dunsford and then down towards the junction with the B3193; the road up from the A38 Exeter – Plymouth road. Edward looked across at his wife as he was enjoying the first stage of the driving. He smiled and said, barely able to contain his excitement:

"We're on our way."

These were the last words she would ever hear her husband say and the last he would ever speak for no sooner were they uttered, then the crash of metal on metal shattered the peace of that early morning air. Out from the B3193 to their right had come the menacing black shape of a powerful 4 X 4, Jeep Renegade. It engine was roaring as it accelerated and smashed into them! Their small utility was hit at right angles; the bull bar fitted to protect the Renegade's sidelights and front bumper ploughing into the driver's door of the red Suzuki. The Andrews', whose vehicle's airbags somehow proved ineffective were thrown violently sideways to their left. Their seatbelts unable to hold them! Their car was pushed brutally off the narrow 'B' road on which it had been travelling and into a farm track. After two complete metal rending somersaults, it finally came to rest on its passenger side. That initial crunching impact causing the driver, Edward to smash his head violently against his wife's headrest on the front passenger seat. So violent and shocking was the contact that it brought on a heart attack and he died almost immediately. His wife was pushed in her turn, against the front passenger door and rendered unconscious. The black, killer car, having stopped, then reversed a few metres back and across the road from where it had shot forth. The driver, switched off his engine, got out and went across to the stricken car whose engine after a few minutes of ominously sounding crunching and sputtering had ground to a halt. Very carefully, not wanting the car perched precariously on its side to roll on him he looked in at the two bloodied occupants. He nodded with satisfaction at a contract fulfilled; put his Glock automatic pistol back into an inside pocket and returned to his own lethal murder machine. Slowly and quite deliberately, his black leather-clad hands re-fastened his seat belt and he looked back across the road at the scene of devastation he had wrought. In a language definitely more Farsi than English he muttered:

"Good!"

***

He switched on the Jeep's engine and set off for Exeter, grateful once again for the car's sophisticated satellite navigation system that was making this phase of his convoluted and dangerous life so much easier. He reached his destination having made very good time. There were few cars around and even fewer pedestrians when he drove through Exeter's streets. Some of these streets he remembered from previous visits and from a very recent one when he had reconnoitred the area to check on the presence of CCTV cameras. He conscientiously observed the speed limit but still arrived at his next destination, a car park a little after 3-45am. A week before he had booked into a bed and breakfast in South Devon to plan that morning's operation but only ventured out when absolutely necessary in order to avoid inquisitive guests. After first carrying out a recce of the Andrews' cottage, he had managed a closer look at their travel plans. The idea to ambush them seemed an obvious one and because of the time of day, an easy option especially after he had managed a few adjustments to their hire car's airbags and seatbelts. The tampering with those safety measures would not be noticeable under normal driving. But what he planned to do at the junction of the B3193 was certainly not normal driving!

He now looked cautiously around him and then reached behind the front passenger seat and retrieved a red, plastic petrol container. Satisfied he was not being overlooked he pulled matches, a small cardboard box, some wood shavings and a small piece of candle attached to a small disc of thick cardboard to keep it upright, from a large rucksack. Before any further action he leaned across to the passenger seat and scooped up a pair of Zeiss binoculars and placed them carefully into his rucksack containing a small printer and several changes of clothes. Forty seven minutes earlier he had used those same binoculars to good effect. He had checked the approach of an oncoming, small, dark red vehicle. Days before, when he had broken into the cottage he had used his mobile phone to photograph every detail of his victims' travel plans so thoughtfully provided by them. This had given him after driving down those same roads listed on the itinerary, the precise moment he would need to intercept them. Now it was time to destroy this potentially incriminating evidence. He placed all the copies he had made of their travel plans across the passenger seat. He opened the Jeep's driver's door and carefully dropped his rucksack a metre or so from the vehicle on to the car park's tarred surface. Then he placed the candle inside the small box and arranged shavings around it and put the matches within easy reach. He liberally poured petrol from the container over the rear and front passenger seats and carpets, reserving just a little for the driver's seat. Very carefully, conscious of the fumes from the petrol, he lit the candle then eased himself from his seat. He grabbed the plastic container and splashed the remainder of the fuel over the seat he had just vacated then lobbed the now empty vessel into the back of the vehicle. Cautiously, he closed the driver's door behind him, gathered up his rucksack and walked purposefully but not too quickly in the direction of Exeter St David's Railway Station. He had covered some one hundred metres from the car when he heard a 'Varrrooomph', as his crude but well tested fire bomb ignited. Within minutes it had reduced the expensive motor vehicle that had been stolen to order, from near Fulham Football Ground ten days before, into a blazing wreck. Years of evading police and para-military forces in many countries across Europe and beyond had honed a variety of skills. Very soon after, he was boarding the 5-10am train to Paddington. Before the passing of many more hours he would be maintaining a very low profile in a flat just off Aspen Way, Poplar. Within a few more hours he would be notifying one of his contacts. He in turn, would be passing on that message to a man whose Albert Embankment office overlooked the River Thames. All he needed to say was:

"Both cars parked. All lights out!"

"Good," said that man, Ranulf Faulkner looking out of his office window as he calmly watched a pleasure craft pass by on the Thames, bound for Greenwich.

"Soon," he thought, "be time after a little job for me to switch his lights off but in the meantime I'll pass the message on."

Shortly after, on the island of Crete one man was delighted to receive news that favours he had called in, had been fulfilled.

***

In Devon, it was almost an hour after the incident before the wrecked Suzuki was discovered and a little more before a dead body was recovered from it.

"One's still alive, just," reported the driver of the police patrol car, diverted from the A30 following a call from a man exercising his dogs before his long shift at Exeter Airport.

It took much care, patience and ingenuity by the combined efforts of the Fire and Police Services, Paramedics and other medical professionals to extract a very damaged Sheila Andrews from the wreckage. No time was lost in rushing her to the high dependency, intensive care unit of the Devon and Exeter Hospital, Wonford where she remains suspended, somewhere between life and death in a deep coma.

***

The day that had begun with so much promise and ended so badly for the Andrews' on a quiet country road in Devon proved to be a very anxious one elsewhere. For Tobias Andrews there had been no pre-flight call to say his parents would soon be boarding the aircraft at Heathrow. Ehlana Stephenson waited in vain for that promised call from her parents to say a fond farewell. Ingrid Saunders glanced frequently at her watch as the morning ticked away wondering when Sheila would be phoning to say they were nearing the airport and exactly where and when she was to meet them for lunch. Neighbours in Chagford speculated as to where in the skies the Andrews' were at various times during the day. Only slowly did news of an early morning crash a few miles away begin to reach the town. There were diversions as both 'B' roads, the B3212 and B3193 were cordoned off for the rest of that day and for the two that followed. By early morning what had been a vague rumour was turning into a discussion in muted tones in the homes and pubs throughout Chagford and the villages beyond, as to the identities of the crash victims. There were really only two people that it could realistically be was the growing conclusion. Then it was confirmed that the Andrews' had indeed been involved in a very serious accident and consequently, many people's plans changed irrevocably. A pall of gloom descended in the town.

By early evening, a stunned, incredulous Ehlana Stephenson was sitting in the office of Mrs Melody Vassallo, her mother's Neurosurgeon at Wonford. Mrs Vassallo had quickly informed Ehlana of the steps already taken by a dedicated team of medical staff to ascertain the full extent of her mother's injuries and to make her as comfortable as possible. A breathing tube, an 'endotracheal' had been inserted in her mother's trachea at the crash site. On arrival at the 'intensive care unit', a neurologist had lifted Sheila's eyelids to check for a response. There was only the slightest of reactions but there was a reaction. Then Sheila was given a CT scan to assess overall damage.

"Will mum recover?" Ehlana asked in a quiet, concerned voice but really frightened of the answer she might receive.

"It's too soon to say with any certainty. At the moment she is in a deep coma. The instant she arrived we checked for two references, two signs; wakefulness and awareness. Put simply and I'm sorry if it sounds so brutal; is she still switched on? Is the patient still able to think and perceive their immediate surroundings? She's received severe blows to the head. The first on impact and others as the car rolled and she was thrown around inside it."

"So is mum still with us?" Ehlana asked, not fully understanding the significance of what had just been said. Once again she dreaded the answer.

"What we don't want to do at this very early stage, is raise or offer false hope. We've also given her an ERG, an Electroencephalograph. This records the activity of the cells, the neurons in the brain. There were indications but I must stress they were only slight but they are there."

"Does that mean she could recover?" though her voice was barely audible.

"It may be a very long haul, months rather than weeks and there is no guarantee that she will recover, either partially or fully," the surgeon replied but making every effort to smile reassuringly.

Ehlana, on arrival had asked for frankness and thanked the surgeon accordingly but even if she had prepared for the worst then the information she had been given still came as a shock. The one hundred and thirty mile drive from Portsmouth to Exeter had gone very quickly. Later, in a few quiet moments as she reflected on the events of the day she alarmed herself for there were parts of that journey that she could not remember. Her thoughts had strayed to thinking as she drove West, about what she might find on arrival. This was in part down to shock which had plunged her into a surreal feeling; that none of this was really happening. Now she took a deep breath.

"May I see my mother, please?" She asked meekly.

"Yes, of course but I feel I must warn you. She is surrounded by machines. The main one is a monitor to check mum's heart rate, breathing and any build-up of pressure on the brain. There's a ventilator that's breathing for her, an EKG and a catheter providing her with nutrients."

"Will she be able to hear me?" Ehlana asked nervously.

"Even when a patient is in a coma we believe it's important for them to be included in their surroundings and there's strong evidence that patients can hear footsteps and speech. To what extent though is really rather more difficult to determine," Mrs Vassallo replied then added, "so please, chat away to her."

***

The surgeon led the way and when Ehlana first caught sight of her mother, she gasped. That small, frail looking person in the bed, was that really her mother? She seemed to be covered from head to foot; from a bandage around her head down to white stockings encasing her feet and on up to her knees. Then there were the machines, wires, instruments and catheters. The one that most alarmed Sheila's daughter was the wire from out of the back of her head linking her to a monitor. Ehlana was informed a little later that this was an intracranial monitor, an ICP, to measure pressure on the brain. Those special stockings were to prevent blood-clots from forming. When one of the medical staff had described her mother's condition as 'poorly', the English teacher in Ehlana thought it was an excellent, if unfortunate example of 'litotes', an extreme case of understatement. As she looked down at her mother's face partially hidden by an oxygen mask, a feeling of despair began to creep over her. But she decided that would help no one, least of all her mother. So she sat down and began to talk to her about anything and everything that occurred to her but only after telling her mother that she loved her.

"Mum, please come back to us. We all love you so much," she said as she lightly touched a piece of her mother's arm that was free of wires and tubes.

Ehlana chatted about the family, the weather, walking along Southsea Beach, her home near Fratton Park and that time before Covid when they had all visited 'HMS Victory' and the incredible 'Mary Rose' in its purpose-built housing. Then they had ascended the noiseless lift to the top of the Spinnaker Tower with its magnificent views of the Solent, the Isle of Wight and Portsmouth Harbour; and on the day they visited, one of those huge new aircraft carriers tied up. The family returned to earth and enjoyed beef burgers and coffee for the adults but colas for the children with their burgers and fries. Yet it was when she talked about the family cat that everything suddenly caught up with and overwhelmed her ; just the sheer ordinariness of it releasing a stream of pent-up emotion. She burst into tears and it was some minutes before she could regain any measure of composure and resume the one-sided conversation. Covid-19 had reminded the world just how precious but transitory life can be. Many millions of people had suffered every inconvenience, ill health and issues of every kind. Hundreds of thousands had died leaving distraught and bewildered loved ones behind. Now here before Ehlana was another but very personal reminder of that fleeting condition.

After an hour of almost constant babble Ehlana rose, kissed the small portion of her mother's face that remained mask and tube free, promised to return the next day and left the room. She knocked on Mrs Vassallo's office door. She entered in response to a voice inviting her to 'come in' and thanked the Surgeon for all that was being done for her mother. Slowly and thoughtfully Ehlana walked back to her car. Then she drove off to Chagford but was forced to go the long way up the A30 before turning into the A382 at Whiddon Down as the

B3212 was closed. This was a small consolation because its closure saved her from having to drive past the crash site undergoing close forensic examination. She had arranged through an earlier telephone conversation to stay with her parent's neighbours, the Lewis's. On arrival that first meeting was very difficult for them all. The neighbours were devastated and that first greeting was stilted with not one of the three of them knowing quite what to say.

Ehlana, with much difficulty eventually thanked them for their kind wishes and briefly described her mother's condition. She accepted a brandy, some cornflakes as it was too late for anything too substantial. It was quite late and as she had been yawning with fatigue since stepping over their threshold, agreed with Janine Lewis that she should turn in. Gregor Lewis collected Ehlana's case from her car and carried it to one of the now spare rooms as both of the Lewis children, now married had moved away. What with the brandy and the milky drink Janine insisted she took with her to bed and having seen her mother so helpless, Ehlana fell almost immediately into a deep sleep. The next morning after breakfast she spoke to her brother on 'Zoom' and brought him up to speed over their mother's condition. This, as well as having to gently remind him that arrangements would have to be made as soon as their father's body was released, for his funeral. Ehlana, as she lived the nearest to their parents had years before been put down as next of kin in the event of an accident. Consequently she had undergone the unenviable task of informing her brother of the accident as well as the tragic news of their father's death. Tobias now planned to fly to England in a few days, hurry down to Exeter so they could face the sad ordeal of organising their father's funeral as well as other formalities, together.

***

The Police showed considerable interest in the badly damaged hired vehicle. They discovered the seat-belt mounting for both front seats showed faint but distinct signs of interference that could result in driver and passenger being thrown to the left if the car was side-swiped. Air bags too indicated some disturbance. Ehlana's brother, soon after his arrival suggested that as doubt over it being an accident was building up then the case should be treated as murder and attempted murder. He added firmly that as a consequence their mother should be put under guard immediately. This as an obvious precaution in case another attempt was made on her life. If any doubt remained over it being foul play this soon evaporated with the discovery of a burnt out vehicle in a car park situated not too many miles from the scene of the Andrews' crash. Any lingering doubt about it being an accident or not, finally dispelled when microscopic traces of paint that had survived the flames that consumed most of the Renegade were discovered by the forensics team. What the killer had not anticipated was a stiff morning breeze springing up and blowing the flames away from a small section of the front of the Jeep before consuming the rest of the car. Those specks matched exactly the 'bright red 5 ZCF' spray paint of the Suzuki.

"It now looks quite conclusive that the Renegade deliberately swept your parents' car off the road so I confirm we are dealing with a case of murder and attempted murder," Detective Superintendent Fleming told Sheila's children.

That evening Fleming made an appeal on television for anyone who had seen the driver of a Renegade or anyone acting suspiciously to contact the Police. All dark Renegades were traced, owners contacted, interviewed and eliminated from the enquiry. That is, with one exception and that had been recovered and transported to the laboratory for further examination.

***

In South Devon, the elderly owners of a bed and breakfast wondered if they should come forward about one of their guests whose stay with them, 'ticked a number of boxes'. He was a tall, taciturn, 'foreign-looking', very well-groomed, including a neatly trimmed beard, quietly spoken gentleman who habitually wore sun-glasses regardless of the weather during his stay with them. He had kept himself to himself seemed to avoid other guests but parked very considerately in the couples' drive but was away before other guests might see too much of him or his car. He had driven away on various occasions, usually very early in the morning, in his large, powerful car that was very similar to the one shown in the appeal. His departure only noticed because Mr Peckham, the co-owner of the business had an enlarged prostate problem, necessitating visits to the bathroom at unconventional hours. This particular guest was always very polite, had paid in cash and just did not look capable of carrying out such a terrible deed, even though he looked foreign.

As Mrs Peckham remarked to her husband:

"No, it can't be him. Far too nice to have done it. Let's not get involved."

Her husband agreed although he was still smarting regarding his view of the police having received a third notification of speeding offences in as many months.

Overlooked too was the fact that the evening before the crash, Mr Jamail Hallet, as he had signed their register, had driven off but not returned; though he had stayed barely seven of the fourteen days for which he had paid in advance.

***

In Exeter, the Andrews' siblings were still agitated over the motive behind the crash:

"Why would anyone want to kill either of them?" Ehlana asked Superintendent Fleming.

"I need to ask but did either of them have enemies or was there anyone they had upset or who bore them a grudge?" the Officer asked

'No, certainly nothing deserving that. Apart from the occasional moan like we all do from time to time about work, mum never talked much about what she did in her professional life," Ehlana replied

Now that she had her brother by her side she felt much more composed. Though when the two of them went off to visit their mother later she would soon reverted to that feeling of tearful helplessness.

"Surely, isn't it more likely to be to do with your line of work than anything else?" Tobias suggested.

"Yes," continued Ehlana, "don't criminals threaten you with all sorts when you arrest them and they end up being put away?"

"Well, with that thought in mind we've begun a comprehensive review of all your mother's recent cases and what we won't easily forget is this is an attack on one of our own. Rest assured Mrs Stephenson, we'll look into everything and we are keeping a close watch on your mother though I suspect her attacker may be long gone by now."

"There is one thing. Could of course be nothing," Ehlana offered. "A short while ago she phoned me asking if we could meet up. She was travelling up to London to a funeral. It was for the husband of a friend, a former police officer. Mum happened to mention she was taking something up with her to give to another woman after she has been to the funeral. It was all to do with something she and Ingrid, her friend had been involved in years ago. Mum wanted to break her journey on the way back and see me in Portsmouth. I had to put her off as I was involved in a school residential week at the time so I never did get to hear the full story."

"Thanks for that. We'll certainly look into that too. You never know," Fleming replied.

***

In a quiet wood, in a water-filled ditch, not too far from the Devon and Exeter Racecourse by the A38 on Haldon Hill, lay a man's body. It was discovered by a party of hikers a week after the crash. Very soon after, it was identified as the body of a detective currently undergoing investigation, Philip McCormack. He had been murdered; shot dead with two 9mm bullets to the brain. Police were now working on the not unreasonable assumption that as he and the still missing Detective Inspector Croft had worked closely together over many years then Croft was almost certainly implicated in some way in the death of McCormack. Croft, it was being further suggested may have killed his long time associate to prevent him from 'grassing him up' in order to save his own skin. They must have shared many dark secrets. If Croft had killed his former partner in crime then he may not have skipped the country as had been the initial police thinking. A second sweep of all Croft's haunts and associates in the South-West was under way and security surrounding Sheila, stepped up in case he had personally carried out or had locally orchestrated not only the shooting of McCormack but the attempt on her life on the B3212.

A possible link provided by the Office of the Devon and Cornwall Police Commissioner was being pursued. This Office had received material from Serena MacDonald, a victim of an assault a decade earlier. Croft, Andrews and Saunders had all worked on Serena's case. The leader of a team which had searched Croft's house for incriminating evidence of corruption, recalled too a very hot, dishevelled and rather bulky Sheila Andrews bringing some evidence to the mobile incident vehicle after groping around in Croft's loft. When other team members searched too they discovered old case notes. What if she had found some similar material from a particular case that incriminated Croft but for reasons best known to herself kept it and then eventually brought it to Serena MacDonald who was now a victim of a very callous murder. There was of course another possibility; that it had not been Croft who had killed McCormack. A third party had carried out that murder and had also killed Croft. His dead body could be anywhere, having been consigned to a ditch or stream in a corner of Dartmoor, never to be found!

***

In a hospital bed over one hundred miles from that sad Hampshire scene where one life had ended so cruelly, another one, interrupted by an assassin's hand was twitching; showing life renewed – perhaps! Her eyes were fluttering, monitors were responding. Intensive Care Staff too were reacting. Were these signs that Sheila Andrews was at last beginning to emerge from her comatose state? More than likely it would be many more months yet but Hospital Staff judged it to be a positive step along the road to some level of recovery. A relapse though could not be discounted but if she did make a full recovery she was not the sort of woman, indeed, police officer to let sleeping dogs lie. There were far too many coincidences for her not to investigate. Her husband had died, not as the result an accident but caused by an act of pre-meditated and cold-blooded murder. Croft had disappeared and a close associate of his had died in mysterious circumstances.

There was a strong link between a London-based drugs' gang, members of a terrorist cell, a Devon drugs operation and police officers under investigation for their involvement in corruption.

There was one common factor; the name of Jamail Hallet had cropped up again. One of the Peckhams' other guests had been travelling back home to Milton Keynes after attending a business conference in Torquay and had not seen the police appeal. Only much later did he hear of the call for information over the Renegade and its driver and remembered seeing a dark vehicle, matching the description pull in behind his own vehicle after wearily returning himself after a long day filled with meetings. He contacted the Police who interviewed the Peckhams, examined the guest house register and quizzed the owners as to why they had not come forward with such potentially vital information. As for common factors, a woman, Serena MacDonald that Sheila had met not long before being brutally murdered. Her murderer, Sefton Mather had been intimately linked with her too. Mather was subsequently convicted of two murders the second of whom Sophie Fortune knew both Mather and Serena.

Sheila would continue to share some of the guilt concerning the first of these women for she had passed material to her that incriminated Croft. Motive enough for the unscrupulous Andrew Croft to seek revenge. There was enough evidence emerging that he had the contacts to arrange murder contracts.

If she did recover and re-examined all the evidence as well as looking into Mather's trial and background she might discover that Croft was not the only one who could have set up the disgraced, former MP. There was a wronged husband who also had many dubious contacts and was certainly capable of engineering the whole thing or contributing materially towards such a conspiracy. There was also Kelvin Fenwick, an embittered former, highly paid professional footballer but he was hardly a 'Mastermind' contender. He may have had a strong motive but blinded by jealousy, lacked the cool head that would have been a prerequisite for such a complicated plot. He had been extremely capable on the football field, particularly around the 'six yard box' but his organising skills would be sorely tested if required to organise 'a piss-up in a brewery', as the saying goes.

***

Somewhere, buried deep within the dark recesses of her dormant brain was the key that could one day, if she ever recovered, unlock a clue to Croft's present whereabouts, if indeed he still lived. That's if she was ever able to retrieve that conversation with Sergeant Croft as they had sat in a van one miserable November night during a 'stake-out' as the rain had poured down!

Chapter Fifteen

A man, formerly well-known but not necessarily liked or trusted in West Country police circles as Detective Inspector Croft sat relaxing under the azure, cyan-blue Cretan sky. That particular colour blue so loved and revered by all Greeks from their national flag to the many domed, whitewashed dwellings clinging to many a hillside town and village all over Greece. For years he had been investing any spare, ill-gotten or legitimate earnings in the several hectares of real estate stretching out before him and covered in olive trees and grape vines.

***

Croft had grown up in Torquay and after leaving school where he had barely employed his ability he managed to gain a place at Exeter University where he read law and found it very much to his taste. After graduating he decided to join the Devon and Cornwall Constabulary. He did his probationary service at Exeter where he rescued a young man from drowning in the River Exe and was given a Royal Humane Society Award. A stint at Newton Abbot followed and fortune seemed to be favouring him for he single-handedly thwarted an armed robber's attempt to seize at gunpoint a shop's takings. For 'his brave action in carrying out his duty and protecting the public' he was presented with a National Police Bravery Award. He took his sergeant's examination and was recommended to join the Detectives. Very soon after he became a member of a detective team under

Detective Inspector Graham Walton based at Exeter Police Station, Heavitree. While investigating a suspected drugs deal he was fortunate enough to assist a colleague during a terrorist bomb scare in the City Centre. While observing the activities of residents of a flat above a shop he noticed a group of men acting suspiciously near the shop and requested back-up. The group was arrested and found to be in possession of explosives and small arms. There was the suggestion of a link between the drugs gang and the terrorists. In the event, drugs were seized but only one of those suspected of drug dealing was found near the premises; he was arrested by Croft to 'assist the police with their enquiries'.

It was however, certainly no coincidence that having done so well, events would lead his career down a very different path. A day after the arrest of the suspect in the drugs enquiry, he received an anonymous phone-call the basis of which was a barely veiled threat:

"Croft, we know where you live and where your kids go to school. You know what you have to do and what will happen if you don't but you'll be compensated for your trouble."

That man fleeing the premises in the centre of Exeter, was according to the single piece of identification found on him by Croft, a driving licence, a Jamail Hallet, of joint British/Iraqi nationality. This single fact was not shared with the other officers in the team. The very confident and rather smug-looking accused, denied any association or knowledge of drugs and terrorist plots. The evidence, the drugs which had soon disappeared and the few witnesses who either withdrew or changed their statements meant the abandonment of any further enquiries. The team, led by Inspector Walton had little choice other than to release the suspect. Sergeant Croft who was in the interview room with Walton had been struck by the very dark eyes of the accused and his quite pale, skin colour. Croft had also been made an offer with threatening undertones that he would have found very difficult to refuse. So with a few adjustments he slipped very easily into a modified but lucrative new way of life.

***

The Croft family moved from their cramped house near Crediton to a large, detached, new build house on an estate between Exeter and Exmouth. The high mortgage, riding and violin lessons for the children, expensive foreign holidays including Cyprus and the Caribbean proved a strain on the Crofts' lone salary earner. His wife, Rosina decided she needed to return to her work in an Exeter estate agency to boost the family income.

Suspicion for a time did fall on Sergeant Croft soon after Hallet's release. Perhaps he was imagining it but there were several occasions when he had wandered into the canteen and moved from the counter towards the tables and conversation had stopped abruptly or changed direction.

During his mid-teens his parents had taken him on a family holiday to Crete and he had been lucky enough to explore some of the more remote parts of that island. Now he decided to put some of the fond memories of that holiday time to a very practical use. At the first opportunity to re-visit Crete alone, he would look for a property, land was so cheap there, and invest for the future. He had perverted the course of justice; once was enough for charges, dismissal and a prison sentence but he had ridden out the storm of accusations and recriminations and emerged much wiser from the experience. He had also been, as that caller had said, compensated and compensated quite handsomely and very quickly turned that to his advantage. Following that drugs debacle he was moved sideways not unexpectedly along with the rest of Walton's team.

Then his career revived thanks to information regarding criminal activity by others provided by a network of villains directed by the man he had originally helped. His arrest rate increased. His success, the result of catching criminals, 'grassed-up' or informed on, by those who enjoyed Croft's looking the other way as to their activities. Senior officers may have winced at his methods but the results ticked all the boxes and so looked very good on crime clear-up sheets. Considerable sums of money were also involved. That caller had been as good as his word when he had promised other favours. A month after the incident Croft had met the man whose driving licence he had managed to 'mislay' and they discussed in detail areas of mutual benefit.

Another facet of the rise in crime at the end of the first decade of the 21st Century was a growth in the numbers of gangs supplying drugs and their distribution that was no longer restricted to the larger towns and cities. This development could also work to Croft and his associate's advantage. It soon emerged that his new friend cast his net widely across Europe and beyond Even the West Country was seeing a rise as London-based dealers looked further afield for new markets. Sadly, even children desperate for easy money to buy the latest 'trainers' were becoming a major factor in distribution as they pedalled their way around run-down estates in small towns and rural areas bringing a variety of substances including, amphetamines, heroin and crack cocaine to that new, growing, circle of users. Drug gangs as the second decade of the century neared its end making a fortune through the exploitation of these so-called county lines (named after phone lines). Police resources to tackle the growing problem were no longer focused solely on the Metropolis and the big cities but dedicated drugs' teams in every police authority were working to cut those county lines. These drug suppliers were well organised and police believed over one thousand of these 'line holders' were responsible for distributing their evil wares over the phone. Many initiatives were launched to divert disaffected young children, said to number at least twenty thousand countrywide, aged from eleven years and upwards from easy money; schools were advised they had a responsibility when suspending children from their premises. Some of whom misbehave solely for the purpose of being suspended so they could make money through drug distribution. Others' more cynical though, realised money from a percentage of this evil trade reckoned to be by around 2020 some half a billion pounds could provide for their future!

***

Not too many weeks after that meeting between Sheila Andrews and Serena MacDonald, Croft upped and went into hiding. The week before his disappearance, his wife, Rosina, growing tired of his moodiness in the face of pending corruption charges and reading about claims of a 'cover-up' concerning police officers in the local newspaper, decided to take herself and the two boys off to her parents in Plymouth. At least until things blew over. She had effectively lost her job though furloughed early on during the pandemic and as the company was yet to return to its pre-Covid level of business had decided to close her branch. An alternative position was offered but she decided a move to Truro at that particular time would be too disruptive for her sons. A week or so after her leaving the marital home, Truro seemed a sensible move! She would be contacting her former employers now that she had been abandoned as she was certainly unable to afford the mortgage on the home she and Andrew Croft had moved to a few years before. At the time of her redundancy the loss of income had much to Rosina's surprise not unduly bothered Andrew whose, 'no need to worry' caused her to do just that as whispers of bribes and corruption began to spread among officers' partners. During those final months while under the same roof he had become even more secretive. He deflected her questions with his standard, 'no need to worry' responses which as before increased her suspicion that there were reasons to worry. Her unease not helped by him regularly paying for their occasional nights out and their sons' school extra-curricular activities, in cash! She would have been more than justified in thinking there was some basis to her concerns had she known that at the end of the week when she taken the children away and just before his disappearance when he may have quit county and country, he had even cleared out the modest amount of funds in their 'rainy day' emergency joint account.

***

Croft, settling comfortably in Crete under his new identity, knew little about the growing of olives or wine. He knew all he needed to know about the latter. Just open a bottle and pour it into a glass, preferably large but he did enjoy a special one. Before he was able to quit his previous working life of twenty plus years leaving all behind him, he had entrusted the building up of what he hoped would be a small but thriving business to a local man. Now he looked with satisfaction at his manager's efforts. Soon, especially now with even the Greek economy showing Lazarus-like qualities, his produce would be accepted by the local co-operative. Greece, particularly in those grim years had suffered the full consequences of shrinking markets, high unemployment and despair that had forced many to seek their fortunes abroad. This sun-drenched land together with the converted farmhouse behind him he shared with his girlfriend, Acacia Dimitriou. To describe his partner as a 'girl' would stretch credulity too far but neither of them was in the first flush of youth either. Youth and good looks had departed a while ago but they got on well enough. On several occasions each month she would lay on her back on one of the twin beds in the main bedroom after placing a pillow under her buttocks to make his entry more comfortable for her; arms at her sides. Her more than bountiful breasts, resembling plump, round cushions spilled down in a warm embrace over those inert arms. If, before mounting her he bothered to take in the naked body before him, the face serene, the eyes closed, the lips parted slightly, he would have more than appreciated her smooth, olive skin. From beneath those dark brown nipples, above a very round areola, down and across her ribs, her curves rose to meet across her middle at the navel. Then it fell away, the covering of body hair from below her belly forming a dense growth as it reached her pubic mound before dipping down at the tell-tale split above her slightly parted thighs. Usually the two comfortable companions waited until the sun's rays began to form soft shadows on the walls of the bedroom. Then, her partner also completely naked advanced towards those dark 'valley sides', poised to plunge deep into that wet, pink flesh. Soon he was in and grunting. Before he lay full length upon her, those comforting breasts with their stiff nipples rising from a very deep tan-colour areola, wobbled jelly-like until squashed under his sweating body. Then it was over. There was no pressure. She was a widow with two sons who had left Greece during one of that country's habitual financial downturns and they had met and that was that. The sons had begged their mother to join them in Germany but this she could not do. She could not bear to leave Crete; there were just too many memories. The family had lived there for many generations. Her grandfather had bravely fought the Nazi invaders and, so the storytellers in the villages maintained, had helped capture a German General, Kreipe. This story was turned into a movie, 'Ill Met By Moonlight' and she had for one of the very few times in her life visited a cinema in Heraklion to see it. Not all of her grandfather's extended family had been so fortunate as to escape Nazi vengeance: many were shot for harbouring British, Australian and Greek soldiers after the 'Fallschirmjager', the German paratroops just fell on the Allies and pushed them back to the sea where Royal Naval ships strove to take as many as possible off the island.

Now the two middle-aged people who shared that white-washed farmhouse lived very comfortably and were content enough. Not every relationship could boast that!

***

Earlier that same gloriously hot summer's day, so typically Greek and so sought after by hundreds of thousands of tourists who were once more beginning to make up for Covid-lost time and flock back to the island, he had driven to the old town of Rethymno in his rugged Toyota 4 X 4 Hilux pickup truck. After sharing coffees and Metaxas with a group of elderly locals he had returned home with a batch of two-day old, English newspapers. Feeling extremely pleased with himself he settled into a hammock slung between two gnarled trees. On his left was a table with wine, a glass and a mouth-watering Feta-topped Greek salad. After pouring a generous measure of the wine he reached for the first of the papers. This was a 'tabloid' whose headlines almost screamed back at him. They seemed also to be gleefully announcing that justice had finally caught up with a now disgraced member of parliament. For weeks the media, particularly the printed variety had been focussing readers' attention on the wrongdoings of Sefton Mather. One tabloid in particular described how not only had he let down the people who had voted for him but his family too. In great detail they told of his lifestyle and the subsequent murders of two women, they hinted at more revelations to come and how his greed had ultimately brought him down. Several women had volunteered their stories (for a price) of wild nights spent in Mather's company. The first of the unfortunate murdered women the papers reported was Sophie Fortune. One of the 'Sundays', he would discover shortly had devoted a whole supplement to her work as a campaigner for many good causes. Now she was dead at the hands of a heartless, brutal killer. The tabloid reported how Mather had forced himself upon her and twisted her neck back and broken it in a drink and drugs' sexual frenzy. Such a cruel end the magazine declared for one who had striven so long to protect women from the violence of men!

***

It was the second victim's death however that was giving him the most satisfaction that almost bordered on enjoyment. Also, according to the newspaper reports, Serena MacDonald had fallen victim to Mather's lustful and vengeful disposition. She too had been his lover having first met him when offering escort services. There were also lurid details of her other businesses including the sex lines and Gemma's Gems. Then, it was disclosed an involvement in several cases of blackmail involving Serena's business partner and former co-escort, Jemima. The latter's victims included several highly placed persons once the two women had set up their own escort agency. Readers of the tabloids who not long before had been forced to live frugally during years of cut-backs closely followed by the pandemic were devastated to read the scale of fees charged by the agency; the newspaper quoted figures ranging from five hundred pounds for escorting a client to dinner, to two thousand pounds to sharing bed and body. Generally unknown to the men who paid for these services they had a co-starring role in movies of their performance. It was revealed that Serena MacDonald had known and entertained her killer and others, for years but this could not excuse her being shot through the head after she had undergone a brutal attack.

"The most savage assault I have seen in my twenty years as a police officer," Detective Superintendent Gareth Valentine had said in one of those newspaper reports.

Mather, having been told it was alleged, of the presence of a camera behind one of the mirrors in her bedroom by Serena, had forced his way in and after searching the house for incriminating evidence and doubtless drugs but finding none of the former, had launched himself at her. The violence of the beating was her punishment for not revealing the hiding place of the photographs and dvds showing incriminating and very revealing scenes of his sexual activity. Items relating solely to Mather's activities were recovered by police following an anonymous tip-off. Then, according to newspaper accounts a frustrated Mather had shot her in cold blood.

***

The man known to just a few of the people of the little village nearby as Eathan Drysdale and not as his former colleagues of the Devon and Cornwall Police Service knew him, Detective Inspector Andrew Croft began to laugh.

"Gotcha!" he snarled and poured himself another glass of Vidiano, dry, Greek white wine and settled back in his hammock.

Life was grand!

Also by Tony Foot

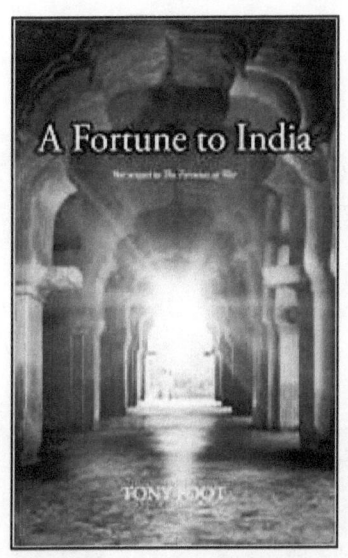

*Available worldwide from
Amazon and all good bookstores*

www.mtp.agency

@mtp_agency

www.ingramcontent.com/pod-product-compliance
Lightning Source LLC
LaVergne TN
LVHW091532060526
838200LV00036B/577